BETTY
THANK YOU F[illegible]
SUPPORT. [illegible]
ENJOY THE [illegible]
FREEDOM IS NOT FREE!
B

BETTY
THANK YOU FOR YOUR
SUPPORT. ENJOY THE READ!
FREEDOM IS NOT FREE!

THE SECRET EYE

BRAD HANSON

The Secret Eye

This is an historical fiction book. Every attempt has been made to accurately represent historical characters and events. Any discrepancies to historical events or misrepresentations of historical figures living or dead, is not intentional.

Brad Hanson
PO Box 675
Celina, Texas, US 75009-0675 www.bradhanson.net

Ordering Information:
For details, contact bradhansonauthor@gmail.com.

Print ISBN: 9781098379773
eBook ISBN: 9781098379780

Printed in the United States of America on SFI Certified paper.

First Edition

This book is dedicated to Charlie Stainer, thanks for all the great stories

My mother, Carol Stainer, what a great love story
with her soul mate Charlie

All of the men and women who served during World War II,
truly the greatest generation

Julie, my wife, my love, and my best critic

PREFACE

Many countries worked to develop Radar technologies during the 1930's. This story follows the groundbreaking developments of Robert Watson-Watt in Great Britain and the sharing of their technological advances with the United States after the attack on Pearl Harbor. The Rad Lab at MIT, working with their British counterparts, developed the technology that propelled America to victory over the Japanese and Germany. The technological advances made during the war have created some of the most important products and systems we use today.

Charlie Stainer, born in February of 1925, was the inspiration for this story. As one of the first Radar operators in the Pacific Theater, his stories about his time on the USS Lexington-CV16 and USS Yorktown-CV10 entertained our families over the years but also taught us so much about what it took to keep America safe from tyrannical forces. It is vitally important that we remember the men who fought during World War II and the people who stayed behind to support the war effort.

We must always remember that freedom is not free, and we must be prepared to defend our way of life from those who wish to take it from us.

ACKNOWLEDGEMENTS

The first book for any author is a monumental task requiring technical expertise in publishing and the financial means to afford the experts. So many people worked tirelessly to bring my vision to print. I am forever grateful to the following people for their knowledge and support.

Tim, Joe Don, Carol, Kip, Tom, Jeff, Richard, and Bert

INTRODUCTION

Over millennia, the treacherous waters of the English Channel in the North Sea afforded the island of Great Britain some protection from invaders. Attacking the island required many ships for transporting every instrument required for war over water. With the discovery of flight, Britain's physical isolation from the rest of Europe vanished. Germany could now send bombers to destroy their beloved homeland.

In early 1934, British military leaders raised concerns that potential enemy airplanes could approach their coast at greater altitudes, out of the reach of their anti-aircraft guns. Bombers from German airfields, only twenty minutes across the English Channel, could wreak havoc on London and other important military locations before the first fighter planes could respond. There was no defense. In response to this threat, Britain created the Committee for the Scientific Survey of Air Defense (CSSAD) and asked Henry Tizard to be its chair.

Born in Gillingham, Kent, in 1885, Henry Robert Tizard studied mathematics and chemistry at Westminster School and Magdalen College, Oxford. After World War I, Tizard experimented with the composition of fuel to reduce their volatility and make them resistant to freezing through the addition of chemical compounds. He also devised the concept of toluene numbers, or the modern fuel octane rating system that is used today.

1. DAVENTRY, ENGLAND

Robert daydreamed as lush rolling meadows dotted with sheep scrolled by his window. The crisp morning air prickled across his face, and a glorious sense of pride swelled within him for what he had done and would do for his country. The February morning was unusually clear, and he was satisfied the conditions were favorable for the demonstration. He had checked the equipment more than once before they departed and was sure his demonstration would go as planned. But was it too late? The fate of his King was in his hands. Robert Watson-Watt—son of James Watt, the father of the steam engine—was the superintendent of the radio department at the National Physical Laboratory (NPL) in Teddington.

"How much further?" Mr. Rowe asked. Only three people knew of this demonstration. Jimmy Roe had been on the CSSAD since its beginnings over a year ago and had the trust of Tizard to vet the potential of Watt's proposal and its value to the war they knew would come.

"Not long now, sir," Arnold said. The road led to a meadow about ten kilometers from the nearest person, a suitable location to prevent interruptions and ensure privacy, he thought.

Arnold Wilkins, Skip to his friends, was driving a 1930 Flatnose Morris Van, modified in earlier weeks to conceal their top-secret cargo. It had been a short fourteen days since his boss Watson Watt sent a secret memo proposing their system to the CSSAD.

"Robert, Mr. Tizard is keen to hear my report on your system. It is vital that we can detect those Gerry planes before they reach our coast," Jimmy said. A physicist and researcher, Jimmy was Tizard's choice to oversee this demonstration not only for his technical skill, but also his sturdy sense of mission.

"Slow down, Arnold!" chided Watson-Watt. "What we are about to reveal is too important to bugger it up by your carelessness." He could hear his cargo rattling in the back, wondering if he had secured it well enough. He knew his design would meet the mark, as long as Arnold did not break their equipment before they could complete the demonstration. "Stop here," he instructed.

The memo Watson-Watt sent to the committee securing this demonstration had stemmed from a suggestion Arnold made earlier that month about using radio waves to detect incoming aircraft. After validating his premise, Watson-Watt designed a system, and his team worked around the clock building and testing his design. It was long hours, but he was very proud of his team and what they had accomplished in such a brief time. But had the Germans already designed a better system? Would their boys be able to penetrate the German defenses when war returned to these shores?

Skip opened up the back of the truck and began setting up the equipment.

Jimmy looked at the jumbled pile of equipment with wry expectations.

"Based on my understanding from your memo and presentation, you intend to show how radio waves will reflect off of an incoming plane to provide accurate distance from our shores. Does that about sum it up, old boy?" asked Jimmy. "So how does your system detect incoming planes?"

The discovery of RDF, radio direction finding, had happened accidentally. It was observed that radio signals were interrupted when large metal objects (ships or planes) passed across a transmission beam. Researchers theorized that the radio waves were reflecting off of the ships or airplanes, and this could allow the detection of these objects. The possibility of providing accurate direction and distance to a detected object would give England a needed advantage if they could make this model work. The technology would have commercial and military applications.

Watson-Watt explained, "We intend to prove that pulsed shortwave radio signals will reflect off of an incoming RAF bomber. We will setup two receiving antennae here and catch the reflection of the incoming object on our cathode ray oscilloscope. The cathode ray oscilloscope represents detected images through waveforms displayed on a green screen.

"Using the Daventry BBC shortwave transmitter as the signal source, the radio waves will reflect off of our Heyford bomber flying a predetermined route between the transmitters at Daventry and Weedon. If all goes well, we will follow the progress of the bomber as it passes between our two transmission towers," Watt added.

"We will connect the equipment in our van to our dipole antenna, which we will string between these four tripods." Arnold pointed at four tripods made from three-inch wooden poles lashed together to create a perfect tripod. Arnold had set up the eight-foot-tall structures ten feet apart, creating a dipole antenna.

Jimmy understood the technical aspects of a dipole antenna, as he remembered studying Hertz during his time at the Royal College of Science in London a long fourteen years ago. Heinrich Hertz, a German physicist, first discovered radio waves in 1887 using a dipole antenna. A dipole antenna is two equal-length metal wires connected via feeder wires to a signal source. For this demonstration, the BBC transmitters would act as the signal source emanating radio wave pulses toward the bomber. The radio receiver modified by Arnold the night before would receive the radio waves reflected off of the RAF bomber and display them on the cathode ray oscilloscope.

Arnold completed stringing the wires between the two pairs of tripods, creating the dipole antenna, and connected the feeder wires to the radio receiver and a DC power source. They were ready.

• • • • •

"Turning to heading one niner three degrees, altitude three eight zero zero feet, beginning my run." Flight Lieutenant R. S. Blucke was a war hero, having served with the Dorsetshire Regiment during World War I. Blucke now enjoyed his attachment to the 63rd Squadron as the signals officer at the experimental section of the Royal Aircraft Establishment. Lieutenant Blucke's briefing did not disclose the nature of his mission. He was only told he was part of an experiment and was to fly one of the Heyford bombers on a training mission following a specific course and speed.

The Heyford bomber, built at the Handley Page factory in Radlett, had two 575 horsepower Rolls-Royce Kestrel III engines. The biplane airframe construction used aluminum, perfect for radiating the radio signal back to the receiving station. Blucke took a skeleton crew comprising himself, a copilot, and a navigator. His commanding officer stressed that he was to fly this mission with minimal crew members and radio chatter. The instruction was explicit: no discussion of this flight with anyone, period.

"Navigator to pilot, continue course and speed."

"Roger," Blucke said.

"We are ready, Mr. Rowe," Watt said as he surveyed their equipment, hoping there would be no malfunctions. There was so much at stake, so many lives they might save! He hoped their calculations were spot on. This had to work.

The team huddled around the oscilloscope and waited.

Watson-Watt looked at his watch. "I expect to see our plane any minute," he stated. As soon as the words left his mouth, the inaudible hum of the bomber was heard in the distance. The hum increased in volume over the next ninety seconds.

"There it is!" said Arnold, a bit too animated for a British scientist. The oscilloscope showed a faint but noticeable blip, and then a vertical line filled the screen and glowed with a slight movement to the left. "That is our bomber flying over the BBC tower near Daventry," Watson-Watt said. "We will know if this experiment is a success if the signal continues moving left, the direction to Weeden."

The team watched for another forty-five seconds as the signal showed a steady movement across the screen. Then, as fast as it had appeared, the line disappeared from view. It was over. They had done it!

"Bloody good show, old boy!" said Jimmy. Each man in the van knew that they had just witnessed history. Britain was now safer. "Now comes the tough part. You have proven that we can detect a plane, but it was not very far away. I heard the hum before the signal showed on the oscilloscope. You must be able to identify our enemies far over the English Channel for this to be of any use to our country. We must report this news to Mr. Tizard straight away." Jimmy was sure the results would cause quite a stir in the committee. *So much more to do before we are safe!*

As Blucke touched down at the airstrip after completing his mission, he wondered what this was all about. Why was he selected? Why was he asked to fly such a quick mission, and over two BBC towers? His skills as a pilot were unmatched, and he was confident there was more to this mission than flying in a straight line over two BBC towers. Little did he know that he had just become the first plane detected using radio waves, a discovery that would save his country from complete annihilation in the coming years.

"Britain is now an island again, Mr. Rowe," stated Watson-Watt.

With this successful demonstration, they would once again have the upper hand against their enemies. They would be able to *see* them coming before they ever reached his shores, he hoped.

The ride back was quiet, with each man pondering the magnitude of what had just been accomplished. How would they meet the needs of their country with this new capability? Could they track planes headed toward their coast and save thousands of their countryman?

Absolutely, they all thought.

2. KAWAGUCHIKO, JAPAN

On a frosty crisp morning, Hadaki Yamatsumi gazed across Lake Kawaguchi toward Mount Fuji, the highest and most revered mountain in his beloved homeland of Japan. The sunrise over the lake at the foothills of Fuji-san compelled Hadaki to make this journey almost every day while the moon hung over the nighttime sky. Most days, he came alone, but today, a very special guest was by his side, his youngest sister Yoshi.

"Why are we here so early, Hadaki?" complained Yoshi, rubbing the sleep from her eyes.

"You turn five today," Hadaki stated evenly, "and it is time for you to learn about your family."

"I know my family," stated Yoshi. "I have a mother, two sisters, and you!"

Absent from her list was their *chichi*, or father Kaisu, who gave his life in honor of the emperor two years previously while fighting in China. Yoshi had a brief memory of her *chichi*, but Hadaki, now fourteen and the oldest, remembered the charge his *chichi* gave him before he left for war, preparing himself to care for his family. This was a job his father would have done, but . . .

"You see Fuji-san across the water?" asked Hadaki. "I come here often to gain strength and wisdom from our forefathers, especially from our *chichi*. Fuji is a very special place. This is where the spirits of our forefathers live and watch over us each day. Fuji-san provides life-giving water for our rice patties. And when you get older, you too will make your journey up Fuji-san to meet our forefathers and learn your place in this world."

"We are so lucky," continued Hadaki, "to live so close to this most sacred mountain."

Mount Fuji, 12,389 feet tall, is a dormant volcano; its last eruption was in the early 1700s. It is one of three *sanreizan*, holy mountains, in Japan, where pilgrims journey each year to gain insight and inner strength.

"Next year, we will come here for *hatsuhinode*," said Hadaki.

Hatsuhinode is the maiden sunrise seen on the first day of the new year. The ancient people of Japan believed the sun was one of the most important Gods and witnessing the *hatsuhinode* was a sacred act.

As the sun loomed behind Mount Fuji, Hadaki and Yoshi saw the summit transform from darkness into a gleaming diamond on top of a perfectly molded cone of the volcanic crater. The transition was especially beautiful today, showing hints of orange as the sun kissed the summit and crested over the eastern edge, coloring the snow-covered peak with deep purple hues.

"It is time we return home," Hadaki said with a sigh. "*Haha* (mommy) will be up soon, and she may have a surprise for you!"

As they turned to walk away, Yoshi turned for one last look. She remembered what her brother told her and wondered about her *chichi*. She missed him deeply and often looked at his picture and asked her mother to tell stories about him. Soon, Hadaki would bring her to meet him once again.

• • • • •

Hiranuma Kiichiro waited on the veranda of his Tokyo home, expecting and hoping his destiny was now within reach. The cherry blossom trees, once full and beautifully ordained, appeared stark as they lay dormant, waiting for winter's cold to release its grip.

The son of a samurai, and soon, perhaps, a leader to honor the memory of my okaasan (mother), Hiranuma considered.

Graduating with a degree in English law, Hiranuma had served as the director of the Tokyo High Court and public prosecutor of the Supreme Court early in his career. Known for his ferocious crusades against corruption and immorality within the political hierarchy, Hiranuma soon grew concerned by outside political influences such as communism, socialism, and liberal democracies.

America and Great Britain are weak, but Russia is a worthy adversary. Japan must be ready to protect herself from this aggressor. The Chinese leader will soon bow down before the emperor, as will Russia one day, he swore.

Hiranuma believed his people were superior to every nation in Asia and expected his military to cleanse those who were not pure. Japan was completing its war against China, which would allow his military to focus on new military crusades.

If Japan is to create an alliance, it is best to forge one with Germany and the Italians. They believe in a master race. We are worlds apart, so their ambition will not interfere with our plans, he knew.

The door to the veranda swung open, and his assistant appeared. "Word from the palace. The emperor summons you to appear," he stated.

The excitement Hiranuma felt swelled within him—he would be the prime minister.

. . . . .

Takijiro Onishi sat at his desk on the aircraft carrier IJN Hiryu. As the rear admiral, he was reviewing tactical plans during the initial cruise of Japan's newest aircraft carrier. The Hiryu was 746 feet long, powered by eight Kampon water-tube boiler units with four geared steam turbines providing 153,000 horsepower to its four shafts.

Onishi grew up in a tiny village in the Hyogo prefecture and had graduated twentieth out of 144 cadets from the Imperial Japanese Naval Academy. He had advanced quickly through the ranks from midshipman to sub-lieutenant, where he helped develop the Imperial Japanese Navy Services. He learned about combat aircraft tactics while dispatched to England and France after World War I. Today, he was preparing to become the chief of staff of the 11th Air Fleet, a position he felt honored to accept.

Onishi looked up to see the ensign assigned to serve him.

"Yes," Onishi said curtly, "what is it?"

"Message from the admiral, sir," the ensign said sheepishly.

Onishi scanned the message quickly. He fumed. *How can they even think this is doable? Do they not know who they are poking? There is a rumor of an unjust embargo against us, but what fool is contemplating this action? Our Navy is superior to any in the world, so any conflict would be as easy as the Mongolians*, he thought. Japan had swiftly handled the Chinese, but he was unsure Japan would survive this plan.

3. LITTLE ROCK, ARKANSAS

On an oppressively hot and muggy day, Charles Edward Brand II, Charlie to his friends, sat crouched behind a hedge at the bottom of a steep hill. He and his best friend Ed Steiner were ready to execute their prank. Charlie and Ed grew up together, meeting in grammar school and quickly becoming lifelong friends.

Charlie was lanky with dark brown hair cut above his ears that protruded from his head like Dumbo the elephant. He was still growing into his six-foot-one-inch frame, and he could put away more food in one sitting than boys twice his size. Ed was about two inches shorter than Charlie and had a square head with a powerful jawline and broad shoulders. As tenth graders at Little Rock high school, they had no issue finding dates.

"The four-twenty-eight should be coming over the hill any minute," Charlie said as he watched, hoping their prank would work.

"Do you think we used enough soap?" asked Ed as he stuffed the soap bars into his pocket in case anyone noticed them.

Just then, at 4:28 p.m., a car on the Pulaski Heights line crested the hill and applied its brakes.

The longest line of the system, the Pulaski Heights line ran from downtown to White City, navigating a steep incline from downtown, which took thirty minutes to complete. The car was preparing to navigate the last hill in the system, the longest and most difficult. At the bottom of the hill, the tracks turned right onto Main Street, completing the last stop on the line.

"Are you sure about this?" Ed asked warily. "What if we get caught?"

"The worst that can happen is the car will derail. We will hurt no one," Charlie said. "We put the soap at the bottom of the hill, not at the top, so the car will not be going too fast."

At the top of the hill, the driver applied the brakes: wooden blocks that pressed onto the rails to cause friction and reduce the speed of the car. The car slowly descended the hill. At the halfway mark, the driver pulled back two clicks on the brake lever and prepared to take the last turn of his shift. Just as the car approached the turn, the driver felt the car speed up. The driver pulled back sharply, applying as much braking power as he could.

"What the Sam Hill!" yelled the driver. Just then, he saw two teenagers poking their heads up over a hedge to his right.

As the wooden blocks hit the soaped rails, all friction between the wooden brake pads and the rails vanished and the car's speed increased. To safely navigate the last turn, the car could not exceed two miles per hour. At the time the car entered the turn, its speed was three-and-a-half miles per hour. The wheels jumped the rails and the streetcar lurched to a stop as it scraped over the cobblestone streets, almost tipping over.

The sudden stop caused some passengers to find themselves sprawled on the wooden floor of the streetcar. The boys ran.

"Come back here, you two!" screamed the driver.

"I told you this would work!" Charlie huffed as they ran to avoid the driver who had jumped from the streetcar and was heading toward their hiding place.

"I have not had so much fun since Hector was a pup!" yelled Charlie as they rounded the corner of a building two hundred yards away. The boys stopped, creeping to the corner, carefully peering to see the effects of their handiwork. The driver stopped his pursuit, and instead decided to concentrate his efforts on his passengers' safety.

"That was too much fun," whispered Ed. "I need to get home or my Pa is going to whoop me." The boys congratulated themselves and promised to meet at the watermelon patch the next day after school.

Charlie entered his home just in time to wash up and sit down for dinner. His sister Doris Ann, five years older, was preparing to marry the grocer's son, a man she had known since they met at church camp four years earlier. His dad, Charles Senior, was a conductor with the Memphis and Little Rock railway, so this left Charlie to his own devices most days. Charlie's mom, Mary, died from a sudden heart attack when he was fourteen. Charlie was still having nightmares from finding her on the kitchen floor that horrible day after school. Life was tough for him without his mother, but his sister tried to keep the family together. Now she would leave in a few short months.

"Where have you been, Charles?" asked Doris Ann sternly.

Doris Ann called him Charles, especially when she sensed he was up to no good. Her senses heightened.

"Nowhere special," claimed Charlie. "Me and Ed were just over watching the streetcars."

Doris Ann glared at Charlie like she already knew what they had done. "I just got off the phone with someone from the streetcar line, and they said they saw two boys running away from downtown after a car derailed on the line," she stated evenly. "You wouldn't know anything about that, Charles, would you?"

"Uhhh . . . we uhhh . . ." stammered Charlie. Composing himself, he said, "Why would you think *we* had something to do with *that*?"

"Because the driver described the exact clothing you are wearing right now!" Doris Ann said with great emphasis. "So, here is how it *will* go. After dinner, you *will* go back to the scene of your crime, and you *will* scrub those rails like you have never scrubbed before! Daddy will not be home for another day, but be sure he will have something to say about this!"

Charlie slumped in his chair. He knew it had been worth every second of cleaning to watch that streetcar jump the tracks. He knew that it would be difficult to sit for a long while after his father returned from his latest trip, a problem he had not experienced in many years. He would miss Doris Ann.

. . . . .

"How long before you are ready to test?" asked Handly, captain of the USS New York.

"Shouldn't be too much longer," the junior lieutenant said sheepishly.

"We set sail for trials tomorrow and I want this boat shipshape," the captain said curtly.

"Yes, sir," said the lieutenant.

The USS New York was just being fitted with the latest radio detecting and ranging (radar) system from the Naval Research Laboratory in Anacostia, Maryland. In the early 1930s, Albert Hoyt Taylor and Leo Clifford Young had completed early experiments where their oscilloscope detected passing ships using a 60-megahertz radio transmission signal. Later, Robert Paige and Robert Guthrie joined the team, leading to further discoveries and refinements of what would become the first shipboard aircraft detection system using radar.

The captain abruptly turned and descended the ladder to the bridge.

"Captain on bridge!" announced the officer of the deck (OOD).

"As you were. Report," commanded Handly.

"We have just completed refueling, and the last load of supplies were just craned into the hold. The crew has been having a field day preparing for our embarkation at 0700 hours tomorrow," said the OOD.

Field days are times of preparation where crew members or swabbies clean and protect the ship from the effects of saltwater. They must scrape any metal surface clean of rust and apply a protective layer of paint to resist the corrosive effects of the salt air. They swab the decks of the ship with saltwater to prevent the growth of fungus on the wooden planks and to keep the planks moist, creating a watertight deck surface. They oil the guns regularly, ensuring smooth operations in the event of a firefight.

"Very well," said the captain. "I will be in my cabin."

Handly moved aft to his quarters, passing the officers' mess. He had much reading to get through before they embarked in the morning. He felt honored that command had chosen his ship for the first testing of the top-secret radar system. His crew did not know the exact nature of the equipment being installed, but scuttlebutt had mostly nailed what they would test over the next week. He had a capable crew, and he knew they would perform their duties with distinction.

4. CAMBRIDGE, MASSACHUSETTS

Dr. Alfred Loomis stared in horror at the headlines of his morning paper.

BRITAIN, FRANCE, AUSTRALIA AND NEW ZEALAND
DECLARE WAR ON GERMANY.

"I thought we had saved the world after the great war," he said out loud to no one in particular.

Loomis had served in World War I, where he rose to the rank of lieutenant colonel, inventing the first instrument that could gauge the velocity of artillery shells. Following the war, he became a preeminent investment banker specializing in public utilities. Using the wealth he gained through shrewd investments during the stock market crash, he funded research in microwave and radar technology.

Loomis knew of Britain's research on using radio waves to detect planes coming from Germany, as he had been to England the previous year to meet the scientists working on radar and see the Chain Home network for himself. The Chain Home RDF network was the culmination of the Watson-Watt and Wilkins' research; it was a network of RDF towers stretching from the Shetland Islands in the north to South Hampton in the south. With war breaking out in Europe, he knew his research at Massachusetts Institute of Technology (MIT) would be crucial in keeping the United States safe and out of the war.

The phone rang, jarring him away from his horror.

"Hello. Loomis here," said Alfred.

"Loomis, Henry Stimson here in DC," Stimson said in great haste. Stimson had just returned to government service to lead the war department. "Listen, I need you down here in Washington in two days for an important meeting. I cannot tell you the nature of the meeting right now, but it is vital you are here by Wednesday. Can I count on you?" Stimson asked.

"Of course, Henry! I will make plans to be in Washington, as you have requested. See you in two days. Goodbye," Alfred said.

Alfred wondered if this could have anything to do with the network of RDF towers he had seen in England the previous year. Time would tell.

Built between 1917 and 1918, and having opened on November 23, 1918, just days after the signing of the armistice with Germany, the Wardman Park Hotel was about three miles from the White House. The hotel was expanded in 1928 to include an eight-story structure known as the Wardman Tower, or the annex as people called it. Wardman had hired Mihran Mesrobian to design the annex, one of his top architects. Shaped like a twisted hub-and-spoke wheel, the annex provided each guest an exquisite view of Rock Creek Park and became a DC landmark because of its prime location at the corner of Connecticut Ave and Woodley Road.

Alfred entered the hotel.

Decorated in the Adamesque style, an obelisk sat in the center of the lobby under an impressive rotunda dome with an elegant periwinkle blue ceiling. As he moved to his right, the staff ushered him into an interior hallway lined with arched windows on each side of the mahogany-paneled walls. At the entrance to the designated meeting hall, a large marine corporal with a side arm challenged him for his credentials.

"Alfred Loomis from Cambridge," Loomis said. He provided his credentials, and entered an enormous room with four tables arranged to create a box. Directly above the center of the room was a dome inset into the ceiling clad in what appeared to be a gold leaf. Already seated was Vannevar Bush, head of the National Research Defense Committee (NRDC) and the man who had asked him to lead the Microwave Committee.

"Dr. Loomis, I want you to meet Henry Tizard and Dr. Edward George Bowen," Bush said, motioning to each man.

"Taffy. My friends call me Taffy, Dr. Loomis," Bowen said, shaking Alfred's hand.

"So good to meet you, Dr. Loomis," Tizard said. "I think you will find what we have to share of great value to us both."

The remaining introductions completed, the men took their assigned chairs.

Bush spoke. "Gentlemen, with war breaking out in Europe," he began, "Winston Churchill requested that this delegation from England come to the United States to meet with us. Let me remind our English delegation, our country is in no position to take sides in this conflict, but we in this room are very concerned about your predicament. Mr. Tizard, the meeting is yours."

Henry Tizard arose and began a monologue he had been writing since he had met with Churchill seven days earlier. He explained the dire position Britain was in, and summarized the work performed by Watson-Watt and Wilkins in the previous years.

"Through the work of Watson-Watt and Wilkins, we have created a network of RDF towers capable of detecting German aircraft assembling over France at a distance of fifty kilometers. We call it our Chain Home network. This network is unlike anything in the world," Tizard claimed.

"Well, Mr. Tizard, we just completed a shipboard test of our own on one of our destroyers using microwave radar and had similar success detecting and tracking airplanes," Loomis said.

"Alfred," Bush stated evenly, "we must be fully transparent here. We are to share completely with our British friends our successes *and* our shortcomings."

"Ok," said Alfred. "We *could* detect a plane, but we are struggling to gain enough power in our system to reach over twenty kilometers," admitted Loomis.

"Perhaps we can assist," stated Tizard.

Tizard reached for a nondescript metal box that looked like it had been used for decades to carry important papers while traveling. Opening the box, Henry Tizard took out a device and held it up for all to see.

"Gentlemen, I believe this device could save Britain from total annihilation," announced Tizard.

Tizard spent the next twenty minutes describing the device, including technical specifications and detailed production drawings.

"Incredible," Alfred said. "This device will transform our shipboard radar installations and give us an immense advantage over our adversaries. Do you think we could make it smaller to fit in a fighter plane or a bomber?" Alfred asked.

“That is the reason we are here, gentlemen,” Tizard said. “Our prime minister believes our two countries should join forces for the betterment of us *both*. Your manufacturing capacity would reduce the time to produce our device by half,” he concluded.

“Alfred,” interrupted Bush, “we need to take our friend’s device and share it with the rest of your team. In fact, we have been kicking around an idea that I would like for you to consider.”

Bush described the new role he wanted Alfred to consider. After another five hours of sharing technology secrets and strategy, the meeting was adjourned, and Bowen accompanied Alfred back to Cambridge, where they had an enormous amount of work ahead of them. Alfred’s mind was spinning with the breakthrough that was just shared with them and what it meant for both of their countries. He was sure his team would be equally excited, and soon the radar used in the United States would rival any the world had ever seen. He knew that Britain needed the United States, but he was just as sure they would be indebted to Britain for this extraordinary gift for many years to come.

5. TOKYO, JAPAN

Admiral Isoroku Yamamoto looked blankly at the blooming cherry blossom trees outside his office. He wondered if the political changes in his country would lead Japan into war with the United States.

Yamamoto found a voice in the naval establishment and had been a proponent of the war with China. This had made him many enemies, and a fair number of assassinations had been attempted over the years. Yamamoto took all of this stoically and commented to a friend that it would be the highest honor to die for his emperor and the empire.

Preparing for war with the United States would not be an effortless task given the raw industrial power they possess. We would be wise not to underestimate this adversary, thought Yamamoto. But he knew there could be a way to dispose of this foe in one quick, decisive blow. The United States had been sparring with Japan for years in the Pacific Ocean, and many of his contemporaries and other politicians wanted a strategy to engage, even to stalemate, this foe so the empire could realize its expansion plans in the Pacific Ocean.

A knock at the door interrupted his thoughts.

"The Supreme War Council (*Gunji Sangiin*) is ready for you," said his assistant.

The War Council had been renamed to the Imperial General Headquarters-Government Liaison Conference (*Daihon'ei seifu renraku kaigi*) three years before, but his staff still referred to it as the War Council. Yamamoto contemplated if he should share the plan he had devised over the past month with the council. "I am ready," Yamamoto said.

"Hai," responded his assistant.

Moments later, he entered the room, and the council stood. Ornately ordained with paintings of famous Japanese samurai warriors, the room watched over each meeting.

Prime Minister Hiranuma Kiichiro spoke first. "How are the plans for disposing of the Chinese coming along?" he asked.

Yamamoto stood to address the prime minister. "Sir, our Manchurian offense has borne many fruits, and Shanghai has now fallen. We have moved to cut off China from all outside help by seizing Indochina as we discussed in our last meeting. Soon, Chiang Kai-shek will beg us for a *mujōken kōfuku* (unconditional surrender). I have another matter I wish to bring to the council for consideration," said Yamamoto, taking a deep breath in anticipation of sharing his plan.

"Proceed," said Kiichiro.

"Our *kaisen junbi* (preparation for war) with the United States is fraught with danger, and I would warn the council that these *kichiku Beitei* (bestial American imperialists) are very cagy and we must not engage them in open seas," Yamamoto cautioned knowing this would create great strife in the room.

"What? You, who lead the great Japanese Navy, are afraid of these *kichiku* (demon-creatures)?" admonished Hideki Tojo, Minister of War.

"Not in the least, sir," responded Yamamoto. "Our forces are more than capable of defeating the *kichiku*, but I would suggest that taunting this dragon will only get us burned by its fire. The best way to kill a dragon is to distract it and attack its vulnerable underbelly. The United States has exposed its underbelly to us. Most of their carriers were moved to the harbor at Oahu, Hawaii, and no one would ever consider that Japan would attack them at this safe harbor," Yamamoto concluded.

"How are they vulnerable at this harbor?" enquired Tojo.

Yamamoto prepared to respond, but Tojo cut him off. "They can hear us coming and launch a counteroffensive against our fleet with complete support from their ground forces. This is a foolish idea spoken by a fool," he taunted.

Yamamoto felt the anger burn within him. He knew this plan would work, but he must have Tojo on his side or the council would not allow him to proceed.

"Please let me continue, Tojo-san," Yamamoto said evenly. "I am sure you will see a way to victory through my vision."

Tojo waved his hand motioning him to proceed.

"The key to our success is to make the Americans believe that we are not where they believe us to be. We must use their technology against them," Yamamoto said passionately. He continued to explain his plan, including referring to a detailed map showing how the Japanese fleet would deliver a knock-out blow to the Americans in one attack.

At the conclusion of his presentation, Tojo spoke.

"Yamamoto, perhaps I was too quick to discount your intellect in this matter. I believe we should move forward with this plan. But let me be very clear. The fate of Japan is in your hands, and I will watch every step you take to prepare for this attack. One wrong move, and I will kill you myself," threatened Tojo.

"Hai! Thank you to the council for your consideration of this plan," said Yamamoto.

Within minutes of adjournment, Yamamoto was back in his office. "Get me Onishi," he demanded.

"He is on the line," said his assistant a few moments later.

"Onishi, we have success with the council! They have accepted our plan. We must begin quickly to put our deception in place so it will confuse the Americans," said Yamamoto.

"Hai! I will begin as you command," Onishi said.

"How much time do we need before we can attack?" Yamamoto asked.

"I believe we can be ready by the end of the year," Onishi said confidently.

"Very well. The fate of the empire is in our hands. We cannot fail!" reminded Yamamoto.

"Hai! This plan will work as designed; the Americans will not know what hit them! They will beg us for *mujōken kōfuku*," predicted Onishi.

"They better! Your life is at stake here. Any mistake and you know what you must do," warned Yamamoto.

The Japanese culture had for years worshiped their warrior class. With that worship came substantial wealth and respect, despite the meager life most Japanese experienced. In the past, people feared and respected the samurai above all others.

They were fierce warriors, but they also followed a strict honor code allowing no failure or surrender. If a warrior broke this code, they expected him to commit *harakiri* or disembowelment by sword. This would be the only way to atone for his mistakes with honor. Yamamoto and Onishi knew this would be their fate should they fail.

6. WASHINGTON, DC

Franklin D. Roosevelt sat in the Oval Office awaiting Secretary of State Cordell Hull, a man who had served him and the country since he took office in 1933.

"Good morning, Mr. President," said Hull as he closed the door.

"Please sit down," Roosevelt said. He did not get up from behind his desk. "I am troubled by the lack of movement on an agreement with Japan," he said with some amount of dread.

"I just received a cable from Prime Minister Kiichiro. Japan will not budge. I believe we have no other choice but to go forward with the oil embargo," said Hull, warily.

Japan had limited natural resources and relied on trading partners for many of the raw materials needed to continue their offensives. This was the primary reason for the war with China: abundant natural resources and people they could enslave to serve the emperor. As the United States was flush with oil, an embargo on Japan would send a powerful message that their actions would be met with equally strong consequences.

Roosevelt pondered this for a moment. "We cannot afford to let this go on. We must stand firm, or Japan will begin its conquest of our territories in the Pacific. Hitler and the emperor share many dreams."

"Mr. President," Hull said evenly, "I would suggest it is the military commanders who are pushing this expansion. The Japanese people worship their emperor as a god, but our intelligence suggests he is not the driving force behind the Indo-China war or the threatening posture they have taken with us in the South Pacific."

"Very well then," said Roosevelt. "Proceed!"

Within the hour, Hull summoned the ambassador of Japan to his office at the State Department.

"Mr. Ambassador, thank you for coming on such brief notice," said Hull as he prepared to escalate the growing disagreement with Japan.

"I am always happy to discuss the concerns of your president," said Ambassador Kichisaburō Nomura coyly.

Nomura had risen to the rank of full admiral in the Imperial Japanese Navy, which had afforded him a seat on the War Council. After his retirement from the Navy, the emperor appointed him to his first foreign diplomatic post in Washington, DC.

"Mr. Ambassador, I am concerned by the posture your country is taking in the South Pacific. If you continue this provocation, it will only escalate to a level that neither of our countries will easily recover from," Hull admonished.

"Mr. Secretary, my country is not provoking the United States. Why would we entertain another conflict when we have our hands full defeating the Chinese?" Nomura retorted.

"Mr. Ambassador, I assure you, the US is not interested in escalating our disagreements with Japan. But your aggressive actions in China and Indochina cause us significant concern. I must inform you that the United States will impose an oil embargo on Japan immediately, hoping Japan will temper its aggression in the region," Hull concluded.

"Cordell, we will not receive this news well in my country. I fear that this will further escalate our disagreements and possibly push us to war. I am sure you and your president do not want that," Nomura warned.

"Mr. Nomura," chided Hull, "we are only responding to the actions of your country. We are not interested in a conflict with Japan, but we also will not allow your country to threaten our territory or push us out of the region. Just five days ago, one of your destroyers came dangerously close to our fleet in international waters in what we deem an aggressive act against our country. So, it is your country who is escalating. We are merely responding."

"Cordell, I will deliver this message to my government, but I would hope that we can continue this dialogue in hopes of an agreement," Nomura offered. He was playing chess with Secretary of State Hull. He had been briefed of a potential plan to eliminate the Americans from the region without having to go to war; unfortunately, he did not know the specifics, nor did he believe his government would share them with him.

"Of course, Mr. Ambassador, we can meet any time to avert a shooting war between our two countries. We have many shared interests, and conflict can only cause both of our countries untold loss of treasure and people," Hull said evenly. "Good day, Mr. Ambassador."

"Good day, Mr. Secretary." Nomura stood and went to the door. As he opened it, he turned and said, "I hope your response does not push my government into drastic actions we will both regret."

"Goodbye, Mr. Ambassador!" Hull said tersely.

After the door closed, Hull summoned his assistant.

"Yes, sir?" she said.

"I need to see the president, now!" Hull said, greatly annoyed.

"I will take care of this right away, sir," she said.

. . . . .

"It works. By God it works!" Alfred announced to his team after reviewing the work of the joint English-American engineering team.

His team cheered.

"This new magnetron from Tizard will give us the technical edge we need should the war in Europe spill onto our shores, God forbid," Alfred said ominously.

The exuberance of the moment faded.

"With the proving of the technology, it is now time to meet with our commercial suppliers. Your efforts, men, will save Britain from annihilation and protect our shores from attack!" announced Loomis.

7. OAHU, HAWAII

The Army Signal Corps established the aircraft warning service (AWS) to protect American territories, including Hawaii, from surprise attacks. The installation uses a portable SCR-270 radar, created at the Signal Corps Laboratories in Monmouth, New Jersey. Known as the first long-range radar systems deployed by the United States to protect its territories, the United States deployed the AWS on Oahu prior to the mission by Tizard.

They deployed the SCR-270Bs on the north shore (Haleiwa)—on the northern tip of Opana Point —at Mount Kaala on the northwest side—and at Koko Head in the southeast, creating a ring around the island. The installation provided a radar ring of 150 miles around Oahu, with the Opana Point system having an unencumbered view of the Pacific Ocean.

. . . . .

"We are prepared to begin the deception, Admiral Yamamoto," said Onishi.

"We have kept this from the captains of our ships, correct?" questioned Yamamoto.

"There are only three people aware of your plan," reminded Onishi. He had concern that this reminder would raise the anger of Yamamoto.

Yamamoto had convinced the Supreme War Council to change Japan's long-standing defensive military posture to an offensive posture. He hoped that the United States and Britain would not detect this monumental shift in military policy. Yamamoto then concentrated Japan's core air power into a single tactical formation, the *Kido Butai*, something never done in military world history. No country could now match Japan's ability to project power in the region, and he knew the Americans would be ready to beg for *mujōken kōfuku*. For Yamamoto's plan to succeed, he would have to make the enemy believe that the Imperial Navy was staying close to its territorial waters, while the *Kido Butai* moved to attack Pearl Harbor.

While completing the final preparations for the surprise attack on Pearl Harbor, Yamamoto knew that total operations security (OPSEC) was imperative, and that he would need to leverage the Post, Telegraph, and Telephone (PT&T) Ministry, radio intelligence using RDF, and human intelligence assets in Hawaii to sow the seeds of deception in the West. The most difficult tactical problem to solve was avoiding the detection of his fleet by enemies of the Imperial Japanese Navy when they leave Japanese territorial waters. The American and British radar systems kept track of the movements of the Japanese Navy by intercepting and decoding radio transmissions from ships, official diplomatic communications, and through newly deployed radar installations around the South Pacific.

"Recently, the British listening post in Hong Kong detected our fleet movements and our leadership is concerned this detection may compromise our attack strategy on Oahu," Yamamoto said. "Our deception must be effective, or we will fail."

Onishi shook his head in agreement.

"We must use the *kichiku* eyes and ears against them. Make them believe we are somewhere we are not," concluded Yamamoto. "They must believe we are still in our defensive military posture, not offensive as we have become."

"May I share these plans with our captains so the deception can begin?" asked Onishi.

"Yes," responded Yamamoto, "but you must speak to each captain alone and in person. We do not want to jeopardize this plan by sending written or radio communications. The code name of this operation will be Dragon Fire."

Yamamoto dismissed Onishi and began reviewing his maps to determine the safest route to Tankan Bay.

• • • • •

Henry Simpson entered the Oval Office to provide his daily briefing to the president.

“Good morning, Mr. President, Mr. Vice President.” Stimson was still standing, waiting for Roosevelt’s aid to help him to the chair facing the sofa. The room cleared, leaving Stimpson and Vice President Wallace on the sofa.

“Good morning, Henry. Please sit down,” the president said warmly. “What is new with Japan?”

“Sir, the Japanese are preparing for training exercises in their home waters. Our COMINT folks,” said Simpson referring to the communications intelligence department, “just decoded a message from Tokyo to Ambassador Numara. The letter shows that they are preparing for an exercise to test communications protocols,” Stimson concluded.

“Should there be concern?” the president asked.

“No, sir,” Stimson assured. “From what we can decipher, this is a routine exercise and may last a month or two. We will continue to monitor the exercises closely.”

“How about checking with our British friends?” Roosevelt suggested. “Perhaps they can monitor Japan’s progress and share what they find.”

“Already working on that, sir,” reported Stimpson. “Our team in Singapore and the British listening post in Hong Kong should give us independent data that we can use to verify the Japanese are just having military exercises. Our folks in Hawaii are listening.”

“I do not trust the Japanese,” warned Roosevelt. “We know them to rely on surprise to gain the upper hand. Now that the oil embargo of Japan is fully out in the open, we must observe them cautiously.”

“I fully agree, sir,” assured Stimson. “Our communications people are the best in the world, and now that we can decrypt any message sent to the ambassador, we *will* have the upper hand.”

“How is the present the British gave us working out?” the president inquired.

“Loomis and his team are working on integrating the new cavity magnetron unit into the CXAM sets. The expectation is that our carriers will increase our detection range to one hundred nautical miles from the fifteen nautical miles in previous sets. Mr. Tizard and his team gave us a significant advantage over any adversaries,” said Stimson.

"I hope and pray we will not have to use our radar to protect ourselves, but I fear we have cast our dye in this matter," said the president ominously. "Anything else, Henry?"

"No, sir. Thank you for your time this morning. Give my best to your wife, sir, Mr. Vice President. Good day to you both." Stimson withdrew from the Oval Office.

"What do you think, Henry?" asked the president.

"I agree with you, sir. We should not trust the Japanese; they are crafty bastards," Wallace fired.

"Time is ticking before they thrust us into this conflict, one way or another," warned Roosevelt.

. . . . .

"I have been monitoring the communications of the Japanese fleet, sir," said a petty officer at COMINT. "All I have heard is regular operational training communications with other ships in the fleet."

"Very well then," said the lieutenant, "I will take this report to the captain."

The message quickly rose through the chain of command as the president ordered regular reports on the Japanese fleet and its movements. Admiral Husband E. Kimmel had recently accepted the promotion to commander-in-chief of the United States Fleet (CINCUS) and commander-in-chief of the United States Pacific Fleet (CINCPACFLT) after the forced resignation of James O. Richardson. The previous year, President Roosevelt had moved the fleet to Pearl Harbor as a deterrent to the Japanese without consulting his military leaders. Richardson believed the Navy and country lacked preparedness for war with Japan, and placing the fleet in such a forward position was dangerous and asking for a surprise attack. Instead of being promoted after voicing his concerns, Roosevelt fired him.

Admiral Kimmel read the communications report.

"Just as we expected," said Kimmel. "The Japs should be busy for the next few months. This is the confirmation that shows the fleet is moving forward with the training exercises. I will have to send that bottle of rum to the team in Singapore."

• • • • •

The MIT campus in Cambridge housed the Rad Lab, or the radiation laboratory. They named it so to make people believe that it conducted nuclear research and not research in radar. They appointed Alfred Loomis the director of the lab in December 1940. Taffy Bowen was staying in the United States to help integrate the cavity magnetron into the existing US technology assets. Alfred Loomis entered the lab to speak to his team.

"Gentlemen," Alfred began, "we have an enormous challenge in front of us. The Japanese have been working on radar for years, just as we have, but it does not appear to be as far along. You have been handpicked to work in this top-secret environment, and I must warn you that everything you see, do, or say here *must* stay within these walls. Our challenge is monumental, but through the gift of the cavity magnetron from our British allies, we will not fail. Let me introduce Mr. Taffy Bowen, who has graciously offered to stay around for a while to help us get up and running."

All in attendance applauded.

"Thank you, my Yank friends," said Taffy Bowen. "Our primary focus will be the development of new radar systems based on microwave technologies. Your country has made significant strides in VHF and UHF radar technologies, but power requirements have hampered your system's usefulness to our warriors in the field. That is where our cavity magnetron has made an immense difference in your power output."

Bowen explained the design and inner workings of the cavity magnetron and how it would win the war for the Western alliance.

Invented in 1910 by H. Gerdien, John Randall and Harry Boot enhanced the device the British shared with the US. Previous versions of a cavity magnetron only produced 300 Watts at 3 gigahertz over a 10-centimeter wavelength. The British device produced multi-kilowatt pulses over a 10-centimeter wavelength. Not only was the British cavity magnetron more powerful, it was also much smaller, allowing the allies to create radar for airplanes and smaller ships. Because of the higher power pulses from the new device, short-wavelength radar was now possible, which translated to detection of smaller objects at further distances.

"Wow!" said one of the scientists working on the original CXAM radar system deployed on the USS New York. "This will increase the range we can detect ships to maybe seventy-five miles!"

"I believe we can make one hundred miles, old chap," Bowen said with a wry grin.

During the rest of the meeting, Alfred made assignments of projects to his teams, and the race to save the Western world from tyranny began.

. . . . .

"Mr. Ambassador, what is the word from your country?" Hull asked.

"My leadership is not pleased with the position taken by your government, but they have instructed me to discuss acceptable actions Japan could take to de-escalate this matter," Ambassador Nomura said. The real instruction from his superiors was to make the United States believe that Japan would negotiate in good faith, but they instructed him to ensure that he dragged the negotiations on for months—they were very specific, months. He consciously instructed his face to not show what he was thinking.

"This is delightful news, Mr. Ambassador," said Hull. *Why the change in posture? What does Japan really want here?* he wondered.

"Here is what the United States needs your country to do moving forward . . ." instructed Hull.

8. TANKAN BAY

"Report," demanded Admiral Yamamoto.

"We will arrive at the assembly coordinates in Tankan Bay within the hour," said the OOD.

Tankan Bay is part of the Kiril Islands to the north of Japan. Yamamoto chose Tankan Bay as the assembly point of the *Kido Butai* as it was sparsely populated, providing adequate cover for the training and last preparations for the attack. The *Kido Butai* was organized as follows:

1st Carrier Division		
Carriers:	Akagi*	Kaga
1st Strike Planes:	9 Zeros, 15 B5N, 12 B5N w/torpedo	9 Zeros, 14 B5N, 12 B5N w/torpedo
2nd Strike planes:	9 Zero, 18 D3A	9 Zero, 26 D3A

Destroyer Division 7: Akebono, Ushio

* Flag Ship

2nd Carrier Division		
Carriers:	Soryu	Hiryu
1st Strike Planes:	8 Zeros, 10 B5N, 8 B5N w/torpedo	6 Zeros, 10 B5N, 8 B5N w/torpedo
2nd Strike planes:	8 Zero, 17 D3A	8 Zero, 17 D3A

Destroyer Division 23: Kikuzuki, Uzuki

4th Carrier Division		
Carriers:	Ryuji	Taiyo
1st Strike Planes:	16 Zeros, 18 B5N	16 Zeros, 18 B5N

Destroyer Division 3: Shiokaze, Hokaze

5th Carrier Division		
Carriers:	Shkaku	Zuikaku
1st Strike Planes:	**6** Zeros, **26** D3A	**5** Zeros, **25** D3A
2nd Strike planes:	**27** B5N	**27** B5N

Submarines: I-16, I-18, I-20, I-22, I-24

The IJN Akagi was the flagship of the *Kido Butai* and the home of Admiral Yamamoto. Named after Mount Akagi, a dormant stratovolcano rising above the northern end of the Kanto Plain, the ship was originally a battlecruiser and then retrofitted into an aircraft carrier in April 1925. She was 855 feet long and could carry sixty-six aircraft, twenty-one Mitsubishi A6M Zeros, eighteen Aichi D3As, and twenty-seven Nakajima B5Ns bombers. Driven by four Kampon-geared steam turbines, she had a range of 1000 nautical miles and a maximum speed of 31.5 knots. The main flight deck was 624 feet long and 100 feet wide, but the middle flight deck was only 49 feet long, preventing usage by even lightly loaded aircraft. Admiral Yamamoto knew this could cause concerns should the Americans survive long enough to mount a counteroffensive.

"Has the *Kido Butai* followed the radio communications plan I outlined?" asked the admiral.

"Hai!" responded the OOD. "Each ship has been following the communications script exactly."

"Very well. I want to see Onishi in my stateroom immediately," demanded Yamamoto.

"Hai!" the OOD responded.

Moments after the admiral arrived at his stateroom, Onishi knocked on the door.

"Enter," said Yamamoto.

"I am preparing the briefing room for your final meeting with the flag officers," said Onishi. "We will begin at 0830 hours per your orders."

Yamamoto prepared to divulge the rest of his plan to his flag officers. After the briefing, Yamamoto returned to the bridge.

"Final training exercises are now underway, sir," announced the OOD.

The first wave of Mitsubishi A6M or Zeros launched from the carriers, and assembled at their attack coordinates. The Zero was a long-range fighter of the IJN and had a lethal reputation in a dogfight. With a crew of one, the Zero could attain a maximum speed of 331 mph and a maximum range of 1,162 miles. They provided aerial cover for the B5N bombers. The next wave to leave the flight deck were the B5N bombers loaded with bombs and torpedoes. The Nakajima B5N was the standard carrier-based bomber of the IJN fleet. With a crew of three, the B5N could attain a maximum speed of 238 mph and a range of 608 miles, and could carry up to two 500-pound bombs. The second attack wave of Zeros launched from the flight deck along with the Aichi D3A Type 99 Carrier Bomber. With a crew of two, the D3A had a range of 840 miles and a maximum speed of 267 mph. The plane could carry up to two 130-pound bombs and had two forward-firing machine guns.

The first strike planes lined up on their target and began their bombing runs. They simulated releasing their bombs with exacting precision, maximizing their deadly potential. Immediately after the first strike, the second strike hit their virtual targets with the same deadly precision.

"Training exercise complete, admiral," announced the OOD.

"We are ready. Operation Dragon Fire is ready. We set sail tonight," ordered the admiral.

. . . . .

Takeo Yoshikawa watched from his perch on the Aiea Heights overlooking Pearl Harbor, on the island of Ohau. Japan had sent Yoshikawa to observe the movements of the newly arrived Pacific Fleet. As he surveyed the harbor, he divided the harbor into quadrants to make the intelligence he would gather more useful to Yamamoto and the *Kido Butai*. Area A would include the waters between Ford Island and the Arsenal. Area B would include the waters next to the Island south and west of Ford Island, the opposite side of the Island from Area A. Area C would include the East Loch with the Middle Loch in Area D and the West Loch in Area E. As he observed, he made a note of the comings and goings of the American fleet, noting specific ships and their anchorages. His work was vital to the success of Japan, and he knew he must not fail.

Yoshikawa looked at his watch and hailed a taxi. After a brief ride, he arrived at a nearby teahouse where he had supper and enjoyed time with the local geishas. As the teahouse also overlooked Pearl Harbor, he could continue his surveillance late into the night without being noticed by the locals. It was imperative that he performed his spying within the boundaries of American law as to not draw undue attention to himself or his mission. If the Americans discovered him, Yamamoto's plan would quickly degrade from a surprise attack to a slaughter, the likes of which the Japanese people had never seen.

. . . . .

The *Kido Butai* moved undetected for two weeks, taking a northerly route through the cold North Pacific far away from shipping lanes.

"Admiral, we have a contact about twelve nautical miles from the *Kido Butai*," announced the OOD. "Requesting your presence on the bridge."

Moments later, Admiral Yamamoto entered the bridge.

"Contact holding steady twelve nautical miles traveling a parallel course with the *Kido Butai*," reported the OOD.

"Does it appear that the vessel is aware of our presence?" asked Yamamoto.

"No, sir," replied the OOD. "I am sure that they would not be aware of our presence, but we will continue to monitor the vessel for changes in course or speed."

"Do we have any idea what kind of vessel it is?" asked Yamamoto.

"We have been monitoring radio communications, and it appears to be a shipping vessel from the United States," said the OOD.

"I order its immediate destruction using the I-16 submarine in our battle group," ordered Yamamoto. "This will be the last radio communication. From this point forward, we are under strict COMMSEC per the operational plan. Communicate only using signals for course, speed, and direction of the target."

. . . . .

"Sir, I have been monitoring chatter by the Japanese fleet all morning, but I intercepted a coded transmission and thought you might need to see it," said the radio operator.

"Have this decoded immediately," ordered the lieutenant.

Minutes later, the decoded message appeared.

"BEGIN COMMUNICATIONS TRAINING EXERCISE 7
CONTACT BEARING 45.656, 162.317 heading W NW, TRACK,
AWAIT FURTHER INSTRUCTIONS"

"Let me see a map," ordered the American lieutenant. "This shows their contact is in Japanese territorial waters. They must be in a war game exercise."

It was not a war game, and they were far away from their territorial waters. In fact, the *Kido Butai* was nearly one-third of the way to its target: Pearl Harbor.

The lieutenant went back to catching up on the sports section of his paper and did not report the Japanese communication to his commander.

. . . . .

"Periscope depth," ordered the captain of the I-16, a type C1 submarine of the IJN fleet.

The type C1 was a twin-diesel-powered submarine with electric motor backup capable of cruising up to a maximum range of 14,000 nautical miles at a maximum speed of 23.5 knots and a maximum depth of 100 meters. The submarine had fittings on its top to carry one midget submarine.

"Periscope depth, captain," said the dive officer, "target bearing two one zero degrees, range 1.5 nautical miles."

"Flood tubes 1 and 2. Open outer doors," ordered the captain.

"Doors open. Tubes 1 and 2 flooded, captain," said the warrant officer. "We have a solution plotted and are ready to fire."

The captain of the I-16 listened to the counterfeit training radio communications, which provided the exact location of the American merchant ship that he was to destroy. They had given him a secret order and calculations that he would use in the event Yamamoto required the destruction of a target. The calculations provided in the order placed the American merchant ship well out of the Japanese territorial waters.

"Fire 1, Fire 2!" ordered the captain.

The captain watched as his instruments of death silently stalked their unsuspecting prey through the clear icy water. Suddenly, there was one bright flash, followed almost immediately by another bright flash. Direct hit! The captain watched the American vessel sink after three minutes into its cold, deep grave. He saw no survivors to betray his nation, nor did anyone detect a mayday radio message. The I-16 returned to its cruising depth of 50 fathoms.

"The I-16 reports target destroyed," reported the OOD.

That is one less ship to alert anyone to our presence, thought Yamamoto. Later that week, an Australian merchant vessel reported to maritime authorities some debris in the water, but the report did not get shared with anyone in the United States. Later, the American owner of the Merchant vessel reported to maritime authorities that they had not heard from their ship for a week, and they requested help to locate the vessel. They never found the ship.

9. WASHINGTON, DC

"What the hell do they think they are doing?" yelled President Roosevelt.

"I am as concerned with their response as you are, sir," assured Secretary Hull.

"Our position was apparent," stated the president emphatically. "Withdraw forces from Indochina and we will remove the oil embargo. It is just that simple! Read that response again."

Hull began reading: "The Japanese government acknowledges and thanks the United States for their response asking Japan to remove forces from Indochina and in return America will lift the oil embargo. However, our national interest must supersede this proposal. The Japanese government will provide a more detailed counter proposal within 24 hours."

"Why the delay, Hull?" asked the president. "What are they up to?"

"Damned if I know, sir," stated Hull.

"You call the Japanese ambassador right now and get him the hell over here!" ordered the president.

"Right away, sir," responded Hull.

It was after 8:00 p.m. in Washington, DC, and Hull knew the ambassador was attending an event at the Russian Embassy; Hull's schedule had him attending the event before being summoned to the White House. *I will call the ambassador at home after the event*, thought Hull.

. . . . .

Hadaki watched with great admiration as his *haha* tended to the children. She was always up before everyone in their modest A-frame thatched roof house. His family had lived in the town of Kawaguchico for generations. His forefathers had constructed his home over seventy-five years ago and had been farming their land for over hundred years.

Hadaki was proud of his *minka*, house of the people, and the family history it held. The bamboo posts of his *noka* or farmhouse told a story passed down through the generations through the oldest child. His forefathers had traveled substantial distances to the great bamboo forests of Fuji-san to harvest the bamboo needed to complete their *noka*. It is said that, during their trip, the mythical bamboo cutter met them.

Japanese folklore tells of an elderly bamboo cutter who found a shining stalk of bamboo. When he cut into the stalk, he found an infant the size of his thumb. He brought her home to his wife, and they raised her as their own. Thereafter, each time he cut down a stalk of bamboo, he found a nugget of gold, which eventually made him a very rich man. As his adopted daughter grew to normal size, so too did her beauty. Many princes wished to marry her, but the bamboo cutter created impossible tasks to prevent each suiter from meeting his demands. Finally, the emperor met her and wanted to marry her, but she could not marry him because she was from another world. Those from the other world sent the bamboo cutter the gold he found over the years to take care of his daughter while she, the princess from the moon, was on earth. When it came time for his adopted daughter to return to her birthplace, a group of heavenly beings arrived at the bamboo cutter's house and took her back to live on the moon. Before she left, she wrote a letter apologizing to her adopted parents for leaving them. Upon reading it, her parents felt immense sadness. The emperor also felt sad after reading the letter and knew he did not want to live forever if he could not be with the princess. He asked his servants, "Which mountain is closest to Heaven?" To which one replied, "The Great Mountain of Suruga Province." He instructed them to take the letter from the princess and the elixir of immortality to the top of the majestic mountain and burn them, hoping the princess, now with her people on the moon, would hear his message. It is said that the word *fushi*, meaning immortality, became the name of Japan's most famous mountain: Fuji.

As Hadaki's forefathers harvested their bamboo on Mount Fuji, the bamboo cutter spoke a blessing over them saying, "Your family will be strong and bring great honor to the emperor. You will have many children who will honor you and your memory, and all will know your family name."

Hadaki remembered these words as he looked up at the structure of his *noka*, strong as the forests of Mount Fuji. He knew his *chichi* had brought great honor to his family, but how would he bring honor to the name of his forefathers?

. . . . .

The Park Hill theater had just opened up in March, and Charlie was excited to catch the next episode of "Holt of the Secret Service." Although intended for adults, Charlie had seen the first chapter "Chaotic Creek" just after the theater opened. He was hooked. If he had the $.25 for admission, he always sat in the balcony on the first row eating M&M's plain chocolate candies from a bag he bought at Holbert's Candy Store. Holt was such an exciting serial, the best he had ever seen. It starred Jack Holt, who played himself as a secret service agent chasing a murderous gang of counterfeiters led by their ruthless leader Lucky. Lucky and his crew kidnapped the best engraver in the United States, John Severn, and Jack plotted to infiltrate the gang and bring them to justice. He could not wait for the next chapter, "Escape to Peril."

"Charles," said a female voice, startling him out of his thoughts. "Your father will not want another call from Mr. Fox telling him you snuck into the theater again," said Mrs. Henderson, the theater manager.

"Yes, ma'am," said Charlie sheepishly. "Please do not tell my dad again. What can I do for work to help pay for my ticket so I can stay?" asked Charlie.

"Well, I suppose I could have you clean the entire theater again," said Mrs. Henderson. This was a regular punishment for Charlie, and he did not mind it one bit.

"Deal," said Charlie. "Want an M&M?"

"No," she said forcefully, "and stop bringing those candies into my theater! I am losing so much money because of you."

Mrs. Henderson had grown to love Charlie as her own son. Shortly after Charlie's mom died, he began sneaking into the Capitol Theater and then to her theater. Charles Senior needed to be travelling most of the time, meaning Charlie did not have anyone at home to watch out for him. She knew Mary from church and swore that she would look out for little Charlie after she died.

"Yes, ma'am," said Charlie, "I will clean this up right up after I'm done watching Jack Holt; he's the killer diller!"

"Enjoy the serial, Charles," said Mrs. Henderson.

The lights dimmed. Now he would watch the newsreel. Charlie stared in awe as the narrator described the meeting between Winston Churchill and President Roosevelt on the battleship Augusta. He felt pride swelling up inside of him that his country was supporting the British like this. Charlie worried if the United States could stay out of the war with Germany. He remembered his uncle and how he died during the World War in Germany, and he knew he did not want to have to fight in Germany. Charles Senior stated on multiple occasions that their family had already sacrificed for those people in Europe, and they had no more to give.

Charlie knew his dad was right, but he still felt a tingle down his spine as he saw the men on the Augusta. He was only sixteen and had much more time before he would have to decide what he would do with himself after high school.

The newsreel completed, and then the serial began. Charlie could imagine himself fighting the forces of evil, just like Jack Holt. Perhaps he would work for the government, where he might be a secret agent like Jack. Charlie settled back into his seat and reached for another handful of M&Ms.

. . . . .

Admiral Yamamoto surveyed the maps strewn before him and reviewed the battle plan he had so painstakingly prepared months before.

"Sir, the latest weather report from our spy in Honolulu," reported the ensign. "Clouds mostly over the mountains. Visibility is good."

Yamamoto read over the rest of the report. "Excellent!" he exclaimed. "The attack will go forward in the morning. Deploy the midget submarines. Complete preparations of our planes and briefing of the crews."

They sent the order to the submarines I-16, I-18, I-19, I-20, and I-22 to deploy their midget submarines to their appointed attack coordinates. Yamamoto assigned each aircraft carrier a midget submarine to provide stealth lethality and protection. The type A *Ko-hyoteki* were 78.5 feet long and 6.1 feet at its beam. They carried two

17.7-inch Type 93 torpedoes and could attain a maximum depth of 330 feet. At a maximum speed of 25 knots, the two-man midget submarines would arrive just before sunrise. Even though the midget submarines had a hull number, the Japanese referred to their midget submarines using the mother submarine that carried it.

• • • • •

"Ambassador Hull here," said Hull.

"Yes, Mr. Secretary," said Nomura.

"We have read your response and my government is not at all pleased. We view this as a direct rebuke and an escalation to an already tenuous situation," explained Hull.

"I understand your concern, Mr. Secretary, and frankly I had misgivings providing you this response," Nomura said apologetically.

Hull paused before answering. So much was running through his head. *What is the game the Japanese are playing here? Is Nomura genuine in his sympathy for our position? I must be careful with my next response.*

Nomura had just received new orders to prepare to leave the United States for Japan, and his travel plans were well underway. The secure communication had told of the upcoming attack on Pearl Harbor, with explicit instructions to make the Americans believe that Japan would negotiate, and to string them along.

"I believe that my country needs to improve our relationship with the United States," Nomura bluffed. "You have raw material we need for our people, and I am sure I can soften the stance of my prime minister."

"What are you trying to pull here, Mr. Ambassador?" Hull said sarcastically. "First your prime minister all but rebuffs our position that you withdraw from Indochina because it is in your country's best interest, and now you tell me you think you can sway your prime minister to soften his position? I am not buying it, Kichisaburō."

Nomura tried to remain in control of the conversation.

"Level with me and let's see if we can de-escalate this before we both regret the consequences," Hull implored.

"I assure you, Cordell," Nomura lied, "my country does not want war with the United States. Your oil embargo is placing great strain on Japan, and there are those in the cabinet that want to avoid conflict with your country at any cost. Let me communicate with the prime minister and tell him the United States does not want to escalate this disagreement further. Give me time to help him understand that this hard line will only increase the wedge that has grown between us. A peaceful end to this disagreement is in the best interest of both of our countries."

Hull weighed Nomura's statement. "Our position on Indochina is firm, Mr. Ambassador."

"I am fully aware of your country's position, Mr. Secretary," Nomura said with veiled disdain. "We will speak further on this tomorrow morning if that is acceptable to you, Mr. Secretary."

"Good night, Mr. Ambassador," said Hull.

"Good night, Mr. Secretary," Nomura said, and he hung up the phone.

As Nomura was packing his bag to prepare for his departure, he prepared a message for his prime minister:

Americans waiting for counter proposal.

They suspect nothing.

Leaving embassy tonight for Japan.

"Encode this message immediately and send it to Prime Minister Tojo without delay," ordered Nomura.

"Hai!" responded the communications officer.

Nomura quickly completed his packing, and headed for the harbor in Baltimore, where a Japanese cargo ship awaited his arrival. Manned by an elite crew, they had orders to ensure the safe extraction of Ambassador Nomura from the United States.

10. PEARL HARBOR

SUNDAY, DECEMBER 7, 3:42 A.M. HONOLULU TIME

"What the hell is that?" said the OOD of the USS Condor. "Look for me, about 1100, 50 yards ahead off of the port bow."

The Condor, a minesweeping ship, was completing her sweep for underwater ship killers outside of the entrance to Pearl Harbor.

"I believe it is a periscope, sir," said the sailor.

"You better damned sure know about this before we report this up the chain," demanded the OOD.

There had been many false sightings over the past year, and Admiral Kimmel made it known that anyone who thought of waking him better have the entire damned Japanese fleet on his doorstep.

"I am positive, sir," stated the sailor. "It was a periscope."

"Comms, send a flash to the Ward. Tell them about this contact," ordered the OOD.

The Condor sent a blinker message to the destroyer USS Ward, patrolling the area:

SIGHTED SUBMERGED SUBMARINE ON WESTERLY COURSE, SPEED 9 KNOTS.

The signals officer on the Ward acknowledged the blinker message and set an intercept course for the contact.

Midget sub I-20, unaware of their detection by the USS Ward, proceeded on their assigned course and speed, ready to approach the entrance to Pearl Harbor.

6:45 A.M. HONOLULU TIME

"Approaching the contact, sir," reported the OOD. Awaiting your orders."

Captain Outerbridge had only been in command for two days, but he did not hesitate. "Set the first depth charge for 50 feet and the second for 75 feet. Prepare to deploy," ordered the captain. "Prepare to fire on the target on my command!"

Destroyers and planes deploy depth charges to disable or destroy submarines. A direct submarine hit is unnecessary for depth charges to be effective. A properly placed depth charge can damage the watertight compartments of the submarine with catastrophic consequences. The Mark 6 depth charge was twenty-eight inches long and eighteen inches in diameter. The cylindrical-shaped charge held three hundred pounds of TNT and could preset detonation at an optimal depth in the water.

"Depth charges deploy now, now and open fire," ordered the captain.

After thirty seconds, the first charge detonated, causing a plume of water to shoot twenty-five feet in the air. Five seconds later, the second charge detonated, and the submarine turned on its side and sunk to the bottom of the harbor.

"Got 'em!" exclaimed the OOD. Then the gravity of the situation hit every man on the bridge. If there is one so close to the harbor entrance, there must be more.

"Comms, send a message to the 14th Naval Headquarters at Pearl Harbor Naval Air station," ordered the captain.

WE HAVE ATTACKED, FIRED UPON, AND DROPPED DEPTH CHARGES UPON SUBMARINE OPERATING IN DEFENSIVE SEA AREA

7:02 A.M. HONOLULU TIME

As the sun crested the horizon to the west of Opana Point on the northern end of the island of Oahu, two privates were preparing to shut down their SCR-270 radar set after a three-hour duty.

"Contact, uh, I mean a bunch, uh—holy shit that is a huge pattern on the screen!" exclaimed one of them. "Hey, can you look at this?"

The second private looked at the oscilloscope. "Damn, that is huge," he said. "That must be fifty airplanes! We need to call this in."

Just north of Honolulu is Fort Shafter, the hub of the radar network. Twenty minutes later, a new lieutenant to the island finally picked up the phone.

"We have a sighting of fifty airplanes heading toward the island," reported the private. "This is the biggest sighting I have ever seen!"

"Really," said the lieutenant with not much enthusiasm. "You realize that we have a squadron of B17s headed to Hickam," said the lieutenant. "I am sure it is just them. Do not worry about it."

"Roger that, sir," responded the private, and he disconnected the line.

"Guess it is time to get some grub," said the other private. "I cannot wait for some of that fresh pineapple."

The privates left their post, got into their jeep, and sped off to commune with their long-awaited breakfast.

7:32 A.M. HONOLULU TIME

The midget submarine I-18 entered Keehi Lagoon when an overhead anti-submarine warfare (ASW) plane spotted the periscope wake.

"Periscope spotted 1100 low," said the co-pilot.

"Prepare to drop depth charges. Set for seventy-five feet," said the pilot. "I am making my run."

The pilot began his descent and lined the aircraft parallel to the small wake thrown by the periscope. On his mark, two depth charges deployed two seconds apart. The plane pulled up just in time to see the fruits of their efforts. The periscope disappeared as the hull protruded above the waterline, only to begin a rapid descent under the water. The AWS plane circled the area for five minutes looking for survivors. None appeared.

7:40 A.M. HONOLULU TIME

The first wave of 183 dive bombers from the *Kido Butai* were minutes from beginning their bombing runs. Commander Fuchida could plainly see the north shore of Oahu's Kahuku Point. He banked his aircraft to the west and began flying down the northwest coast, preparing for the attack.

"*Tenkai* (take attack position)," ordered the commander. He looked to the left and saw their target, Pearl Harbor. He felt a sense of pride as it appeared—they had arrived undetected. The commander slid back his canopy, grabbed his flare gun, and fired a single black dragon into the air.

The black dragon is a dark blue flare used to signal an air squadron during flight. One flare was to signify readiness for the attack.

"Petty officer, send signal *To, To, To* (to charge)," ordered the commander.

Fuchida looked to his right. Thinking the Zeros had missed the black dragon, he fired a second black dragon.

Unfortunately for his squadron, the leaders of the dive and torpedo bombers saw both flares. Misunderstanding the intended message, all the bombers eased into attack formation.

7:53 A.M. HONOLULU TIME

"Signal the Akagi, *Tora, Tora, Tora*," ordered the commander.

"Message sent and acknowledged, sir," said the petty officer. "We have achieved total surprise!"

World War II was about to begin on American soil.

On the northwest side of Oahu is Wheeler Field, the initial target of the Japanese attack. The bombers lined up on the field and released their deadly cargo. Fifty-four planes were immediately hit, preventing the Americans from waging any counterattack against the Japanese forces. Fuchida watched as his country began an attack, one like none in his command had ever experienced.

On Ford Island in the middle of Pearl Harbor, Commander Logan Ramsey was enjoying his second cup of coffee while surveying the fleet when he saw a low-flying plane headed for Battleship Row from the northeast.

"What does that yahoo think he is doing?" the commander asked with great disdain. "Another stupid fly-by—" He stopped mid-sentence as he saw an object drop from the underside of the airplane. "What the hell!" he exclaimed. "That is a fucking bomb!"

He dropped his coffee and ran to the radio room fifty yards away. As he ran into the radio room, he nearly knocked the radio set off of its table. Out of breath, he ordered the radioman to send out an encoded message to the entire fleet:

"AIR RAID ON PEARL HARBOR THIS IS NOT DRILL"

Commander Fuchida took an over-watch position over the harbor as he watched the attack take shape.

11. BATTLESHIP ROW

Midget submarine I-19 left the task force with a malfunctioning compass and found its way to Oahu just after its partner midget submarines. Unfortunately, as the submarine attempted to enter the harbor, she ran aground on a coral reef. The submarine tried multiple times to free herself but was unsuccessful, and the USS Helm detected her and deployed two depth charges. The charges did not damage the submarine, but it dislodged her from the reef. The shock wave of the exploding depth charges hit the I-19 with such force that the crew became unconscious, damaging the periscope. The I-19 lost power to the submarine, and she drifted around the southern end of Oahu into Waimanalo. When the crew regained consciousness, they saw it was night becoming disoriented. They attempted to beach the submarine, but again, she ran aground. They scuttled the submarine. Only one of the surviving crew could swim to shore where, on December 8, he became the first prisoner of World War II in the Pacific Theater.

With the detailed harbor plans provided by Takeo Yoshikawa, the Japanese pilots were well prepared to attack specific targets in the harbor. Unfortunately for Fuchida and his squadrons, the carriers USS Enterprise, USS Lexington, and the USS Saratoga were out to sea, so the prime targets were spared the fury of the Japanese attack.

Pearl Harbor is a lagoon deep-water harbor of the United States and has been a naval base since 1887 after the ratification of the Reciprocity Agreement of 1875. In past years of the port, it was inaccessible to deep water ships as the entrance to the harbor was too shallow. Dredging provided the depth needed to allow deep water access, and the US Navy built facilities to support its presence in the Pacific. The natural divisions of the harbor have created lochs surrounding Ford Island. To the northeast of the island is East Loch, to the west are Middle Loch and Pearl City, and to the southeast is Southeast Loch, home to the US Fleet Headquarters in the Pacific.

Ford Island sits in the middle of Pearl Harbor and is the home of the Naval Air station. Around the island are the tenders for the US Navy when they are in port. On the northeast side of the island were the moorings of the USS Nevada, followed to the southeast by the USS Arizona and the USS Vestal, with the Arizona on the inside mooring. Next down the island were the USS Tennessee and the USS West Virginia, with the Tennessee on the inside mooring. Next were the USS Maryland and the USS Oklahoma, sitting at the mid-point of the island. Next was the USS Neosho, followed by the USS California and then the USS Avocet. Across the harbor to the southeast was where the USS Shaw was in the dry dock facility along with the USS Downes, USS Cassin, and USS Pennsylvania. Directly to the northeast of the dry docks was the USS Cachalot moored to the pier with the USS Ogala, and the USS Helena to the northeast moored at the same pier. The USS Helena was on the inside mooring.

On the northwest side of Ford Island, moored from northwest to southeast, were the USS Detroit, USS Raleigh, USS Utah, and USS Tangier. The ships moored at the entrance to Middle Loch included the USS Curtiss and USS Medusa. The runway for the Naval Air Station was in the middle of the island, flanked by plane hangars on the island's most southern tip. The fuel and oil storage depot for the harbor sat to the east of Southeast Loch.

7:53 A.M. HONOLULU TIME

"Starting my run," said the strike team leader. "I see no enemy airplanes so we will make sure they never get off the ground."

"*Hai*!" was the response from his team.

The Aichi D3A dive bombers hit the southern tip of Ford Island, destroying most of the planes and hangars on the field.

7:55 A.M. HONOLULU TIME

The sixteen torpedo bombers from the IJN Hiryu and IJN Soryu began their attack runs from the northwest.

"No carriers," the Soryu strike team leader said to his team. "Break off and prepare to engage secondary targets."

Only the leader and wingman broke off the attack. The remaining six torpedo bombers continued their attack run. Mistaking the USS Utah for a capital ship, the remaining bombers engaged their target and eight torpedoes hit the water. Only two struck true and the remaining torpedoes missed the Utah, but one torpedo hit the USS Raleigh.

Chaos ensued as the first torpedoes hit the Utah and the Raleigh. The captains of both ships ordered Damage Control below deck to immediately assess and close watertight compartments to prevent further flooding. Despite a valiant effort by her Damage Control team, the captain of the USS Utah gave the order to abandon ship at 8:02 a.m. By 8:12 a.m., the Utah had capsized, trapping hundreds of men who could not escape the rising waters that would soon be their grave. Shortly after capsizing, rescuers heard knocking sounds from the men who were still alive. After hours of cutting through the hull, they saved only four men. The Raleigh fared much better, and the Damage Control teams could save her from a similar fate.

Rounding the southern end of the island, the strike leader found a worthy target.

"Target straight ahead," declared the Soryu strike leader.

He dropped his torpedo on a direct course to what he thought was a carrier. By the time he realized what he had done, his torpedo went under the keel of the USS Ogala at her stern and hit the USS Helena, damaging both ships. His wingman realized that the target chosen by his leader was not a carrier as they thought, so he moved north to attack Battleship Row.

The strike leader of the eight Hiryu torpedo bombers also realized that there were no carriers, so he rounded the southern end of the island to target Battleship Row, followed by his wingman. Four of the remaining six D3A bombers also attacked the Helena, but all of their ordinances missed their target. The remaining two bombers headed for Battleship Row.

7:57 AM HONOLULU TIME

Because of the unique topography of Pearl Harbor, the torpedo bombers only had one attack path to Battleship Row. Attacking up Southeast Loch, flying in a single file, was the only way to avoid the turbulence created while flying low over the buildings. This limited their targets to those moored in the middle of Ford Island.

Twelve torpedo planes from the Akagi began their run over Southeast Loch. Suddenly the air around the planes lit up with anti-aircraft fire, shaking the bombers. The Americans had recovered from the first attack on Ford Island. All the Akagi planes survived to release their deadly payload into the lagoon below. Two torpedoes hit the USS Oklahoma and two hit the USS West Virginia with devastating effect. One plane banked left toward the USS California. As it released its torpedo, it hit the California in the back third close to her stern.

The four Hiryu torpedo bombers followed the Akagi attack team, dropping their torpedoes on the disabled Oklahoma and West Virginia. With thunderous explosions, the torpedoes struck the flailing ships. Minutes later, the torpedo bombers from the Kaga flew the same course and attacked the Oklahoma and West Virginia, sealing their fate. During the attack run, the remaining Soryu bomber came down upon Battleship Row from the northeast and almost collided with a Kaga airplane. Both pilots skillfully avoided each other, and launched on their targets. The Soryu plane also hit the California, increasing her damage. The Kaga plane banked hard to the right, and released its torpedo on target for the USS Nevada, hitting her amidships. The American forces on the undamaged ships shot five of the last seven D3As down by anti-aircraft fire, saving further damage.

8:03 A.M. HONOLULU TIME

A squadron of B17s scheduled to land at Hickam shortly after 8:00 a.m. approached Pearl Harbor, when they saw Japanese planes attacking the fleet. To reduce the cost of flying to Pearl Harbor, they had taken all offensive armaments off of the planes, leaving them defenseless.

"Pearl is under attack!" exclaimed the squadron leader. "Get these planes the hell down on the ground and away from Pearl!"

The formation peeled off for safer airspace. Some pilots found airstrips where they could safely land, while one pilot landed on the sixth fairway of the Royal Hawaiian Golf Club. Each pilot knew there was no chance of surviving a direct enemy attack without their defenses, and each said a silent prayer of thanks that they could fight another day.

At the conclusion of the torpedo attack, Japanese forces hit the USS Oklahoma five times, capsizing her in just fifteen minutes. They hit the USS West Virginia seven times, but she avoided capsizing because of the quick action of their Damage Control teams. Flooding the lower compartments counterbalanced the water rushing in from the gashes inflicted on her port side, and she gracefully settled to the bottom of the harbor. The USS California was preparing for a fleet inspection when two torpedoes struck her amidships. Because her hatches were open, a devastating flooding ensued, and she sank.

High above Pearl Harbor, the high-level bombers prepared to execute their attack. They were to attack the USS Tennessee, USS Maryland, and the USS Arizona, all moored on the inside next to Ford Island. Five planes in each group formed a "V" as their bombardiers sighted their prey.

"Releasing bomb, lieutenant," said the bombardier.

Each plane in the ten groups had a single 1,760-pound armor-piercing bomb designed to breach the deck of the battleship or cruiser; crashing through many decks, the explosion would destroy the target. Of the forty-nine bombs deployed, only ten hit their intended target, with many breaking up on impact or not exploding at all.

Gunner's Mate Henry Simms awoke from a heavy sleep to the sound of an alarm and the message "General quarters, general quarters. All hands, man your battle stations. This is not a drill" sounding from the hailer aboard the USS Arizona. Even though his crew berthing compartment was deep within the ship and next to the second turret, there was still an expectation for him to be at his battle station in less than three minutes. Having practiced many times before, he had proven to be the most proficient crewman in his section. He could drop from his third level bunk and pull his pants on within thirty seconds, have his shoes on in another fifteen seconds, and be out the door on his way to his station while he pulled on his shirt. He was right on time when he heard and felt a loud explosion forward of his compartment. The explosion caused him to slip a rung on the ladder, and he almost fell fifteen feet below. Just as he regained his footing and began his ascent, he heard another loud metal ping hit the wall to his right. That was the last sound he would ever hear. The second bomb went down the second turret, and the ammunition magazine exploded causing the Arizona to break into two pieces, sinking her to the bottom of the harbor. The ship went down with her 1,177 sailors. The Maryland, Tennessee, West Virginia, and Vestal suffered two bomb hits, causing the captain of the Vestal to beach her to prevent sinking.

8:40 A.M. HONOLULU TIME

The midget submarine I-22 entered the harbor unnoticed during the dive bomber attack. Heading toward Middle Loch at periscope depth, the pilot noticed the USS Curtiss.

"Contact bearing two eight five degrees and is coming about. I think they may have spotted us," said the pilot. "Flood tube 1 and prepare to fire on my command. Come to course two eight five. Fire torpedo!"

As the torpedo left the tube, the submarine shook. The Curtiss, seeing the submarine, made a hard turn to starboard, causing the incoming torpedo to miss to the left of the ship.

Hundred yards away, the USS Monaghan saw the ripple of the periscope and increased speed. "Increase speed to flank and come to course three five seven degrees," said the captain. "We will not let this one get away! Sound the collision alarm. We will ram her!" The captain's orders repeated through the bridge, and the Monaghan quickly closed the distance to the Japanese midget. Just as the Monaghan came within fifty yards, the midget crew fired another torpedo. The captain quickly determined that the torpedo was wildly off target to his port side. He knew his prey was out of torpedoes, and he decided a glancing blow to the hull could probably sink her. Despite the actions of the midget pilot, the Monaghan struck to the port side of midget submarine I-22. To ensure the submarine could not leave the harbor, the captain strategically placed two depth charges. Because of the shallow depth of the harbor and the closeness of the target, the two depth charges exploded with such force that the Monaghan's stern lifted out of the water, causing the ship to lose control.

"All reverse full!" ordered the captain. But it was too late. The USS Monaghan hit a nearby barge. Damage to the Monaghan was minimal, and she got underway quickly. Submarine I-22 was not that lucky. Twenty-five seconds after the second depth charge exploded, the hull breached, and she sank to the bottom of the harbor with her crew.

8:54 A.M. HONOLULU TIME

A second wave of Japanese aircraft—171 of them—approached from the northwest, prepared to concentrate their attack on the carriers, cruisers, and destroyers in port. By this time, the American anti-aircraft fire was so heavy in the air that it was like flying through a field of large shitake mushrooms.

The USS Nevada had escaped its mooring and fled the harbor at 8:40 a.m. As it neared the southern end of Ford Island, two groups of Japanese pilots attacked the Nevada from two directions. The dive bombers hit her nine times, causing massive flooding. To prevent sinking in the middle of the channel and blocking all access to the harbor, the Nevada beached herself on Hospital Point at the Navy Yard just across from the southern end of Ford Island. Despite a valiant effort by the Damage Control teams, the Nevada settled into the shallow area of the harbor.

The California also suffered another hit from a dive bomber. The USS Pennsylvania was in the berth next to the dry dock when nine dive bombers attacked. But she only suffered one hit. Docked forward of the Pennsylvania, the destroyers USS Cassin and USS Downes took the brunt of the bomb attack. Two bombs hit the Cassin and one bomb hit the Downes, heavily damaging both ships.

Most of the remaining bombs missed their targets, but fifteen planes trained their bombs on the USS Shaw, which was in a floating dry dock at the Navy Yard. Three bombs hit her, causing uncontrollable fires. As the dry dock was flooded about half an hour after the attack ended, the forward magazine exploded and ripped the bow off of the Shaw.

Near Middle Loch, the USS Curtiss was trying to get underway. "Captain," shouted a young seaman, "dive bomber attacking!"

The guns of the Curtiss breathed fire and .50 caliber shells attacked the incoming plane.

"Bombs away . . . miss, miss!" reported the seaman.

However, the seaman spoke too soon as the plane lost control and crashed into the bow. As the Damage Control parties fought the raging fire, a bomb hit the Curtis amidships killing nineteen of her crew.

As Fuchida and the planes of the second wave flew back to the *Kido Butai*, he knew Japan had dealt a lethal blow to the American naval fleet. They had done their job, and once again, all would fear the Japanese fleet.

Ninety minutes after the attack began, Pearl Harbor and the US Fleet were in shambles: 2,335 men were dead and 1,178 wounded, 8 ships sank, and 160 planes were destroyed. Japan lost 29 planes and all 5 of the midget submarines. As Yamamoto welcomed back his triumphant warriors, he knew his plan was a total success. He knew it vindicated him, and all of Japan would consider him a glorious hero, even Tojo. As the *Kido Butai* steamed home to Japan, everyone knew that the Imperial Japanese Navy was unmatched by any country in the world. Japan would shape the destinies for all nations, and now, the Americans would bow down to the emperor and sue for peace. Yes, this had been a monumental success.

12. KAWAGUCHIKO, JAPAN

Hadaki stared in awe at the headline on the front page of the *Japan Times*:

WAR IS ON!

Japan's Navy Planes Attack Hawaii, Singapore, Davao, Wake, Guam Isles

He read every word of the story in the paper, and felt great pride swelling within him. He was sure that this must be how his *chichi* felt when he left to fight the Chinese. His family knew what it meant to sacrifice for the emperor, but he wondered how many more families would need to make this sacrifice?

. . . . .

Ed and Charlie left church for the candy store to buy some M&Ms. On the way to the show, Charlie and Ed saw the news in the *Arkansas Gazette*:

HUNDREDS KILLED AS JAPS ATTACK U.S.

The boys immediately said their goodbyes and left for their homes. Charlie's emotions raged through his body as he tried to make sense of this tragedy. *Why would Japan do this to us? My dad tells me we have taken no stand on the war in Europe. We have been neutral on the matter. Will Japan be coming to Arkansas to kill me or my friends?* He rounded the corner and saw his house. As he flung open the door, he saw Doris Ann crying at the kitchen table.

"Our world will never be the same," she said. "I am positive we will declare war on Japan. No one knows how long a war would take. I was just a little girl during the war to end all wars and that went on a long time."

"This is horrible news," said Charlie as he hugged his sister. "Why would they do this to us?"

"I do not know," she sobbed.

"When will Dad be home?" asked Charlie.

"He will be on the 4:10 train from Memphis," Doris Ann said just loud enough. "He will know what we must do; he always does."

The 4:10 from Memphis was right on time, and as the last passengers left the train, Charles Senior jumped off of the last rung of the caboose ladder and headed for his home.

As they all embraced, Charles lingered longer as he hugged his youngest son. He could sense how the day's events traumatized him.

"I am sure all of you heard of the horrific news," said Charles Senior. "We have much to discuss. The president speaks tomorrow to a joint session of congress. We will know more after his speech."

On the drive back to the house, Charles Senior had contemplated how he would approach his son. He was sure Charlie was struggling to cope with news and was scared of how this might impact him in the coming months.

"Charlie," his dad said, "come on over here and tell me how you are doing."

Charlie sat down on the floor next to his dad and said, "I just do not understand why, why they would do this to us. What have we done to them?"

"Charlie, you know how I feel about war. I lost my brother in the trenches of France, and I was bitter for so many years. I could not accept that my family had to give up my brother because Europe could not get along. I swore that I would not lose another member of my family to protect people in another land I have never even seen or ever will!"

"Are you scared I will have to leave for war, Dad?" asked Charlie.

"Yes, son," Charles breathed, "but this is different."

"How?" Charlie asked.

"They attacked us," Charles said evenly, "and we cannot let that go unanswered."

"Will I have to go to war, Dad?" Charlie asked again.

"We will wait to see what the president has to say tomorrow, son."

• • • • •

Secretary of State Cordell Hull walked into the Oval Office ready to work on the speech to congress with the president.

"Good afternoon, Mr. President," said the secretary.

"Afternoon," said Roosevelt. "Let us get right down to it."

"Cordell, have you heard from those bastard Japs?" the president asked with great disdain.

"Yes, sir," said Cordell. "The minute they began the attack, Ambassador Nomura sent me an official communication declaring war on us."

"I am so damned mad I could spit," the president seethed. "You told me that the Japs wanted to negotiate further. How could we have missed this plan?"

"Mr. President," said Secretary of War Henry Stimson, "we had no advanced warning that this attack would take place. Initial word from Hawaii is that we picked up some planes approaching from the north, but it coincided with a scheduled delivery of some B17s from California and our boys there missed the sign."

"All communication with Ambassador Nomura were cordial, and he even apologized to me on the phone last night," said Hull.

"Apologized," the president said tersely, "for what? The upcoming attack on us?"

"No, sir," Hull said evenly. "He was apologizing for the response Tojo made to our demand that the Japanese withdraw from Indochina."

"Hell of a thing," injected Henry Wallace. "Make it look like you're taking the side of your adversary and then get clobbered with a hard right to the jaw. They need to pay."

"I have a rough outline for the speech tomorrow," began Roosevelt. "I plan to avoid the strategic angle as a reason for war, unlike Wilson did when he asked for his declaration."

"I believe that is a mistake, sir," interjected Hull. "The American people need to understand what we did to prevent this act against us."

"Go on," said the president.

"We have taken a very strong stand against the expansionistic policies of the Japanese," stated Hull. "Even the opinion columns in the papers have been on our side."

"That may be true," cajoled the president, "but my American people need a stronger approach to move them to action, to mobilize our great American might to fight."

"What do you have in mind, Mr. President?" asked Stimson.

"I believe that we should use the same framework used after other great American defeats," began Roosevelt, "like the battle of Little Big Horn in 1876 and the sinking of the USS Maine in 1898." The president continued to outline the speech for the next two hours, and then adjourned the meeting.

. . . . .

The next day, every radio in the United States tuned in to listen to President Roosevelt's address to the nation. Charlie and his family waited with great anticipation to hear what the president would say to the joint session of congress.

Roosevelt pushed himself up from his wheelchair and stood with the help of his trusted aids. They escorted him to the podium as the applause roared from both sides of the isle. He surveyed the room, knowing what he was asking for was both just and right for the American people. The chamber quieted. The president spoke.

> *Mr. Vice President, Mr. Speaker, Members of the Senate, and of the House of Representatives:*
>
> *Yesterday, December 7, 1941—a date which will live in infamy—the United States of America was suddenly and deliberately attacked by naval and air forces of the Empire of Japan.*
>
> *The United States was at peace with that nation and, at the solicitation of Japan, was still in conversation with its government and its emperor looking toward the maintenance of peace in the Pacific.*

"Then why would they attack us?" exclaimed Charlie.

"Shhhh!" scolded Doris Ann. "Listen to what the president has to say. We will find out."

Charlie listened intently.

The president continued.

And while this reply stated that it seemed useless to continue the existing diplomatic negotiations, it contained no threat or hint of war or of armed attack.

It will be recorded that the distance to Hawaii from Japan makes it obvious that the attack was deliberately planned many days or even weeks ago. During the intervening time, the Japanese government has deliberately sought to deceive the United States by false statements and expressions of hope for continued peace.

The attack yesterday on the Hawaiian islands has caused severe damage to American naval and military forces. I regret to tell you that very many American lives have been lost. In addition, American ships have been reported torpedoed on the high seas between San Francisco and Honolulu.

Yesterday, the Japanese government also launched an attack against Malaya.

Last night, Japanese forces attacked Hong Kong.

Last night, Japanese forces attacked Guam.

Last night, Japanese forces attacked the Philippine Islands.

Last night, the Japanese attacked Wake Island.

And this morning, the Japanese attacked Midway Island.

An audible gasp came from those listening.

Japan has, therefore, undertaken a surprise offensive extending throughout the Pacific area. The facts of yesterday and today speak for themselves. The people of the United States have already formed their opinions and well understand the implications to the very life and safety of our nation.

As commander-in-chief of the Army and Navy, I have directed that all measures be taken for our defense. But always will our whole nation remember the character of the onslaught against us.

No matter how long it may take us to overcome this premeditated invasion, the American people in their righteous might will win through to absolute victory.

I believe that I interpret the will of the congress and of the people when I assert that we will not only defend ourselves to the uttermost but will make it very certain that this form of treachery shall never again endanger us.

Hostilities exist. There is no blinking at the fact that our people, our territory, and our interests are in grave danger.

With confidence in our armed forces, with the unbounding determination of our people, we will gain the inevitable triumph—so help us God.

I ask that the congress declare that since the unprovoked and dastardly attack by Japan on Sunday, December 7, 1941, a state of war has existed between the United States and the Japanese empire.

Charlie sat spellbound by the speech. His president was addressing him. He felt the stir of a call. He said nothing to anyone else in the room.

13. LITTE ROCK HIGH SCHOOL

Charlie and Ed finished their fourth period class and left for lunch. As they rounded the corner toward the lunchroom, they heard crying and racial epithets voiced softly so the teachers would not hear. They stopped.

"Hey, John," greeted Charlie.

John Grayson was the son of the local butcher and was also the quarterback on the football team. His team and classmates revered him. The team had floundered since they won the state championship in 1938, but everyone believed that John could bring them back to a championship this year.

"Hi, Charlie, Ed," said John. "Can you believe what the Japs did to us?"

"I am in shock and really having a hard time coming to grips with what this means," Charlie confessed. "I do not know what will happen to us; will there be a draft? Will we have to go to war now?"

"I will tell you what I will do, boys," bragged John. "I will not wait for Uncle Sam to ask me to fight; I will volunteer. I have already spoken to my parents about it, and they gave me their blessing." All the girls swooned at this news.

"Wow," said Charlie, "that is a big step. Why are you not waiting six months till you graduate?"

"Nope, my country needs me," concluded John, "and I will not let her down."

Charlie thought for a moment about what he had just heard. Was this what was stirring inside of him? He knew he had to do something. He could not just let the Japs hit them hard and not respond. How would his dad react if he were to volunteer?

Charlie spent the rest of the day thinking about it, and quickly made his way home after school.

"Dad, Dad," called Charlie.

"In here, son," responded Charles Senior.

"I need to talk to you," Charlie said sheepishly.

Charles Senior had seen how the events of Pearl Harbor had affected his son. He had seen the same response from his brother before the World War. Service ran deep in his family, and he was sure he knew what his son wanted to talk to him about.

"Come sit next to me," Charles Senior said warmly. "What is on your mind, son?"

"My mind has been going a hundred miles a minute trying to make sense of the attack on Pearl Harbor," Charlie began.

"Son, it is a tragic day for the United States," Charles stated gravely. "Our country will respond, and the Japanese will be sorry they messed with us."

"I have been thinking, Dad," began Charlie. "I was at school today and saw John Sawyer at lunch. He announced to everyone there that he would drop out of school and volunteer to fight. The captain of the football team wants to fight!"

"How does that make you feel, Charlie?" his father asked.

"I have had something stirring inside of me ever since we heard the president speak last night. I need to do something, Dad. I cannot just let what they did to us stand."

"Do you want to enlist, son?" Charles asked warily.

"I am thinking about it, Dad," said Charlie. "I am only sixteen, so I could not enlist until I am seventeen in a few months."

Charles Senior paused before responding, and then began. "I never told you the full story of your uncle Henry," he said. "Shortly after the United States entered the World War, I overheard my brother having a similar discussion with our father. He had some sage advice for him I think you should hear."

"Ok," said Charlie.

"In the good book, in John Chapter 15, it says 'Greater love hath no man than this, that a man lay down his life for his friends'. What you are feeling is the need to serve something greater than yourself. The question you have to answer, having lost your mother and uncle is, are you willing to lay down your life for your country?" Charles asked.

"Before you can make such a decision, your first adult decision," Charles continued, "I want you to pray to God for his gentle nudge on your life. If this is the right decision, you will know it and I will support your decision either way. One other thing to consider, you still need a high school diploma to get a job digging ditches. I really feel it is very important that you finish school before going off to fight in a war."

"Thanks, Dad," Charlie said, and reached across to give his father a hug, something he rarely did. Then he got up and went to his room.

Doris Ann entered the room. "He wants to enlist; I just know it."

"I believe he does, Doris Ann," Charles whispered.

Doris Ann and her father spent the next few hours thinking and reminiscing about Uncle Henry, a man she had only heard about as he died before she was born.

"He has a lot of his uncle in him, Doris Ann," said Charles. "We will see what he is thinking in the morning."

"I am scared, Dad," Doris Ann said, almost in tears.

"I know you are, honey," her father said. "He is almost a man, and I am proud that he is even considering such a sacrifice."

Charles hugged his daughter, and she left to prepare dinner.

. . . . .

Everyone in Kawaguchico was buzzing over the glorious victory Japan had over the evil Americans. The propaganda machine was in full swing with newspapers and flyers posted on every building and every lamp post. The flyers called all to serve the emperor in whatever manner they could. Some would be conscribed into service in the Japanese Navy, much like Yamamoto's father had been. The government expected women and children to work every day in the rice paddies, sew uniforms for the fighting men, or work in the factories to replace the men fighting for the emperor.

Admiral Yamamoto entered the grand hall to prepare for another War Council meeting.

"You have brought great honor to the empire, admiral," said Tojo, newly installed Prime Minister of Japan. "Your attack plan against the Americans worked exactly as you stated. But why did you not destroy their mighty carriers? How could you not have known the carriers were not at Pearl Harbor?"

Yamamoto had expected this question from Tojo and struggled to not allow the fury he felt to show on his face.

"Prime Minister, the spy we had on the island provided excellent intelligence, and we knew the location of all the important targets before we began our attack," Yamamoto said calmly.

"Then how could you not know the carriers were not there?" Tojo retorted sharply. "How did you not know they were on their way to port? Why did you attack on December 7 when the carriers would have been back in port on the 8? Just one more day and we could have destroyed the entire fleet! This mistake may allow the Americans a slim chance of rebuilding, a chance to fight back."

"Prime Minister," began Yamamoto, "I assure you, the Americans are in such disarray that they cannot assemble a fleet in time to stop our expansion in the South Pacific. We have already captured all the important American bases, and we are fortifying the islands on the way to our homeland. We have captured Wake Island and Guam. Before the Americans can mount any resistance, our forces will be impenetrable. Now that we have declared war on Britain, these two soft democracies will not have the stomach to fight for their former territories. Britain already has its hands full with our German friends, so this will leave the Americans alone to fight. And with what? The Americans are too soft, and they lack the courage to mount any significant offensive against us. It will take them at least two years to respond with any serious threat to our fleet. How can they rebuild so many ships we destroyed?"

The prime minister listened closely and allowed Yamamoto the time to let his ego display fully to the other War Council members. If he was right, then the Japanese empire would be the dominant force in all of Asia. If by some slim chance he was wrong about the Americans, his ego and his words would leave him entirely responsible for any dishonor Japan would face.

14. PEARL HARBOR

As the grim task of rebuilding America's navy at Pearl Harbor began, many took stock of the fact that most of the people killed just two days earlier were the enlisted men who had bunked on the ships while in port. Most of the naval officers lived in off-base housing, thus preserving the experienced fighting force the United States would need to battle her way into war with the Japanese.

"Report," demanded Admiral Kimmel.

"Sir," said the vice admiral, "after some initial assessment, our froggies and engineers have determined that we should be able to save the Pennsylvania, Maryland, and Tennessee. However, the Nevada, California, and West Virginia will take considerably more work to bring them shipshape."

"How long before we can use the Pennsylvania, Maryland, and Tennessee?" asked Kimmel.

"Our estimates are within six months," offered the vice admiral.

"Make it three months," barked Kimmel. "How the hell does anyone expect me to fight a war in the Pacific with such a degraded fleet? We *need* these destroyers back here ready to deploy in three months, period!"

"Aye, aye, sir!" responded the vice admiral automatically.

Within three months, engineers raised the USS Pennsylvania, USS Maryland, and USS Tennessee from their watery graves and returned them to Pearl Harbor to join the fleet.

. . . . .

Charlie awoke after a restless night of sleep. He knew his dad was right, but it would be so long until he turned eighteen and forever until he graduated from high school. He threw on a shirt and headed to the kitchen for breakfast.

"Morning, sunshine. Looks like you barely made it out of bed alive," teased his father. "Your decision kept you up last night?"

"Sure did, Dad," Charlie said sleepily.

"Let me know when you want to talk, son," Charles said warmly.

"I will, Dad," Charlie said as he poured his bowl of corn flakes.

"How long do you think the war will go for?" asked Charlie.

"Tough to say, Charlie," his dad said. "The World War took us over four years to beat the Germans, and now we have to fight them again *and* the Japanese. Our boys will need every bit of prayer and all the resources we can give to win *this* war."

"As I was delivering the paper early this morning," Charlie recalled, "I saw a story that mentioned rationing would come back to our country."

"I remember what it was like during the World War and also the Depression," Charles said, his voice fading slightly. "It was tough, real tough, but our country can meet the challenge. Your sister has been canning all summer and we will rely on this store of food for some time. I am sure that my hours away from home will be greater because we will move lots of men and equipment to the East and West Coasts in preparation to ship to Europe and the Pacific."

"Dad, I did not even think of that," said Charlie. "I guess you *will* need me around home to help out, and watch after my sister."

"I am sure I will, son," said Charles. "Have you decided about enlisting?"

"I think I just did," said Charlie, and focused his attention on his cereal that was now resembling mush.

. . . . .

Roosevelt, sitting at his desk, looked up from the communication he was reading to see Henry Stimson enter the Oval Office.

"I do not remember a scheduled meeting, Henry," Roosevelt said. "What is the latest on Japan's movement in the Pacific?"

"Sir," began Stimson, "you know that the Philippines, Guam, Hong Kong, and the Solomon Islands are under Japanese control."

"Yes, continue," Roosevelt said warily.

"As we feared," Stimson gravely reported, "Singapore has also fallen. Our British allies held off as long as they could, but Japan overwhelmed their forces, and they just surrendered."

"Damn!" Roosevelt cursed. "When will we get some good news around here?"

"It is only a matter of time, sir," offered Stimson. "We are just coming up on three months of war and it is tough out there. The Japanese are making headway everywhere they go. We are just getting our battleships back to fighting condition, and the Yorktown and Enterprise have launched air attacks on the Gilbert and Marshall Islands."

"I am concerned, Henry," confided Roosevelt. "What if we have bitten off more than we can chew here?"

. . . . .

Admiral Kimmel watched as the USS Tennessee slowly moved free from the dry dock where she underwent repairs on the wounds she had suffered during the Japanese attack. He now had his three battleships back and ready to fight, and not a moment too soon, he thought.

. . . . .

"This is crazy!" shouted Tojo who stood and showed unusual emotion. "You really want us to approve this action?"

"Yes, Prime Minister, I do," responded Yamamoto quietly.

"You believe that you can surprise them again?" asked Tojo.

"Yes, Prime Minister, I do," Yamamoto said confidently.

"This is entirely on you, admiral," Tojo said warily. "I will not oppose this operation. But be sure you achieve the same success."

"Hai!" responded Yamamoto.

15. THE MARSHALL ISLANDS

"I have signals traffic, sir," reported the ensign. "It is an encoded Japanese message."

"Get that to our code-breakers immediately," ordered the lieutenant.

After fifteen minutes, the message came back to the lieutenant.

OPERATION K APPROVED. PROCEED TO FRENCH FRIGATE ISLANDS TO RENDEZVOUS WITH SUBMARINES

"Get this to fleet headquarters immediately," ordered the lieutenant.

He couriered the message to the Pacific Fleet headquarters at Honolulu, where a lieutenant junior grade, responsible for routing messages to the various department heads received the message. Just as the message was delivered, a seething captain entered, and the lieutenant stood to attention.

"Where is my intelligence report, lieutenant?" screamed the captain.

"I am sure it is right here on my desk, sir," said the flustered lieutenant. "I just received it minutes ago." As the lieutenant flipped through the stack of papers on his desk, he moved a pile onto the decoded message traffic delivered moments before the captain arrived.

"Here it is, sir," the lieutenant said excitedly.

"I better not have to come back here again!" chided the captain.

And with that, the signals message disappeared for ten days.

. . . . .

The War Council agreed to support a second raid against the Americans at Pearl Harbor. The plan called for another sword to the gut of their vulnerable adversary. War planners identified that the first attack had left a crucial strategic asset intact—

the 1010 dry dock. If the dry dock remained intact, it could allow the Americans a way back into the fight. The mission would be to destroy the dry dock and bring the Americans crying to the peace table.

The Kawanishi H8K was an amphibious plane with a 124-foot wingspan. Capable of a top speed of 300 miles per hour, the heavily armed airplane was sitting in Wotje Atoll in the Marshall Islands waiting for approval to begin *Kē-Sakusen* (Operation K). Each of the two H8K planes had four 550-pound bombs, the same used to destroy the USS Arizona.

Lieutenant Hisao Hashizume was the mission commander, with Ensign Shosuke Hisao flying the second plane.

"All systems flight checks complete, lieutenant," reported Hisao.

"Very well," stated the commander. "We are cleared to take off."

The two H8K planes pushed through the clear sparkling Pacific waters. As the planes achieved takeoff speed, the pilots expertly pulled back on the yoke and the planes eased into the air.

"Heading set, commander," said the navigator.

"Stay alert, men," said the commander. "It is almost two thousand miles to the French Frigate Shoals, and I do not want any detection before we can complete our mission. We have no Zero escorts, so our eyes are the only thing between us and failure."

"Hai!" the men responded.

As a big flaming orange sun extinguished over the Pacific Ocean, the two planes glided through the air at fifteen thousand feet on their way to their refueling stop. Seven-and-a-half hours later, the two amphibious planes touched down on the waters of French Frigate Shoals and met their submarines. Each submarine carried enough fuel for the trip to Pearl Harbor and back to Midway Island. The pilots took off for their almost six-hundred-mile flight to deliver more terror to the island of Oahu.

• • • • •

On the Island of Kauai, Lieutenant Anderson and Ensign Fredrick were manning their SCR-270 radar set. Given the results from the attack on Oahu, their commanding officer emphatically stated they should send any contact to his office for verification and action.

“Sir,” said Ensign Fredrick, “I have two contacts bearing two one zero degrees headed directly for us.”

The lieutenant came over to look for himself. “I concur two contacts bearing two one zero degrees. I will call this in,” he said. “Oahu station, Oahu station, I have two bogies incoming about two hundred miles northwest of Oahu bearing two one zero degrees,” he reported.

They scrambled two Curtiss P40 Warhawk fighters to intercept the incoming planes. Despite the recent advances of the Radar Lab, radar was not present on the P40s, and they lost the incoming planes in the thick cloud deck covering the southern half of the island. The P40s continued to perform an intercept pattern based on the bearing provided, but they could not find the incoming bombers.

“I-23, I-23, this is H8 Leader, over,” called the lieutenant. They dispatched mini submarines to support the mission and attack any targets that may try to escape the lagoon during the attack.

Silence.

“I-23, I-23, H8 Leader, can you read me? Over,” the lieutenant called again.

Silence.

As the sun rose over the island and Hashizume and Hisao approached the Western edge of Oahu, the thick blanket of nimbus clouds obscured all landmarks that would guide their attack.

“I see Keana Point Lighthouse and I am making my attack run from the north. Ensign, acknowledge,” ordered the lieutenant.

Ensign Hisao did not hear the communication and turned to the south to follow the coast to Pearl Harbor.

After the attack of December 7, the island of Oahu was under martial law. The military had imposed a complete blackout, thus preventing Hashizume from seeing any noticeable landmarks. He was flying blind with two thousand pounds of bombs ready to deploy.

Having lost sight of his wingman, Lieutenant Hashizume struggled to see anything through the thick cloud cover blanketing the island. Estimating his location based on his course and speed, he prepared to drop his payload.

"Prepare to deploy bombs, now! Now! Now! Now!" ordered the lieutenant.

The bombs deployed, but the lieutenant could not determine if he hit his mark. The four bombs exploded on the southern slope of Tantalus Peak about one thousand feet from Roosevelt High School, creating craters six to ten feet deep and twenty to thirty feet across. Citizens in nearby Honolulu reported hearing the blast, and fortunately, the school only suffered some shattered glass.

As Hisao hugged the coast, he was also having trouble finding his target.

"Deploy bombs now! Now! Now! Now!" ordered Hisao.

Like his commander's, his bombs missed their target, falling safely into the ocean. One bomb came close to the 1010 dry dock, but landed in the middle of the harbor and burrowed deep into the sea bottom. It never exploded.

Lieutenant Hashizume and Ensign Hisao flew back to Midway Island without a single shot being fired at them. They landed at separate harbors and proceeded to their debriefings.

16. WASHINGTON, DC

On February 9, 1942, the United States created a new organization to execute the wars in Europe and the Pacific. The Joint Chiefs of Staff (JCS) had been formed at the Arcadia conference in December 1941, where Roosevelt and Churchill met to establish the overall plan to defeat Germany in Europe and Africa. Britain invited the United States to become a member of a new committee called the Combined Chiefs of Staff (CCS) that had the overall responsibility and authority to prosecute the war for both countries.

A month later, General George C. Marshall, representing the Army, Admiral Ernest J. King, representing the Navy, and Lieutenant General Henry H. Arnold from the Army Air Corps entered the large conference room in the Blair House where President Roosevelt, Vice President Wallace, and Secretary of War Stimson were waiting.

"Good morning, Mr. President, Mr. Vice President, Mr. Secretary," said the JCS members as they entered the room.

"Please sit down, gentlemen," the president said warmly. "Our purpose today is to better understand where we are in our preparation to respond to the threats posed by the Germans and Japanese. Secretary Stimson, please proceed."

Henry Stimson opened his briefing folder and described the overall readiness and strength of the current armed forces of the United States. He then spoke to the major progress the Rad Lab had made in radar technology.

"As all of you know," began Stimson, "our Rad Lab has made significant progress toward giving the United States and our allies supreme primacy in all radar technology."

Stimson spent the next twenty minutes describing the recent advancements in radar technology created by the Rad Lab.

"The new and upgraded technology from the lab includes P-Band, 30 to 100 centimeters, 1 to 0.3 gigahertz; L-Band, 15 to 30 centimeters, 2 to 1 gigahertz; and S-Band, 8 to 15 centimeters, 4 to 2 gigahertz.

"The P-Band radar covers aircraft and shipboard gunfire control. On the battleship California, the aircraft carriers Yorktown and Lexington, and the heavy cruisers Pensacola, Northampton, Chester, and the Chicago, we still have installed our older CXAM radar, or the Bedspring. This radar has been very effective at detecting aircraft at ten thousand feet altitude, smaller planes up to fifty miles, and larger ships and destroyers at twelve nautical miles. We will replace this with our new S-Band radar, which I will describe shortly.

"Using the P-Band gunfire systems increases the range and target acquisition accuracy of our guns. Testing of the Mark 3 system on the USS Philadelphia was completed in October of last year to replace the Mark 2 system. Testing of the F-Series anti-aircraft fire control system known as the Mark 4 on the destroyer USS Roe was successfully completed in September 1941. Our newest system called the Mark 8 can successfully engage enemy targets at forty thousand yards with an accuracy of fifteen yards. We will deploy this system over the next two years as we have an abundant inventory of the Mark 3 systems to manage our deployment schedule.

"The L-Band early warning radar systems are in early development, but the lab has high expectations for the technology. Their goals are to increase capabilities to detect large airplanes at a significant distance, perhaps up to a hundred miles. The Rad Lab codename for this effort is Project Cadillac.

"To support shipboard search applications, the Rad Lab invented the S-Band radar. The SG radar can discover large ships at fifteen miles and a submarine periscope at five miles. We will begin sea trials in a few short months. We expect this technology to reduce the number of reconnaissance missions needed during air operations.

"The team is continuing to develop new radar technologies and at subsequent Joint Chiefs' meetings, we will discuss their efforts. One more time, we must acknowledge the work of our British allies in the enhancement of the cavity magnetron, without which we could create none of these systems," Stimson concluded.

Applause echoed throughout the room.

"Admiral King," said Roosevelt, "please update us on the state of the Pacific Fleet."

"As you are all aware," stated King, "our Navy took heavy losses, but our men are resilient and so are those working to rebuild our Navy. I am fully confident that, by this summer, all the ships damaged during the Pearl Harbor attack will steam back to join the fleet."

King knew that this was a nearly impossible task, but he had great faith with the shipbuilders in Seattle and his team in dry dock 1010. They had already improved the expected timeline for repairs to the fleet by weeks, and he knew he would have to drive them to improve their timelines even more.

"During engagement with the Japanese last month, we lost the carriers Langley and Houston. They scuttled the Langley after she could not evade the third attack run of the Japanese while on her way to Java. The Japanese adapted to our standard evasive maneuvers and bracketed the Langley during their last attack. The Japanese hit her five times, causing the captain to abandon her. The destroyers Whipple and Edsel were delivered their final mortal wounds on February 27.

"During the Japanese march through the Dutch West Indies, the Houston was part of the attack force sent to stop the invasion force headed toward Java. Her men fought bravely during the battle, but had limited success scoring any direct hits on the Japanese invading force. We only had one ship equipped with radar, but superior force overwhelmed us. We delayed the invasion force by one day."

"Was the radar on one of our ships, Admiral King?" asked the president.

"No, sir," replied the admiral. "It was on one of the Australian ships."

"How was the Houston destroyed?" asked the vice president.

"After the initial battle," Admiral King continued, "we ordered the Houston to Tjilatjap, where she accidentally encountered the Japanese invasion force. With almost no fuel or ammunition, the Japanese fleet surrounded her, but she fought valiantly. The reports are still coming in, but multiple torpedoes hit her, and she finally sank on February 28."

"Were there any survivors from either ship, admiral?" asked the president.

"Mr. President," King said gravely, "sixteen men died on the Langley, and we do not have any definitive numbers on the Houston. Some survived, but they may be in enemy hands right now."

"Admiral King," said Stimson, "please report on our enlistment numbers."

"Our current enlistment is up to almost two million sailors from just one million at the end of last year. We project that we will be up to over three million by the end of the year. Our fellow Americans are answering the call to service," concluded King.

General Marshall and Lieutenant General Arnold provided their updates, and then took their seats.

"Gentlemen," began Roosevelt, "these are tragic days we are in with much grievous news to endure. However, I am confident that we will soon turn the tide of this horrible war and drive our enemies into submission. The American people are sturdy, and we have proven we can fight if the cause is just. Japan attacked us, and the American people want justice. You, the men of the Joint Chiefs, will be the weight behind the spear that will guide and direct our forces to victory. Your vision and planning will light our path to victory—of this I am sure. Now we have two more topics to discuss.

"Regarding General MacArthur, we must move him out of Corregidor. I agree with the recommendation from General Marshall and believe he is the right man to lead our Southwest Pacific Theater. Based on the recommendation from Admiral King, I also agree that we should promote Admiral Nimitz to commander-in-chief of the US Pacific theater," Roosevelt concluded.

. . . . .

"Admiral Yamamoto," stated Tojo, "you have made substantial progress executing this war against the Americans."

"Your support and counsel have been invaluable," Yamamoto lied.

"I have significant concerns that the former British colonies may impede our progress to total victory," said Tojo, knowing that the admiral had a plan. An internal spy had briefed Tojo earlier in the day on the plan.

Yamamoto paused at the preciseness of the query hidden in Tojo's statement. "Yes, prime minister," said Yamamoto with great confidence, "we have a plan to address this concern." Yamamoto held his emotions in check as he described the details of the plan. He worried that Tojo had infiltrated his command. This would be the only way he could have known of this operation.

"At the completion of our offensive, named Operation MO, we will have full control of the Australian territory of New Guinea. We will begin by establishing a seaplane base near Guadalcanal in the Solomon Islands to support our operations in the Coral Sea. Our South Seas Detachment will take Port Moresby to establish another seaplane base. Finally, we expect to crush the American forces in the South Pacific as our superior naval forces depart Truk through the Eastern Solomon's meeting with our Westerly forces to cut the supply lines to Australia. Our intelligence also reports that we expect to engage the mighty aircraft carrier USS Yorktown," concluded Admiral Yamamoto.

"When do you expect this operation to begin?" asked the prime minister.

"We expect this operation to begin in early May," answered Yamamoto.

As the briefing completed, Yamamoto took an inventory of his command staff. Who could have leaked this information to the prime minister? He swore he would discover this traitor in their midst.

17. USS LEXINGTON CV-2

"We have two hours to launch, captain," said the executive officer (XO).

Captain Frederick C. Sherman, or Ted as the officers knew him, surveyed the battle plan as his ship prepared to strike the Japanese base at Rabaul on the island of New Britain. A graduate of the Naval Academy, Captain Sherman was best known for his constant companion, Admiral Wags, his family's black Cocker Spaniel that accompanied him on all official duties.

"Very well, XO," stated the captain. "Notify the ready room and prepare the deck for launch."

The XO relayed the orders to the pilot ready room and the plane captains as they prepared the F4F Wildcats for battle. Built by the Grumman Corporation, the Wildcat began service in early 1940, but the faster Japanese Zeros had an advantage. At a maximum speed of 331 mph for the Wildcat, the Zero was faster and more maneuverable. However, the Wildcat had self-sealing gas tanks, making the Wildcat harder to shoot out of the air. Even if multiple rounds pierced her fuel tanks, she would still continue to fly.

"Captain," said the XO, "the deck reports ready for flight operations on your command."

"Very well, XO," said the captain.

Radarman John Tenner was sitting at the controls of the Lexington's new CXAM radar, sweeping the horizon, looking for enemy activity, when he saw a huge spike on his scope. He trained the bedspring antennae until he could see what appeared to be a single plane headed toward the ship.

"Oh, boy!" exclaimed Tenner. He pressed the button on his communications headset. "Plot, Radar."

"Plot, aye," was the response from the Air Plot.

Prior to the use of radar, reconnaissance missions were the only method to detect enemy task-force locations. Now they could test the CXAM radar in battle.

"Air target bearing three fiver one, range five two nautical miles," relayed Tenner.

"Anderson, validate we have no friendlies in the area," ordered Lieutenant Junior Grade (JG) Watson.

"Checking . . . No friendlies reported in the area. Recommend identifying the target as a bandit," reported Anderson, a bandit implying a hostile aircraft.

"Bridge, Plot," called Watson.

"Bridge, aye," responded the XO.

"We have a bandit bearing three five one, range five two nautical miles. Contact Sierra-1," reported Watson.

"Captain," reported the XO, "we have a bandit reported by Air Plot. Recommend we launch a welcoming party, sir."

"Agreed. Launch six Wildcats, intercept, and notify the Commander, Air Group (CAG). I want him up here during this engagement," ordered the captain.

Within minutes, they dispatched the orders, and six F4F Wildcats were in the air, led by Lieutenant Commander John S. "Jimmy" Thach.

"Plot, Radar," called Watson.

"Radar, aye," responded Tenner.

"I want updates every minute on the bearing and range of Sierra-1," ordered Watson.

"Aye, aye, sir!" responded Tenner.

"Plot, Radar, Sierra-1 still bearing three five one, range four eight nautical miles," reported Tenner.

"Jimmy, come to heading one seven one and proceed to Angels ten. Expect visual contact in ten minutes."

"Wilco," responded Jimmy.

"Plot, Radar, contact Sierra-1 still bearing three five one, range four zero nautical miles," reported Tenner.

"Jimmy, do you have visual?" asked Watson.

"One, Plot, I have visual. One snooper bandit," said Jimmy. A snooper was a plane performing a reconnaissance mission. "Two and Three, engage on my mark," ordered Jimmy. "We need to splash this seaplane before they see us and report our position to the enemy."

Two—call sign "Ginger" because of the color of his hair—and Three—call sign "Charmer" for the list of girls sending him letters from home—were Jimmy's wingmen.

"Roger wilco," responded the wingmen.

"Two, Three, ready and tally-ho!" ordered Jimmy.

The three Wildcats broke off from the formation at ten thousand feet and dove to engage the Japanese seaplane. Jimmy took the lead and lined up his guns on his target. His plane breathed a burst of fire, hitting the forward fuselage, just missing the fuel tank. Ginger and Charmer followed the same line, with Charmer getting the final kill shot.

"Splash one snooper, Jimmy!" reported Charmer.

"Plot, One," called Jimmy.

"Plot, aye," responded Watson.

"Contact Sierra-1 confirmed killed," reported Jimmy.

"Roger, One," responded Watson.

"Radar, Plot," called Tenner.

"Plot, aye," responded Watson.

"We have another contact bearing three three niner, range five two miles," reported Tenner.

"Confirmed contact Sierra-2, bearing three three niner, range five two miles," responded Watson.

The second leader of the team was Lieutenant Junior Grade O. B. Stanley. His call sign was "Bluffer," because he was from Pine Bluff, Arkansas. Bluffer's wingmen

"Sawyer"—his family owned a sawmill—and "Razor"—his last name was Rasinski—were handling overwatch when radar discovered the next contact.

"Four," Jimmie said, "you and your team go after this contact and we will fly overwatch for your team."

"Roger that," said Bluffer.

"Plot, Four," called Watson, "come to course one five niner, and keep your eyes open for our friend."

"Roger," said Bluffer, "coming to course one five niner."

It took only minutes before Razor got confirmation of the other snooper. "I see Sierra-2 one o'clock low," announced Razor.

"Follow my lead. Tally-ho!" said Bluffer.

The Wildcats banked right and began their dive. This time, the snooper was ready and made a hard banking turn to the left to protect his fuel tanks. Sawyer and Razor split from Bluffer to the left and right to box in their prey.

Bluffer continued to dive and let go a burst from his guns. He hit the back of the seaplane, but she was still flying. Within seconds, Razor lined up to fire and let go a long burst from his guns, creating a perfect line down the side of the fuselage. Sawyer was in position just as Razor fired, and let go a barrage from his guns just as Razor pulled up. Razor's aim was true, and he hit the seaplane causing an impressive explosion. The seaplane dove to the sea—gone forever.

"Plot, Four," called Bluffer, "confirmed kill of Sierra-2. Headed home."

The six planes flew back into formation and plotted a course back to the Lexington. Once aboard, the team assembled in the pilot ready room for their debriefing. The CAG entered.

"Attention on deck!" announced the captain.

"At ease," said the CAG. "Have a seat, boys." "First," he began, "great shooting, everyone! I want you to know that you have just taken part in history."

The pilots looked around at each other and did not understand what the CAG meant. Sure, they had killed the enemy, but this was not the first recorded enemy kill of the war.

"You are the first pilots directed to an enemy engagement using our latest weapon." The CAG did not mention the word radar because it was still top secret and most people on the ship did not know the function the bedspring mounted on the front stack performed, but they had heard some scuttlebutt surrounding a new technology able to "see" over the horizon. Most pilots did not understand how Air Plot could direct them to their intercepts, but they believed the reconnaissance missions contributed to their target selection.

"Our weapon is secret," continued the CAG, "but it has proven an invaluable asset for taking the fight to the enemy. With this weapon, we will be able to more accurately direct you to your targets. Soon we will share more about this weapon and you will meet the men responsible for delivering you your prey this morning."

Some pilots wanted to ask about the bedspring but knew the CAG would not divulge this knowledge, and they knew not to ask too many questions. The CAG had kept them safe so far, and there was no reason to push the topic.

The CAG completed the debrief, and the pilots shared stories about the morning's events complete with hand motions showing how they completed each kill. The air wing left for chow, and then assembled back in their ready room to wait for something to happen. To pass the time, the pilots played cards and listened to their newest pilot play his guitar.

As the pilots settled in for what they hoped would be a quiet afternoon, the call to general quarters came over the ship's hailer.

"Report," ordered the captain.

"Captain, we have a group of nine large incoming bogies, course bearing three two eight, distance five one miles," reported the OOD.

"Captain, I recommend we launch six Wildcats," offered the CAG.

"Make it so," ordered the captain.

As the last Wildcat left the flight deck, Air Plot provided an intercept course just as it had that morning. The combat air patrol (CAP) met the enemy at the directed location.

"Plot, One," called the CAP leader.

"Plot, go ahead," responded Watson.

"Visual on contacts," reported the CAP leader. "Nine Bettys heading three two eight. However, I am sure they have spotted us as we are at Angels ten and the Bettys are running at Angels fifteen."

The Betty was the Japanese Mitsubishi G4M1 attack bomber. The bomber had little armor plating, which increased its range. The fatal flaw, however, was the lack of self-sealing fuel tanks, making the Betty vulnerable.

"OK boys, break and climb to Angels eighteen. Pair off and engage the enemy. Watch out for any Zeros flying overwatch," instructed the CAP leader. "Tally-ho!"

The CAP teams broke left and right, and climbed to Angels eighteen and prepared to engage. As the first team of three began their attack run, they split off three of the Betty bombers from the formation. With the Bettys exposed, each pilot took on one Betty. The Wildcats dispatched each Betty with lethal accuracy, including the lead plane from the formation who they assumed to be the squadron leader. The second CAP team engaged two more Bettys with the same lethality of their squadron members. After the first engagement, all five Bettys were sinking into the Pacific Ocean below.

While the first engagement was underway, Captain Sherman ordered the launch of another six Wildcats to provide overwatch. As the last Betty splashed below them, the remaining four Bettys lined up to begin their bombing runs.

Petty Officer First Class John Wilkinson leapt onto his battle station to search for the incoming Betty bombers. He was part of the team calling elevation and distance coordinates for the 1.1-inch anti-aircraft guns providing the last defense he and his crew had against these dive bombers. He looked into his telescope and acquired his target.

"Set your elevation to one eight degrees, distance two zero thousand yards," ordered Wilkinson.

"Elevation one eight degrees, distance two zero thousand yards, aye," was the response.

"Fire, fire, fire, fire!" ordered Wilkinson.

The 1.1-inch guns exploded, firing one hundred fifty .917-pound projectiles toward the incoming Bettys.

Wilkinson watched and shouted corrections in elevation and distance as the Bettys streaked closer and closer to his ship. Suddenly, he saw an explosion and ordered his team to hold fire. He trained his telescope to his next target. As he was about to order his team to shoot, the target fell from the sky in a ball of flames.

"Plot, Radar," called the operator.

"Plot, aye," responded Air Plot.

"We have another set of eight bogies incoming bearing three zero one, range twelve nautical miles," responded the operator.

"Bridge, Plot," called Air Plot.

"Bridge, aye," responded the bridge.

"Eight incoming bogies twelve miles out!" called Air Plot.

"Bridge, aye!" responded the bridge.

"Captain, we just launched our last two Wildcats, and the remaining air patrol is engaged with the first squad of Bettys," announced the CAG.

Wilkinson found the next target and called his guns into action. His body shook as the guns shot, recoiled, and shot again. The sound was deafening. His team was not hitting the target.

"Correction! Elevation two five degrees, distance one five thousand yards," ordered Wilkinson. "Get that bastard!"

"Vector those two Wildcats to intercept those bombers," ordered the captain.

Just as the guns retrained on the target, a 550-pound bomb dropped from the incoming Betty. The ship broke hard to starboard, and the crew braced for impact. The bomb missed the Lexington to stern, and a Wildcat shot down the Betty.

"CAG, is that Butch and Duff on the way?" asked the captain.

"Yes, sir, it is, captain," said the CAG, and both men shared a look.

"Butch," Lieutenant Henry O'Hare, and "Duff," Lieutenant Marion Dufiho, had just reached Angels eighteen to provide overwatch.

"Tango One, Plot," called Air Plot.

"Tango One, aye," responded Tango One.

"Eight incoming bogies headed your way. Eleven miles out and coming in unchecked. Intercept vector one one one degrees. Make it quick, boys!" ordered Air Plot.

"Tango One, roger wilco!" responded Tango One.

"Come on, Duff, let us give those Japs a little welcoming party they will never forget!" said O'Hare.

Butch and Duff reached the incoming bombers within two minutes. They were in a tight V formation at Angels thirteen. They were nine miles out from the Lexington.

"Break left, Duff, and engage, tally-ho!" ordered Butch.

Duff tried to fire his .50-caliber guns, but they jammed.

"Butch," called Duff, "my .50 just jammed. I am trying to fix it right now!"

Butch was all alone to face eight incoming Betty bombers by himself! He developed a quick plan and engaged.

With only four 150 rounds of ammunition, enough for 34 seconds of firing, Butch knew he would have to conserve every round if he was to save his ship. He made a high-side diving attack on the formation and chose a target. He let go a burst from his .50-caliber guns and hit a Betty on the starboard engine, causing it to fall out of formation. He trained his guns on the next Betty and also hit the starboard engine, causing a fire. The Betty fell out of formation, but the crew quickly put out the flames and proceeded toward the Lexington.

Butch lined up for his second attack run. He chose a Betty on the outside of the formation. With another quick burst of his .50 calibers, he damaged the starboard engine and hit the port fuel tank, causing the pilot to dump his bomb and disengage from the attack formation. He moved his aim to the next Betty in formation, and let go another burst. Another hit, and the Betty burst into flames and began its death spiral to the ocean below.

The six remaining Betty bombers prepared to release their bombs.

O'Hare began his third attack run and targeted the lead plane to remove the flight commander. His first burst hit the Betty in the port fuel tank, and the plane left the formation. Now Butch trained his aim on the lead plane. He concentrated another burst on the port engine, which rewarded him with an explosion so violent that the engine fell from the plane, causing the pilot to begin his death dive. He tried to engage another plane, but he was out of ammunition.

Butch and Duff withdrew from their attack and flew to a safe distance away from the booming AA guns below.

"Plot, Tango One," Butch called, "I am out of ammunition. We have cleared the area for the AA team to engage!"

"Plot, aye!" was the response from Air Plot.

The remaining four bombers released their bombs, but they all missed the Lexington. One plane that Butch had hit lost altitude, and the pilot knew he could not return home. He directed his bomber toward the deck of the Lexington. He avoided the incoming AA gun fire exploding around him, but he could not hit his target. The Betty bomber impacted the ocean to the port side, close to the stern.

"Tango One, Paddles," said the Air Boss. Paddles was the name given to the landing signals officer (LSO) because he directed aircraft using colored flags or paddles to help direct pilots onto the flight deck.

"Landing position is good," said the LSO. "The deck is clear."

Just as Butch was about to answer, he felt his left wing get hit. His airspeed indicator was not working. "Plot, Tango One," called Butch, "cease fire! Incoming friendly!"

Butch landed the plane without further incident. He jumped out of his plane and made a beeline for the gun platform where the offending friendly fire had originated. He found the gunner's mate who he believed had shot at him.

"Son," said Butch calmly, "if you don't stop shooting at me when I have my wheels down, I will have to report you to the gunnery officer."

The gunner's mate saluted and slowly crumbled to the ground.

The remaining Wildcats returned to the carrier. Only one Betty successfully returned to its Japanese base, and the Lexington lost one pilot and two Wildcats.

18. MOUNT FUJI, JAPAN

Hadaki stopped midway up Fuji-san to rest and enjoy the view. He could see patches of bright white dot the countryside below him. The cherry blossoms were just emerging from their long winter rest. He could barely see his village, but he knew his family would be eager to hear how their ancestors would counsel him.

Earlier that week, military officials had visited his village where they had conscripted all the military-age men to fight the demonic mongrel Americans who were spreading their western culture across Japan and all of Asia. The Japanese military had designed rules governing conscription to protect the family structure while ensuring maximum sacrifice from all Japanese families. As Hadaki was the oldest male member of his family and his father was no longer living, they could excuse him from military service. Hadaki was not sure this was his destiny.

Soon I will seek the counsel of my sorei (the spirits of the ancestors of a family), thought Hadaki. *They will guide me to my destiny.*

Hadaki felt the air thin as he continued to climb Fuji-san headed for a specific shrine where he would stop and wait to hear from his ancestors. His father brought him to this shrine before he left for war so Hadaki could understand his purpose and place in his world. Now, he would return and ask his father what he should do.

Hadaki reached the midway point of the traditional climb to the summit, where all pilgrims complete their spiritual journey. He found the shrine his father had taken him to just three years earlier. He laid down the sack with the mementos of his father given to him by his mother the night before. He bowed his head in a prayerful posture as he called on his ancestors for guidance.

He felt a surge of energy pulse through his fingers all the way to his toes. He prayed.

"My ancestors, you have guided my family for ages, and now I must come to you as I feel my country needs me. My mother and sisters daily tend our rice paddies that help feed our soldiers, and at night they sew by candlelight the garments we send to keep them warm. I am the only one who can lead my family, and if I undertake this dangerous course, my family could lose everything."

When his father died, he became the head of the household and the sole owner of all the property. Women could not own property. He fell deeper into a trance-like state.

"The mongrel Americans have threatened my homeland and must pay for their lies and deeds in Asia. I now understand the deep feeling you had with my father as you left our home to fight for our beloved homeland. I now ask for your guidance, great ancestors, on my destiny during this time of war."

Suddenly, Hadaki heard a sound in the distance that startled him from his trance. There, before him, stood a red fox. Hadaki immediately understood what his ancestors wanted him to do. Japanese folklore portrays the red fox as a guardian and protector. They tell of a red fox coming to a village and teaching the elders how to grow rice. Seeing a red fox is a sign of protection. This would mean that his ancestors would protect his family, and he was free to pursue his destiny.

Hadaki now had his answer: he must join his brothers and fight against the Americans. Hadaki gathered his mementos and began the two-hour trip back to his home.

. . . . .

"I thought we had talked about this, Charlie," said his father with deep concern.

"I know we did, Dad," began Charlie, "but I still have this feeling in the pit of my stomach that I need to do something."

"But you are only seventeen, son," said Charles.

"I know, Dad, that is why I am asking you to go with me and sign the papers allowing me to enlist early," said Charlie.

"I don't know, son," Charles said warily. "If I agree, you must complete this school year and promise to finish high school when you get back from the war."

"I promise, Dad," said Charlie.

"This is a big decision, Charlie," his father said. "I am proud that you feel so strongly about your need to contribute to the war effort."

They could hear light sobbing from the other room.

"Doris Ann," called Charles, "you need to be here for this discussion."

Doris Ann entered the parlor where Charles and his son were talking. She dabbed the tears from her eyes and sat down on the sofa next to her father. "I am scared for you, Charlie," she began. "I cannot lose another member of our family to war."

"I know it scares you, sis, but I will be OK," Charlie said warmly. "I need to do this to protect our family from those Japanese. If they can get us at Pearl Harbor, who says they can't come here and bomb us? I will be back before you know it, sis," assured Charlie.

The family came together to hug one another, each person deep in thought about how this decision would change their lives forever.

"How about you make some fried chicken with black-eyed peas and greens for me, sis?" Charlie asked.

"Oh, Charlie, always thinking about your stomach. I will be glad to not have to fill your bottomless pit anymore," Doris Ann laughed as she went into the kitchen, heartbroken and fearful of the days to come.

The next morning, Charles accompanied his son to the recruiting offices off of Main Street.

"Which service do you want to serve?" asked his father.

"I am not sure," said Charlie. "I need to look at their uniform."

"You need to look at what?" his father said incredulously.

"The shoes, Dad," responded Charlie.

"What about the shoes?" his father asked warily.

"Well," explained Charlie, "the Army guys have to wear brown shoes, and I do not want to do that. I want to wear black shoes even if I have to button all of those buttons on the Navy uniform."

Charlie went into the induction center and spoke with the Navy recruiter. He listened as the recruiter completed his presentation.

"What do you think, son?" asked the recruiter.

"This is what I want to do," started Charlie. "Correct that, this is what I must do!"

"You are his father, correct?" asked the recruiter.

"Yes, sir, I am," said Charles.

"And will you permit his wish to join the Navy?" questioned the recruiter.

Charles paused for what seemed like an eternity. "Yes, sir, I will. But he must complete his schooling this year. After that, he has my blessing to join up."

"Are you agreeable to your father's wishes, son?" asked the recruiter.

"Yes, sir, I am," said Charlie as he beamed.

"Very well then," said the recruiter. "We shall begin the paperwork, and you can be on your way."

Charlie completed his paperwork and signed his application. He slid the application to his father for his signature. Charles paused again. He knew this is what his son felt he needed to do, and although he did not like it, he knew he made the deal to let him serve. He signed the application.

19. HONOLULU, HAWAII

"Captain Stillwell," instructed Admiral Nimitz, "the briefing is yours."

Admiral Chester Nimitz was just five months into his new role as the commander-in-chief of the United States Pacific Fleet (CINPACFLT). When Roosevelt appointed General Douglas MacArthur commander of the Southwest Pacific Area, the Joint Chiefs of Staff made Admiral Nimitz the commander-in-chief of the Pacific Ocean Areas. Born in Fredericksburg, Texas, in 1885, Nimitz had applied to West Point hoping to become an Army officer, but no appointments were available. Instead, his congressional representative found an appointment to the United States Naval Academy, where he graduated with distinction in 1905. Early in his career, the destroyer USS Decatur ran aground in the Philippines while Ensign Nimitz was in command. He was court-martialed for dereliction of duty, but served with distinction in World War I where he was Chief of Staff for the Commander Submarine Forces. Prior to his current appointment, Admiral Nimitz was chief of the Bureau of Navigation, where he conducted experiments in underway refueling of large ships.

"Our signals intelligence," began Stillwell, "have been hard at work intercepting Japanese communications, and I believe we have ourselves a real nugget. The Japanese are in the last stages of planning an operation named MO. We believe that their intended target is Port Moresby, New Guinea. If they successfully achieve their operational goals, they will control the entire airspace and shipping lanes to Australia, interrupting the supply lines to our Aussie friends." Once Captain Stillwell completed his briefing, he asked for questions.

"Describe our readiness to respond to the Japanese," ordered Admiral Nimitz.

"Sir," said Stillwell with a sense of uneasiness, "we have the Yorktown. She is the closest carrier able to make it to the Coral Sea in time to engage the Japanese."

"You mean to say that there are no other carriers in the entire Pacific Ocean we can use to thwart this attack?" said a newly minted commander. Nimitz glared at the Commander.

"Sir," said Stillwell with increased intensity, "the USS Saratoga has been in dry dock since January because of a torpedo strike. The Enterprise and Hornet are just returning from the Doolittle Raid, leaving us the Lexington to team up with the Yorktown."

The Doolittle Raid, led by Lieutenant Colonel James Doolittle, had shown that a carrier-launched attack force could hit the Japanese mainland. On April 18, sixteen B-25 bombers departed the USS Hornet to bomb military targets in Tokyo. Although the raid caused minimal damage to Japanese military installations, the morale boost to the United States was immense. In Japan, the citizens expressed doubt that their military leaders could protect their homeland as they had promised.

"The Yorktown has 65 aircraft," continued the captain, "and the Lexington has 69, giving us 134 aircraft."

"What is your recommendation?" asked the admiral.

"Sir, I would order the Yorktown to the Coral Sea immediately and send the Lexington to support the Yorktown," said the captain with great confidence.

"That is our only play here," stated the admiral. "I want Admiral Fitch to run point on this operation as the tactical commander."

"Yes, sir!" responded the captain.

"Draft the operational orders and get them to the Yorktown and Lex immediately," ordered Admiral Nimitz.

. . . . .

"Captain Sherman," said an ensign, "we have a flash communication from CINPACFLT."

"Thank you, ensign," responded Captain Sherman without looking up from his communication.

The captain grabbed the mic and called, "XO to the bridge."

Within five minutes, the XO reported to Captain Sherman. "XO reporting as ordered, sir," said the XO saluting.

"XO, follow me," ordered the captain.

The captain and his executive officer left the bridge for the captain's quarters.

"XO," began the captain, "they ordered our task force to support the Yorktown in the Coral Sea. We need to rendezvous with Task Force 17 on 1 May at 1616'S 16220'E northwest of New Caledonia. The Japanese are planning an attack on Port Moresby, and they ordered us to patrol the perimeter of the Japanese attack force and prevent their landing on Port Moresby."

The XO left the captain's cabin and prepared his crew for their next engagement.

On May 1, the two task forces united as planned and spent the next two days refueling. The Lexington was slow to complete her refueling operations, so the Yorktown headed northwest to engage the Japanese.

. . . . .

The Kawanishi H6K flying boat provided better long-range discovery of enemy targets. With a crew of nine, the flying boat could handle twenty-four-hour patrols and had a range of three thousand miles, making it a formidable asset of the Japanese attack force. The Japanese had established sea bases in Rabaul and Tulagi, but these assets could only find the enemy if they could see them. During inclement weather, a flying boat could not see through the cloud cover to find the enemy.

. . . . .

In June, Charlie reported to the train station where he had seen his father off so many times before. This time his sister, who had not stopped holding his hand, accompanied him while they walked to the station. Charlie would go to Chicago to attend boot camp at the Naval Station Great Lakes. His father had pulled some strings so he could be the conductor on this day.

"All aboard!" called Charles the conductor.

"You be safe, young man!" cried Doris Ann.

"You know me, sis," Charlie assured his sister. "Trouble slips off my back like water on a duck."

Doris Ann held on for one last hug. She had so many things she wanted to say to him about life and girls. She was proud of him, and scared, all at the same time.

"You write me all the time," chided his sister.

"I will, sis," assured Charlie, not knowing if he would have time.

Charlie stepped up onto the train and disappeared from view. Doris Ann saw Charlie walking toward the back cabin of the train where she knew her father awaited.

The train lurched forward and struggled to move. Doris Ann wept as she waved goodbye to the train taking her only brother to war. Her heart was sick, but she knew her country needed men like him to bring the fight to the Japanese. As the train exited the station, she saw a figure stick his head out of the window and look back toward her.

"I love you, sis!" called Charlie.

Doris Ann tried to answer, but could not form the words. All she could do was wave and pray daily for Charlie's safety. She knew it would be a while before Charlie was in any danger, so that thought comforted her briefly. Then the train disappeared around a corner, leaving Doris Ann alone with her thoughts. Doris Ann slowly turned to take the fifteen-minute walk back to their house. As she entered the house, she headed directly to the sofa where she fell face first and cried for hours.

20. CHICAGO, ILLINOIS

The train pulled into Union Station and lurched to a stop. Charlie had spent the past sixteen hours in the conductor car with his father, talking about everything and nothing at all. He had travelled this route many times, with and without his father. As a teenager, Charles would allow his son to travel alone to visit relatives across the South and even those in Schaumburg where his uncle Tim and cousins lived. Everyone on the train line knew Charlie and watched out for him like he was their own. Now, Uncle Sam would send him to war.

Every porter and engineer on the line had watched Charlie grow up, and each spent time with him during the journey to Chicago. One of Charlie's favorite porters even brought him his favorite ice cream, telling him they probably will not have ice cream as good as this where he was going!

But the time spent with his dad was the most special. Charles traveled for days at a time working on the railroad and missed many of Charlie's baseball games, one of his many regrets.

"Any idea what you want to do in the Navy, Charlie?" asked his father.

"Not sure, Dad," said Charlie. "The recruiter said there were lots of jobs for guys good with their hands, so I guess we will see what they say."

"When do you have to report to boot camp, son?" asked Charles.

"By 3:00 p.m. today," Charlie responded.

"How about I buy you a late breakfast," said his father. "It may be your last enjoyable meal for some time."

"I would like that, Dad," Charlie said with a grin.

Charles completed his paperwork and ensured the complete offloading of all the passengers and their luggage from the train. The father and son then left the train station and had breakfast at Lou Mitchells before finally finding their way to

Grant Park for one last visit. At 1:00 p.m., Charlie loaded the bus headed to Naval Station Great Lakes.

. . . . .

Reveille played through the loudspeakers of Ship 2 as the company hit the deck and prepared for the day's activities. Charlie was to report for testing at 0900 hours. He had completed his first few weeks of boot camp where he learned personal hygiene, naval history, and skills he would need while out to sea. Charlie rushed off to breakfast and then to the testing facility five blocks to the south.

"Recruits," began the chief, "today, you will take the Eddy test where we determine your aptitude for radio roles in the Navy. Based on your scores, we will send you to other Navy schools throughout the United States. It is important that you do your absolute best on this test, as the future of our country is at stake. The Japanese want nothing more than to attack our homeland and thwart our preparation to protect our families. You will have five hours to complete this test. We will score this test, and your command will notify you of your next orders. Questions? Fine, then begin."

Charlie completed his test in four-and-a-half hours and felt satisfied with how he did. He had always been inquisitive about how things worked. He was an excellent mechanic, having worked on the family car since he was thirteen. He loved tinkering with items in the house, taking things apart and mostly putting them back together, much to the ire of his sister. He would see what the Navy thought of him soon enough. Charlie headed back to get some lunch and complete his daily training.

Two days later, Charlie entered the company commander's office.

"Brand reporting as ordered, sir," Charlie said at attention.

"Brand, at ease, sailor. How do you feel about the test you took the other day?" questioned the commander.

"Well, sir," began Charlie, "I am not sure. There were lots of questions I was not sure how to answer, so I did my best thinking on them and came up with an answer."

"It is my pleasure to announce that you performed very well on the test." Charlie had the highest test score on the Eddy test of any recruit, informed the commander. "Did you ever study electronics at school in Arkansas?"

"No, sir," said Charlie, "but I sure like to figure out how things work."

"Son," began the commander, "I will send you to a very important school to support the war against Japan. Soon you will get orders to San Diego where we will train you to operate and maintain the most important weapon the Navy possesses."

Pride welled up inside Charlie, and he heard his sister's voice tell him "pride is from the devil; no one gets anywhere following him."

"You cannot tell anyone where you are going, Brand," warned the commander, "not even your family!"

"What can I tell them, sir?" asked Charlie.

"That you are going to a school for eight weeks out west," instructed the commander.

"Aye, aye, sir!" Charlie stood and saluted the commander.

Charlie walked out of the commander's office with so many questions and few answers. The commander was now asking him to kind of lie about where he was going and what he would do for the war effort. Well, he really did not understand what he would do, thought Charlie.

Charlie kept to himself for the last two weeks of the boot camp. He and his shipmates graduated as seamen, and each received their orders. He made some wonderful friends while at the bootcamp, and his friends wanted to know where the Navy would send him next. To ensure the secrecy of the orders, they gave Charlie a second set of orders, sending him to Canada to train with the Royal Navy. His friends were envious that Charlie would go to Canada.

Each of his classmates wished each other good luck as they prepared to leave the training center for some time with their families. When all his friends left, Charlie reached into his seabag and took out his real orders. He carefully opened the envelop and slowly read each word. He would leave for San Diego in ten days. He rushed to make the bus headed for Union Station and a trip back home to see his dad and sister. The course of his life was about to change forever.

. . . . .

Hadaki walked into an enormous room on the outskirts of Tokyo. It had been three days since he left his *haha* back home. He was proud of the decision his ancestors had made for him, and he swore he would do or go anywhere to fight against the imperial Americans. No one would attack *his* homeland, he thought.

"Name," said the clerk at the desk.

"Hadaki Yamatsumi," Hadaki said proudly.

"Fill this out and bring it back to me in five minutes," said the clerk with no interest in Hadaki.

"Hai!" said Hadaki.

Hadaki filled out the paper and brought it back to the clerk. He handed him the paper. The clerk stamped the paper and handed it back to Hadaki.

"Go over there," instructed the clerk.

Hadaki looked to where the clerk pointed to see other men standing in a line, waiting. Hadaki walked over and waited in line. Soon, a military man came to the line.

"I am Lieutenant Ito," began the lieutenant. "The emperor thanks you for your service. Now follow me."

The men followed the lieutenant to a bus. Each man loaded the bus and took a seat, and one hour later, the bus arrived at a military base where a man entered the bus.

"Take your things and follow me," ordered the man.

The men left the bus and lined up in front of the man.

"I am your *gunso*," said the sergeant. "You will address me as *Gunso*, nothing more, nothing less. I will prepare you to fight for the emperor against the imperial Americans. I will teach you to fight like a *samurai*. Soon, you will engage the enemy on our islands where you will kill every last one of them. If you do not kill them first, they will surely rape you and slowly torture you until you die. These Americans are dogs, and we will treat them like the animals they are."

Hadaki smiled to himself.

21. CORAL SEA

MAY 7, 0833 HOURS

Task Force 17 began air search operations with the certainty that the Japanese fleet was nearby.

"Plot, Radar," called the radar operator on the Lexington.

"Plot, aye," responded Air Plot.

"I have a possible bogey bearing two seven zero degrees and only two five miles out," said the operator evenly. "I recommend we launch fighter to intercept."

Air Plot relayed the request to Captain Sherman, who denied the request.

"That is dangerously close! How did we miss this?" the captain steamed. "I need more information on this contact. We do not know if we are dealing with a friend or a foe."

Captain Sherman only had 3 percent of his aircraft equipped with Identification Friend or Foe (IFF) equipment. IFF technology provided the radar operator a mechanism to determine if a contact was friendly.

"Plot, Radar," the operator tried again five minutes later.

"Ploy, aye," responded Air Plot.

"The bogey is still bearing two seven zero degrees, but the distance to the bogey has not changed," reported the operator. "I believe the bogey is circling."

The operator waited for a response from the captain on his repeated request to send fighters to investigate the mysterious radar contact.

The captain finally relented and ordered two fighters launched to investigate the bogey. As the fighter team approached the last known location of the bogey, they encountered decreasing visibility because of cloud coverage in the area and reported back to the Lexington that they could not find the bogey.

At 1050 hours, the CAP reported a sighting of two carriers, sixteen other combatants, and ten transports about 270 miles from the task force. They had discovered the Port Moresby Japanese invasion force. That was what the radar operator had found.

"CAG, prepare to launch," ordered the captain.

The CAG relayed his orders, and within minutes, a combination of fifty-three bombers and dive bombers left the task force headed toward the Japanese invasion force.

"CAP, striker lead," called the squadron leader, "I need a vector to our target."

"Striker lead," responded the CAP, "targets still bearing two seven zero degrees. Climb to Angels twenty and you better put a hurry on your delivery. It does not appear our friends know we are here, and I do not want it to get too crowded up here."

"Roger wilco," responded the leader.

Twenty minutes later, the Port Moresby invasion force was in view.

"CAP, striker lead," called the leader, "we are here earlier than we expected, but we are ready to engage."

"Striker team," called the leader, "form up into attack formation and prepare to engage."

The other group leaders acknowledged.

"Tally-ho!" called the strike force leader.

The bombers engaged first, scoring thirteen direct hits to the carrier below. The strike force would later learn that this carrier was the light carrier Soho, used during the attack on Pearl Harbor.

Next, the dive bombers engaged to finish the Soho. The bombers scored nine direct torpedo hits to the carrier, causing her to break in two and sink in five minutes.

The strike force reformed and flew back, landing at about 1345, minus only one fighter who bailed out and landed on Rossel Island in the Louisiade Archipelago. Friendly islanders found him, and he eventually returned to the task force to fight again.

At 1747, Lexington's radar scope lit up.

"Plot, Radar," called the operator, "I have multiple contacts bearing one four four degrees and range four eight miles."

Air Plot relayed the message to Captain Sherman, who was in his combat state room just off of the bridge preparing for dinner.

Captain Sherman made his way to the bridge. "CAG, I want a large welcoming party for those bogeys," he ordered, "and send a message to Radar that I need to know who is friendly up there!"

"Aye, aye, sir," responded the CAG.

Thirty-eight fighters launched from the Lexington and the Yorktown to intercept the attack force.

The bridge relayed the order to Radar through Air Plot.

The radar operator looked at his A-scope to identify the friendlies in the sky. Friendlies would appear on the bottom area of his scope, and bogeys would appear at the top. The captain was not happy as he still did not have enough IFF equipment on the fighters to be useful in this engagement. He had an idea. There was a CAP already headed to intercept the attack force. Only four of them had IFF.

"Air Plot, Radar," called the operator.

"Air Plot, aye," was the response.

"Recommend recalling CAP three, six, seven, and eight," said the radar operator. "No IFF in these planes."

"Radar, Plot," responded Air Plot, "good idea. CAP, Plot," called Air Plot. "Recalling CAP three, six, seven, and eight to the task force," ordered Air Plot.

"Roger wilco," responded the CAP leader.

Air Plot vectored the remaining four CAP fighters to intercept the bogeys. Eight minutes behind them, twenty-nine fighters screamed to catch up.

"Plot, CAP," called the leader, "contact nine Bettys headed your way."

"Boys," said the leader, "two-man teams. Two, you are with me. Four and five, break right on my command. Tally-ho!"

In diminishing daylight, the two fighter groups broke from the formation and dove to meet the single-line formation of Betty bombers. The CAP leader let go a burst of fire toward the edge of the line of bombers. He saw his target disappear from the formation in a ball of fire. His wingman quickly dispatched the third bomber in the line.

The second fighter group attacked the right side of the line, scoring only one downed Betty. The remaining six bombers sought cover in a cloud bank. The Wildcat fighters did not pursue. The remaining fighters arrived and broke into groups, providing air support as they waited for the bombers to exit the cloud bank.

The last flicker of daylight escaped the battle zone. The Bettys now had the upper hand. Suddenly, the six bombers exited their hiding place in the clouds ten thousand feet below the circling Wildcats. They lined up to attack the task force below. Seven fighters broke from the formation and took the fight to the bombers, downing one Betty and dispersing the rest. The seven fighters broke from their attack formation to chase the remaining Bettys, who were looking for their home carriers to fight another day. The Bettys jettisoned their bombs to gain more speed and better fuel consumption.

Darkness consumed the night, and over the next hour, radar discovered three more bogeys. Each time, Air Plot vectored fighters to the area where they discovered no enemy targets.

"Plot, Radar," called the operator.

"Ploy, aye," responded Air Plot.

"I believe we have a bogey on approach to land," said the radar operator.

"Plot, gunner," called Air Plot.

"Gunner, aye," responded the gunnery officer.

"Bogey in the flight path, ten o'clock," called Air Plot.

The gunnery officer trained his anti-aircraft guns on the target and waited until the flight path was clear of friendly planes.

"Guns two, target bearing one zero niner, range one thousand yards," instructed the gunnery officer.

"I see it," responded the gunner.

"Fire, fire, fire!" ordered the gunnery officer.

The guns breathed fire causing the remaining Betty bombers trying to land to disengage and slink back into the blackness. The Betty on approach disintegrated, causing a great roar to rise from the carrier. The remaining fighters landed safely. They had kept the task force safe today, but everyone knew this was not over. The Japanese now knew where they were.

22. CORAL SEA

MAY 8

"Captain on the bridge," announced the OOD.

"Report," ordered Captain Sherman.

"Intermittent rain squalls and a cloud deck at ten thousand feet," reported the XO. He was about to continue when a message from Air Plot interrupted his report.

"Bridge, Plot," called Air Plot, "bogey bearing three three zero, range two two miles flying very low."

"Splash that bogey!" ordered the captain.

The CAP had launched twenty minutes earlier and was patrolling the area.

Air Plot vectored two fighters to intercept the bogey, but they could not find it as she disappeared from radar. The Japanese knew where they were. Ten minutes later, a yeoman handed the captain an intercepted Japanese communication confirming his worst fears. Earlier that morning, scout planes had found the Japanese attack force about 170 miles to the north of their position. A force of forty-six dive bombers, fifteen fighters, and twenty-one torpedo planes launched to attack the enemy position.

At 1008 hours, lookouts aboard the Lexington spotted a large four-engine flying boat operating at a very low altitude intending to avoid radar. The CAP fighters made quick work of the bogey, but it was clear there would be an attack within the hour. In fact, the Japanese had already launched thirty-three dive bombers, eighteen fighters, and eighteen torpedo planes headed to the American task force.

"CAG," began the captain, "I need more cover to protect our position."

"I recommend we use our Dauntless torpedo planes," offered the CAG, "and let them act as a screen against any Jap torpedo planes that might come our way."

"Agreed," said the captain.

At 1012 hours, ten torpedo planes launched from the Lexington to act as a shield. At 1048 hours, a large blip appeared on the Lexington radar.

"Plot, Radar," called the operator.

"Plot, aye," answered Air Plot.

"Large attack force bearing two four seven, range six eight miles," reported the operator. The CXAM radar had once again been late to identify the contact.

At 1109 hours, three Wildcats visually confirmed the attack force. The Zeros were covering the force at about thirteen thousand feet, the dive bombers were next at about twelve thousand feet, another layer of Zeros flew at about eleven thousand feet, and the remaining torpedo bombers flew at about ten thousand feet. This was a well-coordinated attack force. The dive bombers began their attack. The Wildcat fighters moved to engage the dive bombers at twelve thousand feet.

"CAP, Plot," called Air Plot, "we have fourteen bogeys twenty miles out to the northwest."

"Plot, CAP," called the CAP leader, "we have visual on the dive bombers. They are moving into two groups as they prepare to attack our flat tops."

"CAP team leaders, form into three teams and engage," ordered the CAP leader.

Three teams of Wildcats dove to meet the attacking dive bombers.

Team One screamed to meet the enemy, firing bursts of machine gun fire.

"CAP, One," called Team One leader, "splash one bomber!"

"CAP, Three," called the Team Three leader, "splash three, I repeat three, taking heavy—"

The comms went dead. The CAP leader looked down to his left to witness four Zeros attacking Team Three. One Zero sprayed an extended burst of machine gun fire, slicing off the right wing of his Team Three leader. The Wildcat began a death spiral toward the sea below. Three more Wildcats found their water graves.

"Plot, CAP," called the leader, "dive bombers lining up to attack from all points of the compass. I repeat all points."

The Lexington anti-aircraft guns burst into action, punching holes in the late morning sky. The remaining dive bombers continued unabated, releasing their deadly fish from every compass direction. Captain Sherman was out of options. Any evasive move would put his ship directly in the path of another torpedo. At 1118 hours, a torpedo struck the Lexington just forward of the port forward gun gallery. Two minutes later, another torpedo hit just aft from the gun gallery across from the bridge. Two minutes later, another torpedo hit in the same location.

"Bridge, Damage Control," called the officer.

"Bridge, aye," responded the OOD.

"Recommend we avoid further damage on the port side. If possible, direct any further torpedo damage to the starboard side," requested the officer.

The captain did not receive this recommendation.

Evasive maneuvers prevented the dive bombers from scoring a hit on the USS Yorktown. However, a five-hundred-pound bomb crashed through her flight deck, exploding beneath it, killing sixty-six men.

Just as the crew on the Lexington thought they had dodged a bullet, the shipped visibly compressed into the water.

"Where was that hit?" demanded the captain.

"Looks like they hit us with two bombs, sir," reported the XO. "One looks to be a thousand pounder that hit the after end of the port forward gun gallery. The second looks to have been a five-hundred pounder that hit the gig boat pocket, also on the port side. There might be another hit inside the stacks. I will get Damage Control to verify immediately."

At 1132 hours, the attack was over. The Lexington and Yorktown survived. The Lexington was listing six degrees to port due to the massive explosions suffered during the attack. Damage control parties pumped fuel oil to starboard to right the ship. At 1223 hours, she was making twenty-five knots and could still recover her planes.

At 1242 hours, Damage Control contacted the bridge with a problem.

"Bridge, Damage Control," called the officer.

"Bridge, aye," responded the XO.

"Sir, we have a definite problem here," began the officer. "We have a strong smell of aviation fuel down here near the chief's workroom. We may have a significant leak somewhere."

The XO relayed the report to the captain.

"Evacuate the area as quickly as possible," ordered the Captain, "and find out where that leak is coming from on the double!"

At 1247 hours, a horrific internal explosion rocked the Lexington. The leaking aviation fuel exploded, causing multiple fires throughout the ship.

"Damage Control, Bridge," called the XO, "report!"

"Sir, we still have explosions everywhere on the ship," said the officer. "Every time we get one under control, another aviation gas pipe ruptures and we have another fire. My team is handling the mayhem as best we can, sir."

"I want updates every fifteen minutes," ordered the captain.

Over the next six hours, Damage Control parties throughout the ship fought valiantly to save the Lexington, but to no avail.

At 1707 hours, Admiral Fitch sent word to Captain Sherman to abandon ship.

"Men," said the captain to the crew on the bridge, "I really thought we could save her. My men fought with distinction, but now I must give the worst order any captain can give." The captain reached for the hailer.

"All hands, all hands, this is the captain," called Captain Sherman. "Abandon ship. I repeat abandon ship!"

The captain moved away from the microphone.

"XO," ordered the captain, "supervise my abandon ship order."

"Aye, aye, sir!" responded the XO with a smart salute. The captain returned the salute, and the XO left the bridge.

The ship sprang into action as did the adjoining ships who sent life rafts to accept the Lexington crew. The captain monitored the progress from the bridge. At 1755 hours, the captain left the bridge and began a sweep, looking for stragglers. At 1800 hours, the captain met up with his executive officer who reported the forward section of the ship was clear of survivors. The captain then directed his XO to leave the ship. The XO climbed over the rail grabbing a rope, and let himself to the ocean below where another life raft waited to take him to safety. The captain made one last inspection and found some sailors struggling to get away from the distressed ship listing toward their position. The captain ordered the remaining sailors onboard to move to the starboard side aft of the ship, a safer egress position. As the captain observed the final sailor disappear over the rail, he made one last inspection of the ship and found a rope escaping his doomed carrier. Lowering himself to the ocean, he swam to the closest life raft where they helped him onboard.

The Lexington shook from another explosion. Within ten minutes, Captain Sherman reported to Admiral Fitch, and the magnitude of the situation hit him square between the eyes. Captain Sherman reviewed his former command. The Lexington was listing over ten degrees to port and burning uncontrollably. Admiral Fitch ordered the USS Phelps to sink the doomed aircraft carrier. With a heavy heart, the captain of the Phelps ordered the launch of five torpedoes to finish the work the Japanese began over seven hours earlier.

Three torpedoes hit their target, and the Lexington struggled to stay afloat. As the Lexington sank below the waterline, a tremendous explosion rocked the fleet as the Lexington protested her fate one last time before sinking two miles to her grave.

The after-action report described the following factors contributed to the loss of the carrier USS Lexington CV-2. First, the CXAM radar did not discover the incoming enemy assault early enough to launch an adequate defense. Detecting the incoming forces thirty miles earlier could have prevented the loss of the Lexington. Second, the Air Plot command in control structure was cumbersome and lacked the agility needed to respond to enemy action. Finally, CAPs should have flown at twenty thousand feet to ensure enemy interception prior to any attack of high-flying dive bombers.

23. DALLAS, TEXAS

Charlie looked out the window of the train to see his next stop. He would be on the train for the next fifty-six hours as he headed to San Diego, where he would train in what he did not know. The train lurched to a stop.

Charlie got up to stretch his legs.

"Where are you headed, son?" asked a businessman.

"Off to war, sir," responded Charlie. He followed his instructions and did not disclose the military base or his ultimate destination.

Dressed in a blue pinstripe three-piece suit with a smart tie, he exuded success.

"Are you hungry, son?" he asked.

"Yes sir, always!" responded Charlie.

The businessman brought Charlie to the Club Car where they had sandwiches and chatted about their lives and the war effort. Charlie thanked the businessman and went back to his seat.

Charlie heard the "all aboard" from the conductor and settled in to watch his country go by his window. He had never been west of Arkansas before and had only seen pictures of the world out west. Charlie was deep in thought about his sister and father back in Little Rock when a voice jarred him from his thoughts.

"Where are you headed, good looking?" a very attractive young lady was standing there right before him. At five-foot-five-inches with crimson hair and piercing blue eyes, her milky white face glowed as she stood before him, backlit by the sun shimmering on her back. She was wearing a dress Charlie recognized from a magazine his sister had back home. It was expensive; he was out of his league. He had dated while he was in high school, but nothing serious. He did not leave a girl back home in Little Rock.

"The war, ma'am," responded Charlie, following the same instructions provided by his training commander. The training from his sister was now kicking in. "Would you like to sit down?" Charlie said awkwardly.

"What's your name?" asked the girl.

"Charlie, Charlie Brand," responded Charlie.

"I am Lillian Hope, but you can call me Lilly," she said coyly. "I am from Dallas and headed to Phoenix with my parents," Lilly said. "My father is a businessman traveling to meet with some of his suppliers. That is my family over there."

Lilly pointed to a man and woman at the head of the car. As the father looked up, Charlie could see he was the same man who had bought him some food earlier. Charlie waved. The father smiled.

She took a seat next to Charlie. "Come on now, Charlie," she said flirting a bit, "you can tell me more about yourself."

Charlie spent the next few minutes describing to Lilly his life in Little Rock, trying to leave out items that would make his family look less attractive to his new friend.

"What about you?" Charlie said. "Tell me about yourself and your family."

"I am the youngest of four daughters, and I am getting ready to attend my last year at Ursuline Academy. My father owns a store in Dallas; that is why we are going to Phoenix. He is very interested in learning more about the southwestern states and hopes to find some new products to put in the store," Lilly said proudly.

Charlie tried not to look concerned; he knew families who had money in Little Rock and the daughters of these men were very high-minded and did not look kindly on working people. But there seemed to be something different about Lilly.

"My grandfather Hope was the man who started the store in Dallas in 1901," continued Lilly. "My daddy just took over the store with his brother. He has many fresh ideas to expand the store!" Lilly could sense that Charlie was becoming uncomfortable and steered the conversation back to him. "What caused you to want to fight for America?" she asked.

"Well," Charlie began slowly as he had not fully thought through his reasoning, "when Pearl Harbor happened, something clicked inside of me. I felt I needed to do something, but after my mom died a few years ago, I felt I needed to be at home to help my family."

"I am so sorry, Charlie!" cooed Lilly.

"Thank you," said Charlie. "I was at the movies a while back and saw a serial, Holt of the Secret Service. It was a grand show, but I got to thinking, I felt a stirring in my body that God had something for me to do, something more important than myself. As a Boy Scout, I know about service to others, and I guess I just think I need to do this for all the people who cannot. I guess I believe that God wants me to do this."

Lilly took this in and smiled warmly. "That is the most noble thing I ever heard." She held her emotions in check so she would not seem too forward. "What branch of the service will you be serving?"

"The Navy," said Charlie.

"Do you get seasick?"

Charlie's face sank. He had never been on a ship before.

Seeing the change in his expression, she asked, "What?"

"I have never been on a boat before. I do not know if I will be seasick or not," Charlie confessed with great embarrassment.

Lilly touched his hand. "Oh, Charlie, I am sure you will be fine. I am sure that God would not send you to a ship if you would be sick all the time. You will be fine, Charlie."

Charlie looked at his hand and looked up where he saw Lilly smiling at him. He looked into her eyes and the bottom half of his body went numb. He was lucky he was not standing, he thought.

"Charlie, Charlie," Lilly cooed, "what are you thinking?"

"I am just amazed that I signed up for the Navy and never thought that I might be sick until the war is over. Not very smart of me."

Lilly laughed, which caused Charlie to break into laughter. Her parents looked up to see what was causing the commotion and smiled.

One day later, the train pulled into the train station in Tucson where Lily and her family would transfer to another train that would take them on to Phoenix.

"Lilly," Charlie said shyly, "I have really enjoyed visiting with you. I can't believe we are here already."

"Charlie Brand," responded Lilly, "there is something very special about you. I know that God will bring you back to us and He will guide your steps. He *has* a plan for you, and so do I."

Charlie gulped. "Can I write you while I am gone?" he asked.

"You better!" instructed Lilly, and both of them broke into raucous laughter.

Lilly's father pointed to his pocket watch. "Time to go, Lilly," he called.

"Yes, sir," responded Lilly. "Here is my address so you can write me," she said to Charlie, and paused. "Every day!" giggled Lilly.

They both laughed again.

24. TOKYO, JAPAN

Hadaki recoiled in pain as the cane crossed his back. He was familiar with the ways of his superior officer, who whipped him for any minor infraction of the rules. His understanding of discipline changed during his first three months of service to his emperor. His *chichi* used corporal punishment sparingly to make a point, but Hadaki believed that his superiors basked in the pain they could cause a human being. Hadaki was lucky. Many of his fellow soldiers emerged from their beatings with broken bones and bloodied faces. Discipline was necessary and feared by the Japanese military man.

Hadaki felt welts emerge from his back as he prepared for the next strike. *Whack!* He breathed. His superior officer liked and complimented him most of the time. Completing the first live fire exercise of his Type 97 81-millimeter infantry mortar, Hadaki had misjudged the azimuth and overshot his target by ten meters. His superior officer, so incensed by his careless calculations, beat Hadaki for five minutes, only stopping to switch hands. The beating ceased.

"You will be more careful, private!" screeched the sergeant.

"Yes, *gunso*," Hadaki said, gritting his teeth.

"Do it again," screamed the sergeant. "This time you better not miss."

Hadaki recalculated his azimuth and pulled the cord, launching the seven-pound projectile toward its target. This time, his aim was true, destroying the target and saving his back from another beating. He would be an expert with his weapon, he swore.

. . . . .

Charlie had not stopped smiling since he watched Lilly leave to board another train. He was so giddy he nearly forgot to eat, something he had not done since he had the stomach flu last year.

"San Diego!" called the conductor. "We are arriving in San Diego!"

As the train lurched to a stop, a man dressed in uniform entered the train car. "You Brand?" asked the man. From his insignia, he was a Navy lieutenant.

"Yes, sir," responded Charlie as he stood to attention and saluted.

"Come with me," instructed the lieutenant.

Charlie grabbed his gear and followed the lieutenant to a waiting jeep.

"You are my last pickup sailor," said the lieutenant. "I am Lewis, Henry Lewis."

"Nice to meet you, sir," said Charlie. "Where are we going?"

"Can't tell you," chided Lewis. "They instructed you *not* to tell anyone where you were going, correct?"

"Yes, sir," responded Charlie. "I did not tell a soul about my destination or what I would do."

"Good," said Lewis. "Now sit back and breathe the fresh Southern California salt air."

Charlie sat back as ordered and looked as the ocean passed by. He was now more concerned than ever that he would be sick until the end of the war.

The jeep followed San Diego Bay to the north, and curled around until they arrived at Point Loma, their destination, and the site of the Navy training center.

"Here we are," announced Lewis. "Welcome to the Navy Training Center at Point Loma. This will be your home for the next eight weeks. If you make it out of here, we will send you to the Pacific to support the war effort."

Now Charlie had something else to worry about. He was told he did well on the test that brought him to San Diego, but he was still not sure what he would do in the Navy. They stopped at a building as a newly minted machinist's mate exited a military Jeep.

"Here we are," said Lewis. "Chow is at 1730 so do not be late. The guys inside will show you to your bunk."

Charlie grabbed his gear and thanked Lewis. The exterior of the building was in the Spanish style with yellow stucco and a red tile roof. The interior was ninety feet long and forty feet wide, with bunks arranged in two rows. At the far end of the building was the head, or the bathroom.

"You must be Brand," said a sailor. "We've been waiting for you."

"I've been on a train for the past fifty-six hours," offered Charlie. "I didn't have much chance to ask the engineer to hurry it up for me."

The men laughed. The building could hold ninety men, but there were only thirty men in the building. Charlie introduced himself to his bunk mates and unpacked his seabag.

The next morning, the men loaded onto a bus and rode five minutes to where they would spend the next eight weeks of their lives. The men were anxious. They talked the previous night, but no one had any idea why they were in San Diego. The lieutenant met them as they arrived.

"Good morning, men," began Lewis. "As many of you will remember, I am Lieutenant Lewis, and I will be your liaison officer during your time here at Point Loma. What you are about to see and hear over the next eight weeks has the highest classification. You cannot discuss what is in this building or what you will do for the war effort with anyone. Am I clear?"

"Yes, sir," responded the men.

"Now fall out and move toward the MP guarding the door," ordered Lewis. His hopes for these men grew as he thought of how they would change the direction of the war.

Each man was given a notepad and pencil when they arrived on base. They grabbed their supplies and waited in line in front of the guard as instructed. Before each man entered the building, the guard checked his papers and military ID.

Charlie entered the building and looked up. He realized he was in an aircraft hangar. He looked around and noticed concentric circles painted on the floor like a bullseye and strings hanging from the rafters. Then he saw ten tricycles. *What in the world are they doing here?* he wondered. They escorted the men to their classroom where they saw electronic equipment.

"Welcome, men," began their instructor. "I am Captain Handy. Me and my instructors will train you for your next assignment. But first, I must read all of you into this top-secret program."

Captain Handy spent the next twenty minutes reading the men into the radar program and described how this weapon would change the war effort and give the United States an advantage over all other countries in the world.

"Before we had radar," continued Handy, "we used aircraft to extend the visual range from our ships. These Combat Air Patrols, or CAPs as we call them, extend out twenty-five miles from the aircraft carriers to provide an early warning of incoming hostile aircraft. Even with the early warning, we still had insufficient time to react to the threat, but it was all we had. Later, we split the air patrols into sectors, which limited the visibility of the patrols and this was not effective. The flight control officer had to be airborne so he could see the entire air battle area, but the enemy often drew him into action during dog fights. As a result, he would become distracted and not able to provide tactical direction to his team. Before radar, we handled our air defense with minimal control by one tactical commander without valuable information about the enemy locations and strength."

The men listened intently.

"Radar will win the war for the US," concluded Handy. "You men will be the first line of defense against the Japanese as radar operators. At the conclusion of this course, we will assign you to ships in the Pacific where you cannot tell anyone what you do. As radarmen, you will need to blend into the life of your ship. People will see you working on the radar equipment, but they will not know what it is used for. There will be scuttlebutt amongst the crew about what you do, but you will say nothing. Even most of the officers will not know what you do. You are to keep what you do a secret, or you will be court-martialed and sent to the brig for a very long time."

A brig, short for brigantine, is a military prison. Small two-masted ships were used as floating prisons throughout the nineteenth century.

The men began looking at each other with looks of concern. What had he gotten himself into, thought Charlie.

25. WASHINGTON, DC

"Thank you for coming, admiral, captain," began Admiral King. "We all share your loss."

"We are excited to present our proposal to you today, admiral," said Admiral Nimitz.

"Thank you, Admiral King," responded the captain.

Admiral Nimitz and Captain Sherman had been called to Washington to discuss a new tactical structure to support Air Plot and the radar operators of the fleet. Losing the USS Lexington because of late enemy notifications was unacceptable, and Captain Sherman was there to present the proposed solution to the Joint Chiefs.

"Admiral Nimitz," said Admiral King, "you may begin the briefing."

"Thank you, sir," began Admiral Nimitz. "On 8 May of this year, we lost the USS Lexington and almost lost the USS Yorktown. Captain Buckmaster from the Yorktown and Captain Sherman from the Lexington identified significant concerns with the communications protocols and physical structure of our radar and plotting capabilities during the battle of Coral Sea, and I have asked Captain Sherman to brief this body on our recommendations. Captain Sherman, please continue."

"Thank you, sir," said the captain. "Gentlemen, I am sure you have reviewed our after-action reports so I will not revisit the details of these reports. Let me begin by stating critical components of the tactical situation, the component failures of our current structure, and then I will detail our proposal."

"Very well, please continue," said Admiral King.

"During the engagement on 7 and 8 May," began Captain Sherman, "we experienced communication failure and disruption in our ability to discover the approaching enemy forces using our CXAM radar equipment. Further, the communication protocols used to communicate radar plot information to Air Plot are cumbersome and delay important decision-making abilities of our fighter director.

"As you are aware, information gathering is the critical determining factor for success or failure during battle. The general operation of the CXAM radar requires multiple steps to determine the direction and range of incoming enemy targets. Also, there are dead areas in the radar coverage the enemy exploited during the battle, causing delays in transmitting critical tactical enemy positions to our Air Plot and ultimately to command. This was the largest tactical battle experienced in the war and the volume of radio traffic from the fighters, Radar, and Air Plot overwhelmed the command, reducing its effectiveness."

"Captain, you have succinctly stated the problem. Please proceed with your recommendations," prompted Admiral Nimitz.

"Yes, sir," continued Sherman. "Captain Buckmaster and I developed a new structure for radar plot to increase the effectiveness of information sharing while providing facilities that will promote camaraderie while presenting a complete tactical view to the fighter director and command. Here are our recommendations:

- Provide a unit within the ship to house all elements of detection and fighter direction.
- Have sufficient room to allow radar plotting, communications, and fighter direction to function without interference.
- Isolate the members of the team from noise interference, creating an environment free of distraction.
- Have its own radio communications, capable of transmitting or receiving on any aircraft circuit, and on a super-frequency circuit with other search-radar-equipped vessels and with other fighter directors.
- Provide communications connection to signal the bridge, lookouts, flag officers, and fire control stations.
- Be in proximity to Air Plot to facilitate actual conversations with them.
- Contain plotting facilities capable of supporting two radar stations, one for search activities and one for tracking fighter direction.
- A facility capable of providing a complete tactical situation to the command."

"This is impressive work, captain," congratulated Admiral King. "Do you have a proposed name for this structure?"

"Admiral Nimitz and I propose the Combat Operations Center, sir," responded the captain.

"Well," began Admiral King, "based on your assertion that, information sharing during battle is the key to successful engagements, I would suggest changing the name to Combat Information Center."

"Excellent suggestion, admiral," said Nimitz.

"Decision made," stated King. "Admiral Nimitz, prepare a technical bulletin and we will identify space in our ships under construction."

"Aye, aye, sir," said Admiral Nimitz with a salute.

Admiral King saluted his officers and thanked them for their participation in the meeting.

. . . . .

"Admiral," instructed Tojo, "please provide an update on our Port Moresby invasion."

Yamamoto needed to be careful to not give away any advantage during his briefing. "Sir," he began, "our invasion force encountered Admiral Nimitz's forces south of Port Moresby as we expected. Our spy planes found the enemy, and we sent overwhelming forces to engage their fleet. Our superior air power gave us victory over the Americans, and they have left the area. We sunk four of their ships: the USS Neosho, USS Sims, the USS Lexington, and the USS Yorktown, two of their prized aircraft carriers."

"We did not leave this victory unscathed," reminded Tojo.

His information is accurate; careful here, thought Yamamoto. "You are correct, Mr. Tojo," offered Yamamoto. "We lost the light carrier Shoho and one destroyer."

"So, you say this was a glorious victory, yet we lost two important ships to their four," taunted Tojo. "You are too careless in your planning. We had the advantage of surprise. Yet, you lose two ships. Why should we trust you with more of our emperor's treasure?"

Yamamoto carefully composed his thoughts. He could not allow Tojo to goad him into a mistake. He would not let the venom from this *nihon mamushi* (pit viper) bring shame to the Japanese people and his emperor.

"Tojo-san," Yamamoto said in his most deferential tone, "this council has entrusted me to lead the war effort, and I fully expect that we will crush these demon creatures and send them back to *jigoku* (hell) where we will continue to inflict torture on them."

"We cannot accept further failure," chided Tojo. "You know the penalty. There is nothing more to discuss today." Tojo stood and left the room, followed by the other members of the council.

Yamamoto waited until he was alone, and his anger rose to the surface. *I will see Tojo sent to Jigoku for his insolence. Look at the brilliant victory I created at Pearl Harbor. No one in this room is capable of such greatness. They will cry when I am honored at the palace by the emperor himself for my service while he sends his soldiers to kill these chīsana on'nanoko (little girls) and feed them to the dogs*, swore Yamamoto.

26. WASHINGTON, DC

Admiral King entered the Oval Office where the president awaited him on the sofa.

"Thanks for meeting me this early, admiral," the president warmly said. "Would you like some coffee or danish?"

"Coffee please, black," responded the admiral.

The porter served his coffee and retired through the secret side door.

"This loss of the Lexington," the president began, and his face grew grim. "Every time we seem to make headway, another disaster befalls our cause."

"I know we lost three ships during the battle, sir," offered the admiral, "but we won a tactical victory."

"How is that?" asked Roosevelt.

"The Japanese forces could not establish their base on Port Moresby," countered King. "Our losses were not in vain. In fact, I fully expect our next engagement with the enemy to change the trajectory of the war in the Pacific."

"Strong words, admiral," cautioned the president.

"I say these words with great confidence, sir," said King. "I know our radarmen will come through for us. Our equipment is superior to the Japanese, and we have a righteous cause that our men fight for. I promise you, sir, our men *will not* let us down."

"I know this is true, admiral," said the president.

The men talked for another forty minutes, discussing strategy and the new Combat Information Center.

. . . . .

Tojo entered the room and called the War Council to order.

"Admiral," began Tojo, "we are here to discuss our new offensive plans. I trust that this plan will be more successful than Operation MO."

"Thank you, prime minister, for your confidence," Yamamoto said with an ounce of credulity. "Our next target," he continued, "is Midway Island. We have devised a plan that will lure the Americans from Pearl Harbor to protect their island base, where we will deal a crushing blow to their fleet. At the completion of this operation, we will have complete control of all shipping lanes in the Pacific, and we will have a base of operations where we will launch a massive assault on Pearl Harbor, destroying their navy and ensuring our ultimate victory over the demon creatures."

"Fine words, admiral," taunted Tojo, "but I ask again: why the emperor should continue to trust you with his treasure after our last operation?"

The anger inside of Yamamoto was showing, and a thin smile crept onto Tojo's face.

"Prime minister," assured Yamamoto, "this operation is bold—I will agree—but we cannot deny the strategic nature of this island."

"Agreed," Tojo slightly relented.

"We have always known of the necessity of taking this atoll," continued Yamamoto, "but I must remind this council that our enemy lost two of their precious carriers during Operation MO. Our intelligence reports show we sunk the Lexington, and one of our dive bombers inflicted a mortal wound to the Yorktown. A strike that surely split her in two."

"True," Tojo said, gritting his teeth.

"With these losses suffered by their fleet," concluded Yamamoto, "we must act now. Finish them once and for all!"

The council approved Yamamoto's plans, and he set a date in early June for the attack. *Soon, I will have my ultimate revenge on this council when I crush the rest of the American fleet,* Yamamoto thought.

27. POINT LOMA, SAN DIEGO

Charlie sat mesmerized as his instructor covered the first lessons in radar fundamentals. He was a fiddler, taking the cover off of their radio at home when his sister was not at home. He almost always reassembled the radio before she came home so he would not catch her wrath. But the few times he couldn't, "Charles, how many times do I have to tell you?" she would chide. "I cannot miss Amanda of Honeymoon Hill! Now get that radio back together before my show at three fifteen."

"If you have ever been in a canyon or in a train tunnel," began the instructor, "what happens if you shout hello?"

Johnny Savage raised his hand. Johnny grew up in the Smokies of Eastern Tennessee in a little town called Pigeon Forge. He expressed the same calling to join the Navy as Charlie, although he heard the call later in life; Johnny was twenty years old.

"Yes, Savage," called the instructor.

"I hear an echo," answered Johnny.

"Correct," said his instructor.

"So, when you say hello in this environment," explained the instructor, "a sound wave reflects off of the hard surfaces and comes back to you as your voice, only delayed a bit. Radio waves operate the same way, except we use them to reflect off of planes and ships where we see them displayed on your radar sets in the form of a pip.

"If you shout continuously in the same environment, what happens?" asked the instructor.

Charlie had this. He raised his hand and waited for recognition.

"Brand," called the instructor.

"Well, sir," Charlie started, "I guess you get a mishmash of sound coming back on you."

"That is right, Brand," said the instructor, "which makes it difficult to find anything. So how do you think we should manage your voice so you can hear your distinct location?"

"Maybe use shorter, consistent shouts?" offered Charlie.

"Spot on, Brand." The instructor had spent time in England and had picked up some British slang.

The instructor continued his lecture covering how radar uses short, narrow, directional radio pulses sent at regular intervals to reflect off of objects far beyond your sight. The objects then reflect the pulse back to a receiver, and measurement of the travel time between the object and the transmitter determines the distance to the object. He also explained that radio waves can reflect off of the upper atmosphere or ionosphere, allowing detection of objects below the horizon. The wavelength used, the power of the transmitter, and the sensitivity of the receiver all determined the effective range of any radar system.

The instructor was now speaking about the latest innovations from their British allies. "Our British allies gave us an important tool a few short months ago. What I will share with you now is top secret, and any disclosure will surely land you in Fort Leavenworth for the rest of your life."

The instructor reached into his pocket, and removed a whistle. He held it up high in the air. "What is this?" he asked.

The students laughed.

"It is a whistle, sir," responded a student.

"Correct." The instructor put the whistle to his mouth and blew. It created a tone. "Does anyone know how a whistle works?" he queried.

The room was silent, but most knew that you blew into the whistle and it made a sound.

"You see, boys," began the instructor, answering his own question, "when I blow across the open pipe of this whistle, it generates a wave within the pipe. Our ears hear the generated wave as a musical note. This is also how a pipe organ works. The longer the tube, the lower the musical note. Last year, the British gave us a gift that works like a whistle, but instead of generating a musical tone, it generates a microwave."

A microwave, thought Charlie.

"A microwave," explained the instructor, "is like a radio wave, but it operates at a different frequency. We measure the frequencies in megacycles and break those frequencies into five different ranges or bands, P, L, S, X, and K. Each of our radar uses a specific band that corresponds to its military use. We will discuss each radar set and its associated band in later lectures."

The instructor continued to explain the general theory of the cavity magnetron and radar.

. . . . .

"Admiral Nimitz," interrupted Commander Collins, "I have a report from our code-breaker team you must see."

Commander Collins was the newly minted commander who had raised the ire of the admiral during his last briefing. He commanded all signals intelligence, or SIGINT.

"More news about Japanese battle plans, I hope," desired Nimitz.

"Yes, sir," answered Collins hoping to redeem his last performance. "Our code-breakers have struck gold again, sir. They intercepted a communication from the Japanese describing plans to attack Midway Island."

"Damn, I knew this day would come," swore the admiral. "Any timeline given?"

"The communication gave a vague timeline of early June," said Collins.

"Assemble the command staff immediately," ordered Nimitz.

Within twenty minutes, the command staff was in the conference room next to Admiral Nimitz's office. A large map of the Pacific Ocean hung on the wall behind the head of the admiral, and more detailed regional maps lay on the conference room table.

"Commander Collins, the briefing is yours," said Nimitz.

“Thank you, sir,” said Collins. “We have intercepted Japanese communications outlining plans to attack the island of Midway in June. There were few details of the operation in the communication, but Admiral Yamamoto signed the communication.”

“Based on the high level of this communication,” Nimitz said warily, “we can only assume this will be a major offensive. I need options and what assets we have available to beef up the defenses of the island.”

The command staff provided input over the next hour.

Admiral Nimitz listened carefully to the proposals from his command staff. Most of them were experienced war fighters and tacticians, and he was lucky to have them.

“I agree we need to strengthen our Marine garrison on the island,” Nimitz said, taking back the conversation from the organized chaos, “but we are going to need more planes if we are going to fight off their enormous attack force. Will the Avengers be ready in time, Vice Admiral Anderson?”

The Grumman TBF Avenger had just entered the war effort that year. Manufacturing had begun in 1941 at the General Motors plant in Dearborn, Michigan. Military leaders expected the plane would replace the Devastator dive bombers that had been a staple of the Navy since 1935. Heavier than any other Navy bomber, the Avenger had a range of 1000 miles and could carry four 5000-pound bombs or one Mark 13 2000-pound torpedo.

“Sir,” answered Anderson, “six Avengers just landed on Midway, but we do not expect the remaining ninety-four to be ready in time for any battle in early June. We have eighteen Dauntless bombers we will move immediately to support the effort on Midway, and we have eighteen B-17 bombers stationed on Oahu we can make part of our plans.”

“I expect a complete battle plan for my review by the end of the day.” Admiral Nimitz rose to leave the room.

“Aye, aye, sir,” the command staff rose and saluted.

28. HASHARAJIMA, JAPAN

"Onishi, let us review one more time our battle plans for the Midway offensive," ordered Yamamoto.

This would be *his* battle plan. It was a brilliantly conceived plan filled with deception, and he was sure this would destroy the Americans once and for all.

"You command your battle force," began Onishi, "comprising seven battleships, three cruisers, two seaplane carriers, one light carrier, and twenty destroyers. The *Kido Butai* carriers Hiryu, Soyu, Akagi, and Kaga will depart for Midway on 27 May, escorted by two fast battleships, three cruisers, and eleven destroyers. The Midway invasion force comprises two battleships, four heavy cruisers, one light carrier, and seven destroyers. Five thousand troops will occupy Midway after we crush the American forces on the island."

"Correct," said Yamamoto, "and our Aleutian forces?"

"Those forces originate from Ominato in the north of our homeland," responded Onishi. "One heavy carrier, one light carrier, two cruisers, and three destroyers. The invasion force of one thousand troops and seven battleships will attack Dutch Harbor, Alaska, where we will force the Americans to split forces from our Midway campaign to protect their assets in the Aleutians."

"And our submarines?" queried Yamamoto.

"Twelve submarines will create a picket around Oahu to detect the American departure from Pearl Harbor," said Onishi. "This plan is truly a stroke of genius, Admiral Yamamoto! It is my honor to work beside you."

"Ensure that the submarine picket is in place by 3 June in case the Americans catch wind of our operation," said Yamamoto.

"Hai!" said Onishi.

Admiral Yamamoto and his fleet left harbor on May 30 steaming for Midway.

• • • • •

"Yorktown has just entered dry dock, sir," said the commander of naval operations.

"Very well," responded Nimitz. "How much time do they need to repair her damage?"

"Estimate from the team is three months," reported the commander.

"Three months!" exploded Nimitz. "In three months, the Japanese will occupy Midway, and we can expect attacks on Oahu to follow. We do not have that kind of time!"

"I already made that message perfectly clear, admiral," the commander cajoled. "I told them we need this carrier in one month, sir." The commander believed this would assuage the anger of his boss.

"Did you not hear anything I just said?" Nimitz roared as he pounded his fist on the table. "I want the Yorktown out of dry dock in five days."

"Five days, uh, yes, sir," said the commander sheepishly. "Aye, aye, sir." The commander saluted, leaving the admiral to stew.

Three days later, the Yorktown floated dry dock. Fifteen hundred men worked around the clock to repair the major damage suffered during the battle of Coral Sea, and 150 dockyard workers accompanied the carrier as she steamed out of port to complete the remaining repairs. Task Force 17 left port on May 30, ahead of the Japanese submarine picket, headed for Midway Island.

29. MIDWAY ISLAND

JUNE 3

"Catalina One, you are cleared for takeoff," called the air traffic controller.

"Roger," responded the pilot.

Catalina one, piloted by Ensign Jack Rice, pushed his throttle controls to maximum, skimming off of the choppy seas until he eased his plane into the air and banked hard to the right, climbing to Angels fifteen. Ensign Rice was new to the island, having received his commission only three months earlier in Corpus Christi, Texas. He flew crop dusters back home in Indiana and always carried a picture of his girl Rita with him on every flight. His orders were simple. Patrol the area west and southwest of the island looking for enemy activity. This was the seventh day in a row he was performing this same search.

"Midway, Catalina One," called Rice.

"Catalina One, Midway," responded the radio operator, "go ahead."

"Beginning search pattern Zulu," said Rice. "At least it is a beautiful day to fly."

"Are we bothering you up there, son?" called an unfamiliar voice. "If this duty is too boring for you, I am sure I could find something more interesting for you on the ground. Now get your head in the game!"

Rice gulped. "Yes, sir," he responded. "I am perfectly happy up here flying this mission."

At 0926 hours, Rice looked out of his starboard window to see a large fleet of ships headed toward Midway Island.

"Midway, Catalina One," called Rice with far more urgency, "sighting of a large Japanese force headed toward Midway Island."

"Catalina One, Midway," the strange voice was back, "number of ships, bearing, and distance."

"Midway," responded Rice, "heading three seven degrees, distance two four six miles, twenty-two ships. This looks to be an invasion force. I repeat an invasion force. Over."

"Nice job, Catalina One," complimented the unknown voice. "Looks like you get to fly another day. Now see if you can find anything else out there."

Ensign Rice completed his search pattern, and safely landed, providing a complete debrief to his command.

. . . . .

Vice Admiral Chuichi Nagumo labored over the tactical plans for the upcoming attack on Midway. Nagumo, a graduate of the Naval War college, specialized in torpedo war tactics and recently left his post as the commandant of the Torpedo School to become the commander-in-chief of the First Carrier Striking Force, better known as the *Kido Butai*. Many questioned his appointment as they considered him to be an overly cautious leader. Recently, he had received criticism for not sending a third strike force to Pearl Harbor to destroy the maintenance and oil storage facilities, rendering the upcoming Midway offensive moot.

"Admiral," interrupted one of his commanders, "we are 340 nautical miles from Midway, and our reconnaissance planes have found no carriers in the area. We will have complete surprise as we attack in the morning."

"Our crews are ready?" questioned Nagumo, knowing the answer.

"Hai!" responded the commander. "We will fit half of our planes with bombs to attack the bases at Midway and leave half of our planes here in case the American carriers are foolish enough to engage our overwhelming forces."

"Very well. We launch at 4:30 a.m. tomorrow," ordered Nagumo.

. . . . .

"Admiral Nimitz, a flash communication from Midway," said the lieutenant.

"Thank you," said Nimitz, and he sat down to review the communication.

The communication identified a large Japanese invasion force to the southwest headed toward Midway Island. *But that is not the main attack force*, thought Nimitz. *What route will this force take?* Nimitz stood and put his finger directly on Midway Island on his wall map. He stood back and knew.

"Prepare a comm to Task Force 17," ordered Admiral Nimitz.

Twenty minutes later, Admiral Fletcher received the communication from Admiral Nimitz at CINPACFTL.

The Japanese are hiding in over one million square miles of the Pacific Ocean. I hope the Admiral has intel to narrow this search, thought Fletcher.

"Assemble my command staff," ordered Fletcher.

Three minutes later, Fletcher entered the room and closed the door. "Men, I have received word from Admiral Nimitz," he began. "It is the belief of the admiral that the attack on Midway will come from the northwest. He ordered us to head southwest to intercept the Japanese fleet. Is our radar in good working order?"

"Yes, sir," responded the Yorktown captain.

"We will need surprise on our side this day. Men, be alert and begin combat air patrol operations at 0300 hours. I want that fleet found before they attack Midway," ordered Fletcher.

"Aye, aye, sir!" responded the officers.

30. NORTHWEST OF MIDWAY ISLAND

JUNE 4, 0400 HOURS

Ensign Rice thought himself lucky to be searching in a new zone. He had been airborne for forty-five minutes on a northwesterly heading.

"Midway, Catalina Four," called Rice.

"Catalina Four, Midway, go ahead," responded the operator.

"Midway, I believe I am seeing a large group of lights below me bearing two seven one, range two eight niner miles," reported Rice.

"Catalina Four, Midway," called the unfamiliar voice again, "verify range and bearing."

Ensign Rice verified the range and bearing. "Midway, I see more lights," reported Rice. "Definitely more action now."

"Great job, Catalina Four," offered the unfamiliar voice. "Better get back here to refuel. We may need your eyes throughout the day."

"Roger that," responded the ensign.

The unfamiliar voice was the commander of forces on Midway Island, Jonas Sterns. It was now time to give his Radar team a heads up that company was definitely coming their way. Minutes later, the SCR-270 set sprang into action, probing the skies for the approaching enemy.

At 0430 hours, Nagumo launched his force of 108 planes for another surprise attack on an American base. He knew his forces would devastate the infrastructure of the island, preparing the invasion force for a decisive victory.

At 0440 hours, Catalina Five spotted the attack force.

"Midway, Catalina Five," called the pilot.

"Catalina Five, go ahead," responded the operator.

"Many planes, heading Midway, bearing three two zero, two five zero miles," the pilot said with great urgency.

"Roger," responded the operator.

Two minutes later, the SCR lit up. They had found the attack force.

"Major," called the radar operator on Midway, "I found the attack force. I confirm range and bearing, sir."

Within five minutes, the Brewster Buffalo fighters were in the air along with what few Wildcats the island defense could muster. Radar vectored the planes to intercept the Zeros racing to meet them in battle.

"BR One, lead," called the Brewster squadron commander, "split off high and engage."

"Roger, tally-ho!" responded BR One.

"BR Two, Three, and Four," instructed the commander, "try to split off the Zeros from their formation. My team is going after those bombers."

"Roger," responded the team leaders.

The Brewster Buffalo, introduced in 1939, had a top speed of 270 miles per hour, significantly slower than the attacking Zeros. The Zeros made quick work of the Buffalos, downing seventeen of twenty-eight fighters in the initial engagement. The Zeros continued their air supremacy as they downed seven of the Wildcats. The Japanese lost only three bombers.

A squadron of B-26 bombers flew over the skirmish below, hoping to pass undetected.

"Captain," called the number one gunner, "Zeros, four-o'clock low."

The squadron fiercely defended itself, losing only two bombers to enemy fire. The squadron prepared to rain hell down on the enemy.

At 0620 hours, the Midway anti-aircraft guns spoke angrily as the Japanese bombers released their fiery wrath against Midway's Eastern and Sand islands. Fortunately, all island-based airplanes narrowly escaped the attack as they were airborne by 0600 hours. The Japanese bombers devastated Eastern Island's infrastructure, destroying the power plant, command post, gasoline lines, and the mess hall. However, the Japanese missed critical infrastructure during the bombing as the two runways suffered minimal damage and remained operational.

On Sand Island, direct hits to the oil tanks and water lines ensured the remaining island infrastructure would be ablaze for weeks to come. The Japanese did not escape unscathed. During the attack, the Midway anti-aircraft guns plucked eleven planes from the sky, damaging another fourteen, rendering them useless for future attacks. The Japanese air commander surveyed the damage and realized another strike would be necessary.

At 0700 hours, the *Kido Butai* came under attack from four B-26 bombers, fitted with torpedoes, and six Avenger torpedo planes added two days earlier.

"Evasive maneuvers," ordered Nagumo.

Thirty Zeros engaged the attacking American bombers. The Avengers targeted the Hiryu.

"All right, boys," squawked the squadron commander, "Zeros coming in ten-o'clock high!"

One by one, the Zeros cut the Avengers from the sky until only two remained.

"Release, release, release!" ordered the American commander.

The torpedoes hit the water, streaking toward their prey. The torpedoes missed their targets and fell helplessly into the deep.

The four B-26 bombers dove to meet the Akagi.

"Make them count," called the squadron commander. "Those Zeros will cut—"

The commander and his wingman dropped from the sky. The last two bombers released their torpedoes with the same result: misses.

Nagumo watched in disbelief as a B-26 flew straight for the bridge of the Akagi. The B-26 bomber commander miraculously extracted his plane from its watery grave to make one last attempt to sink his prey.

"I cannot believe this American would be so brave," said Nagumo, almost gushing over his enemy.

"Gotta hold this steady," said the American pilot, gritting his teeth. "Steady, steady, steady! I am going to sink this carrier even if I have to . . ."

The pilot veered to his right at the last second, just before hitting the bridge of the Akagi. *Americans do not commit suicide*, thought the commander as the ocean swallowed his plane.

"Admiral, the Midway strike force commander informs us there must be a second attack," said the Japanese air operations commander.

"Prepare the deck and make ready the reserve planes for the second Midway strike force," ordered Nagumo.

At 0753 hours, a second American attack targeted the Hiryu. Sixteen Dauntless dive bombers formed to make a glide run attack. Nine Zeros descended to protect their carrier, plucking eight bombers from the sky. The remaining eight torpedo bombers released their fish. All torpedoes harmlessly missed their target.

At 0810 hours, fifteen B-17 high-altitude bombers attacked the *Kido Butai* from twenty thousand feet. Anti-aircraft guns stretched to meet the B-17s, but to no avail. The bombs fell helplessly into the ocean, missing the evasive carriers.

The Japanese had survived a formidable attack.

At 0820 hours, Nagumo received news of an American sighting 240 miles to the north of Midway. The communication read, "The enemy is accompanied by what appears to be a carrier."

Nagumo quickly ordered the refitting of the reserve Kate dive bombers to torpedoes from the land-based bombs. With the refit in progress, Nagumo spent the next forty-five minutes landing, refueling, and rearming the original Midway attack force.

Now, he would finish the Americans and silence once and for all those who doubted his fitness for this command.

31. USS YORKTOWN

Captain Buckmaster heard a knock on his stateroom door. It was 0534 hours.

"Enter," said the captain. He had slept little, preparing in his mind for the upcoming Japanese engagement.

"Captain, I have a report you need to see, sir," said the XO, handing him the communication.

"Well then," said the captain, "we now have confirmation. It will happen today. Any news from our Dauntless patrols?"

The Dauntless dive bombers had been in the air by 0400 hours, performing search patterns to look for Japanese activity. Task Force 17 was on course to intercept the Japanese per the orders from Admiral Nimitz.

"Looks like Nimitz was right," said Buckmaster. "The Japanese launched their attack northwest of Midway."

"Great instincts," offered the XO.

"The best," responded his captain. "I will inform Admiral Fletcher."

"Aye, aye, sir!" the XO said as he saluted the captain and retired from the stateroom.

Captain Buckmaster quickly changed into a clean tunic and headed for the admiral's quarters. He knocked on the door and waited.

"Looking for someone," said a voice over his left shoulder.

Buckmaster turned to see Admiral Fletcher before him with a cup of coffee and a piece of toast. The admiral did not eat much before a battle.

"News of the Japanese attack force on Midway," said Buckmaster. The captain provided a quick summary of the report as they moved toward the bridge.

"Admiral and captain on the bridge," announced the XO.

"As you were," said the captain.

"I need the Hornet and Enterprise to dispatch immediately to engage the Japanese forces at our expected intersection point here," the admiral said pointing to their rendezvous position on the map.

At 0745 hours, Task Forces 16 and 17 began air operations for an all-out attack on the Japanese fleet. However, during the fog of launching their large attack force, the Wildcat escort tasked to support the fifteen Devastator bombers from the Enterprise instead broke to support the Devastators from the Hornet, leaving the first wave of Devastators without cover.

At 0815 hours, radar aboard the Enterprise displayed a contact.

"Plot, Radar," called the operator on the Enterprise.

"Plot, aye," responded Air Plot.

"Contact bearing one eight five degrees, range thirty miles. It appears to be a low-flying contact," informed the operator.

"Bridge, Plot," called Air Plot. "Sir, we have a contact bearing one eight five degrees, range three zero miles flying very low."

"We have to splash it," said the captain. "We do not have a choice. Break radio silence and dispatch a team to bring that snooper down before he can relay our position."

Red Section 17 Leader Steven Saunders listened as the Yorktown relayed bearing and range to his Wildcats. To disguise the communications from the Japanese, they used the word arrow instead of a bearing to confuse anyone who might intercept the transmission. The Wildcat pilots converted the true bearing communicated in the transmission to the magnetic bearing of their compass. This masked the correct position of the task force from the Japanese.

Red Section 17 turned to the converted bearing of one seven zero, and began the search for the snooper float plane. Ten minutes later, the team could not find the snooper plane. Five minutes later, the Akagi received and acknowledged a message from their snooper plane. The Japanese knew the position of the American forces.

At 0830 hours, air operations on the Yorktown sent a squadron of Devastators and Wildcats in search of the Japanese fleet.

"Based on our calculations," began the admiral, "we should engage the enemy here." Admiral Fletcher pointed to a position that was sixty miles southeast of the Japanese, a position off by over forty miles because of incorrect intelligence received earlier that morning.

"Plot, Bridge," called the CAG.

"Plot, aye," responded the fighter director.

"Do we have radar contact with the Japanese carrier force?" asked the CAG.

"Radar, Plot," called the fighter director.

"Radar, aye," responded the operator.

"Do you have any contacts?" asked the director.

The radar operator was just completing a sweep of the area. "No contacts to report," said the operator.

The bridge received the report with disdain.

"We should have contact by now," the CAG said with great frustration. "Keep at it."

Within ten minutes, most of the Wildcats ran out of fuel and ditched their planes.

At 0920 hours, the Scarlett section leader found the Japanese carriers.

"There they are, boys," said the leader. "Give 'em hell!"

The section moved into attack formation, but a hail of gunfire met them from the Zeros swooping from above. They lost all fifteen bombers without a torpedo being launched. Fifteen minutes later, the unescorted Enterprise bombers found the carrier force, but they also lost ten of fourteen planes before they could hit a single carrier target. The Yorktown bombers appeared at 1000 hours. This time, a fighter escort led by Lieutenant Commander Jimmy Thatch provided important air cover for the Devastators. Thatch deployed a new tactic never seen by the Zero pilots—the Thach Weave. The team would break into teams of three fighters and move into a beam defense position. Two fighters would fly on the right side of the formation, and a third fighter would fly about thousand feet to the left of the other formation, acting as a decoy to attract enemy Zeros. Once a Zero engaged the lone Wildcat, the team of two and the decoy pilot would turn toward each other leaving the Zero open to attack by the trailing Wildcat. The Japanese lost four Zeros before the remaining CAP overhead of the *Kido Butai* came to engage the oncoming Devastators. Yorktown lost ten out of seventeen planes without a single hit. The American forces struck out again and limped back toward their ships.

At 1005 hours, the shape of the battle changed. The original Japanese Midway strike force and reserve planes were ready to launch the counterattack against the American fleet steaming to meet them. Although the previous attacks did not score a single hit on the *Kido Butai* carriers, the American harassment prevented Nagumo from launching his planned counterattack. The Japanese could not launch their attack force while engaging the enemy.

Thirty-one Dauntless bombers, sucking the last fuel from their tanks, found the *Kido Butai* as they approached from the south. The CAP was still engaging enemy planes to the northeast, leaving the *Kido Butai* uncovered.

Diving from Angels nineteen, the Dauntless bombers targeted the mighty carrier Kaga. Japanese radar was only available on some destroyers in the fleet, so the American dive-bomber attack came as a complete surprise. Finally, American bombs hit their mark when three bombs pierced the deck of the Kaga, exploding within the crowded hangars, causing the fully fueled and armed planes to explode into an inferno that quickly engulfed the ship. One bomb struck the bridge, killing the captain and his staff.

From the north, another team of thirteen Dauntless bombers targeted the Soryu. Three bombs pierced the deck, and just like the Kaga, a deathly inferno engulfed the crippled carrier. Just as the attack on the Kaga started, three Dauntless bombers split from the formation and attacked the Akagi, landing one bomb in her midships hangar. Fire spread slowly through her hangars. But soon, the Akagi would suffer the same fate as her sister carriers.

By 1034 hours, they could see the smoke and flames from their sister carriers on the horizon, shocking the crew of the only remaining carrier, the Hiryu. How was it possible for such a devastating attack on their carriers? The pilots of the Midway attack watched in horror as death slowly engulfed the doomed carriers. The greatest naval fleet the world had ever known was now ablaze. There would be retribution.

32. IJN HIRYU

The men of the Hiryu crowded the rails as they watched their mighty carriers struggle to survive. Each man swore to avenge this savage attack on their great Navy. The pilots of the Hiryu ran to their planes, waiting for the call to return hell on the savage American carriers.

Within ten minutes, eighteen VAL dive bombers and an escort of six Zeros screamed to exact revenge on the Americans. Their chance would come sooner than they thought.

. . . . .

"Scarlett Leader, Four," called Scarlett Four, "I see six Zeros on their way, eight-o'clock."

The Enterprise-based Dauntless bombers broke right to gain better angles against the Zeros. A fully loaded Dauntless bomber would be no match against a Japanese Zero, but the bombers had no bombs.

"Split them off and use the Thach Weave," ordered the Scarlett leader.

The Dauntless bombers held their own against the Zeros, damaging two and causing them to turn back. The remaining Zeros disengaged and moved back into formation. The Zeros were now far behind the VAL attack force—another tactical error.

At 1152 hours, the Yorktown radar lit up.

"Plot, Radar," called the Yorktown operator.

"Plot, aye," responded the director.

"I have multiple contacts thirty-two miles out, bearing . . . directly for us!" reported the operator.

"Target strength?" asked the director.

"Best as I can see, four contacts," said the operator, "but I also see our boys headed back from the bombing raid."

The CXAM radar tracked targets, but it was the scope that provided the clarity if the contacts were friend or foe. The A-scope displayed enemy planes on the top section of the screen, while the bottom portion displayed contacts equipped with IFF. The operator identified two friendly contacts and mapped them to the new contacts he had just identified on his upper screen.

"Bridge, Plot," called the director.

"Bridge, aye," responded the bridge officer.

"We have four incoming contacts, thirty-two miles out, sir," called the director.

"Notify our CAP," ordered the CAG.

"Aye, aye, sir," responded the director.

Eight CAP planes received the bearing of the incoming contacts and raced to close the distance to the targets, trying to prevent an attack on the Yorktown.

The CAP fighters identified the targets as VAL dive bombers three minutes later, and engaged the attacking force. The Zeros lagged behind the VALs, giving the Yorktown CAP fighters an opportunity to deliver the first blow.

"Alright boys," began the CAP leader, "the VALs have no protection. Break into four teams and split them from their formation."

The CAP team scored seven kills before the Zeros appeared just in time to protect the remaining VALs.

"Zeros engaging," called CAP Seven.

"I got this," called CAP Five.

CAP five flew directly through the middle of the formation, taking out the lead Zero before losing his engine, causing him to dive to his death. Two more Zeros disappeared from the formation, along with two more VALs. Seven VALs split into two attack divisions, one from the west and one from the southwest.

The starboard gunner crews opened fire, hitting one VAL. Unfortunately, the VAL continued until it crashed into the starboard #2 elevator of the embattled carrier, killing ten crew. The gunners scored another hit, downing a second VAL that hit the fantail and exploded in a huge flame ball.

"Hard to port," ordered Buckmaster.

"Hard to port, aye," responded the helmsman.

Two more VAL bombs exploded off the starboard side, just aft of the fantail. However, the next bomb pierced the deck amidships, plunging deep inside the hull. The subsequent explosion damaged the stack uptakes, extinguishing all but one boiler. The Yorktown dropped to five knots.

The sixth VAL scored a direct hit on the port elevator, causing fires below the amidships hangar. The final VAL bomb missed to port. The Yorktown had survived, but four minutes later, the Yorktown ground to a halt, dead in the water. The few returning Japanese planes to the Hiryu reported that they had severely damaged an American carrier and probably sunk her. Two carriers remained.

"Damage Control, report!" ordered the XO.

"Sir, we have controlled 85 percent of the fires and we should have all boilers online in fifteen minutes," reported the officer. "I expect control of the remaining fires within twenty minutes."

"Excellent work!" praised the XO.

At 1415 hours, Yorktown radar again picked up enemy activity.

"Plot, Radar," called the Yorktown operator.

"Plot, aye," responded the director.

"I have a large attack force headed our way," reported the operator. "Estimate number at twelve planes, range four five miles."

"Roger," responded the director.

The Yorktown was now making nineteen knots. Unlike Japanese carriers, the Yorktown filled her fuel systems with carbon dioxide during battle, preventing catastrophic explosions like those of the enemy carriers. As the enemy attack force approached the American fleet, the commander of the Kate dive bomber noticed a carrier on his starboard side. *This must be another carrier*, he thought. *There is no visible damage or smoke around the carrier*. The superior US Damage Control parties had concluded their repairs just in time.

"CAP, Plot," called the flight director.

"CAP, aye," responded the leader.

"Arrow two four zero, range four three miles, strength twelve," ordered the director.

The CAP leader quickly performed the calculation and set a course for 259° to intercept the enemy planes. Within seven minutes, he could see the enemy forces below him. Captain Buckmaster instructed all CAP overwatch teams to patrol at Angels twenty. Intermittent cloud cover prevented the CAP from discovering the attacking Kates until they flew past them.

"Tally-ho," called the leader, and his team descended from the clouds.

The CAP team found only the trailing Kate in the formation, cutting it from the sky.

Eight Kate bombers split into two attack teams, one from the north and one from the east.

"Hard to starboard," order the captain.

"Hard to starboard, aye," responded the helmsman.

As the northern attacking force lined up to drop their bombs, a Wildcat fighter streaked toward the lead Kate.

"Who is that pilot?" asked the CAG.

"I think that is Thach, sir," said the spotter. He had seen Thach's call sign on his plane.

It was Thach.

"See if this slows you down, Jap!" said Thach as he let loose a trail of gunfire. The machine gun shredded the port fuel tank, causing a fire. However, the pilot controlled the plane long enough to release his torpedo, missing its target. Each of the remaining three Kates missed the Yorktown.

"That was clo—" the captain began until he saw a streak from his port side. Four torpedoes entered the water, hunting for glory. Two torpedoes hit on the port side amidships, gashing massive wounds to the struggling carrier. She listed to port.

"Report," demanded the captain.

"Damage Control reports water gushing in on the port side," began the XO. "They are not sure they can right her, sir. We lost three boilers and we have no steering control because of a jammed rudder."

The captain surveyed his ship. Time was not on his side, and his crew was in danger.

"All hands, this is the captain," called Buckmaster. "Abandon ship. I repeat, abandon ship!"

The XO left the bridge to supervise the order. As the last sailor left the ship, the XO eased over the side and lowered himself to a waiting boat below. The captain made one last tour of the ship and, finding no survivors, lowered himself off the fantail. After his rescue, Buckmaster reported to Admiral Fletcher onboard the USS Astor.

"Red Lady, Red Search Four," called the search plane. No response. He called again.

Onboard the Hornet, the flight director responded. "Red Search Four, Scarlett, go ahead."

"Last enemy carrier located," reported the search plane. The Yorktown launched a search team forty-five minutes before the torpedo attack to locate the Hiryu. The search plane relayed the bearing and distance to the carrier. She was within range.

"Red Search Four," called the director, "roger. No joy for coming home to Red Lady. Scarlett Letter will host."

The squadron of search planes landed safely on the Hornet.

Thirty-four Dauntless bombers from the Enterprise and sixteen remaining Yorktown Dauntless bombers left to retaliate on the Hiryu.

At 1700 hours, the squadron spotted the Hiryu.

"We attack from the southwest," ordered the strike leader, "Scarlett will take the carrier and Red will hit the battleship."

Coming out of the sun, the Yorktown bombers, aching to exact revenge for their carrier, obeyed the order and formed on the battleship. The Scarlett team dove to engage the Hiryu, which turned violently to port. The first group of bombs missed. The Red team, seeing the evasive maneuver of the Hiryu, broke the attack from the battleship and engaged the Hiryu. Four bombs ripped through the forward section of the ship, exploding gasoline and ordinance.

The greatest carrier force the world had ever known would never again claim supremacy over the skies of the Pacific. The Japanese scuttled the carriers of *Kido Butai* as the sun set on any hope of capturing Midway or dealing a lethal blow to the American fleet.

JUNE 6

The Yorktown continued to list to port, but did not capsize. Captain Buckmaster selected a skeleton crew to save her from a watery grave. The destroyer Hammann came along her starboard side to deliver the salvage party. Lurking one thousand yards away, a Japanese submarine prepared to deliver the final death knell to the carrier. Four torpedoes raced toward the struggling ship. The first torpedo cut the destroyer Hammann in two, while the next two torpedoes hit the Yorktown, inflicting the final mortal wound. The surviving Damage Control parties evacuated, and watched the mighty ship roll and slowly slip below the surface.

The Japanese lost over three thousand men and the carriers of the *Kido Butai*. The Americans lost 362 men, the Yorktown, and the Hammann. The Americans won their first decisive battle of the war.

33. SAN DIEGO

Charlie worked hard to live up to the promise he made to Lilly.

"Dear Lilly,

I am doing well in my class for the Navy. Everyone here is so nice and treat me real swell. Ever since I arrived here, I have had a hard time concentrating on my studies, but I know God has a plan for me and I need to pay attention to my work.

How was your trip with your parents? Did your father find what he was looking for in Phoenix? Maybe someday I can come back to Dallas and you can show me around some. It would be fun.

I hope I am not being too forward here, but I do miss talking to you. Our time on the train was very special to me, and I think you are just swell.

I will write when I can, and I will provide an address for you to write me once I get my assignment. Soon, you will be able to write me.

Your friend,

Charlie"

. . . . .

President Roosevelt waited in the Oval Office for everyone to take their places. The president sat in a chair facing the fireplace; to his right sat the VP and Admiral King.

"Good morning, gentlemen," said the president warmly. "What news do you have for me from the Pacific Theater, admiral?"

"Sir," began the admiral, "the last time we spoke, I promised you that our boys would step up and bring you good news. Today, I am happy to report a significant victory in the war against the Japanese."

"Excellent news!" exclaimed the president. "Please continue."

"As you are aware," explained the admiral, "the Japanese launched a major offensive on 4 June against our base at Midway Island. Our forces were outnumbered, but we prevailed."

The admiral had not been able to provide the president with much good news as of late, and he was going to tell him the good news before he had to break the news that they lost another of his aircraft carriers in the battle.

"On the fifth of June," said the admiral, "forces found and destroyed most of the carriers involved in the attack on Pearl Harbor."

"Hot damn!" yelled the president. "I have been waiting to hear that we exacted revenge on those Japs for their sneak attack on us!"

"Despite overwhelming odds against us," continued the admiral, "the loss of the Japanese carriers will mean that we now have air supremacy over the Japanese. They can still attack our forces from their island bases throughout the Pacific, but they cannot directly engage our carrier fleet with the same strength or experienced forces as they once did. With the loss of the carriers, they also lost their elite pilots and experienced support personnel."

"That is the best news I have heard in some time, admiral," said the president warily, "but I can see by the look on your face there is more to this story."

"Yes, sir, I am afraid there is," said the admiral with much dread. "During the last stages of the battle on the fifth, Japanese planes severely damaged the Yorktown. Unfortunately, we lost her."

"How unfortunate," said the president as he lowered his head to pray. "Were we able to save the men?"

"Yes, sir," said the admiral becoming more animated. "We only lost 362 men to over 3000 Japanese forces to our best estimate."

"As always, admiral," said the president, "make sure you express to the men my sincere gratitude for their hard work and sacrifice."

"I will, sir, thank you for your time."

The admiral and the VP left the Oval Office.

• • • • •

Admiral Yamamoto left the War Council room. It had not been a good meeting.

Onishi met him as he exited the room.

"I am sure this was a difficult meeting, sir," Onishi cajoled.

"How Tojo rose to prime minister, I will never know," fumed Yamamoto. "The plan was masterful," he said proudly, "and the execution of the plan was flawless until the Zeros made their single mistake. They became fixated on their targets, drawing them away from their primary responsibility, protecting the carriers of the *Kido Butai*. The Americans had great luck striking our carriers in between flight operations."

"Nagumo is dead; his ineptness caused this disaster," Onishi offered.

"Tojo did not look kindly on that tactic," Yamamoto said, "but I reminded him that his War Council placed Nagumo in that position. They took all the praise for the attack on Pearl Harbor, but they wanted to blame me for the carrier losses."

"Were they successful, admiral?" asked Onishi.

"No. I still have allies on the council, and they came to my aid," said Yamamoto.

"It was Sato, correct, sir?" asked Onishi.

How would he know that? thought Yamamoto. *Is it possible that this is the traitor in my midst?* Yamamoto protected his reaction. He would know for sure soon, he thought.

"Yes, Onishi," said Yamamoto. "Come, we must prepare for the next attack."

Onishi followed his mentor into his office. He would not have to endure this charade much longer. He was the brains behind these battle plans, and soon all on the council would recognize him for the brilliant naval tactician he was, swore Onishi.

34. QUINCY, MASSACHUSETTS

On July 15, 1941, the Fore River Shipyard laid the keel of the USS Cabot. Owned by Bethlehem Steel, the shipyard began operations in 1883 in Braintree on the banks of the Weymouth Fore River, just upriver from its current location. The shipyard had a proud heritage and had built many naval war vessels, including the USS Lexington-CV2.

Henry Wellington, son of Thomas Wellington, took over the shipyard in 1918 just after World War I. It saddened him when he heard of the loss of one of his beloved carriers in the Coral Sea earlier that year. He still had men in his yard that had worked on that beautiful ship.

"Mr. Wellington," said his secretary over the intercom, "a telegram from Washington, DC, just arrived."

"Bring it in, please," instructed Thomas.

His secretary handed the telegram to her boss, and he saw that it was from the War Department. He quickly opened the telegram.

"Received your request to rename the USS Cabot.

We approve your request.

Frank Knox, Navy Secretary"

"Take a memo, please," ordered Wellington.

"The United States War Department has approved our request
to rename the USS Cabot to the USS Lexington. I know you will
continue our proud tradition of building ships for our country.
We need to ensure this ship does not share the fate of her sister ship.
We cannot lose another ship to the Japanese in the Pacific.

Your hard work and craftsmanship are legendary among shipbuilders, and you should be proud of the work you do to support the war effort. Know that every piece of steel and rivet placed on a ship in our yard brings us one step closer to victory.

I am proud of each of you and thank you for your continued sacrifice.

Henry Wellington"

"Ensure you have this posted throughout the shipyard," instructed Wellington.

"I will, sir," said his secretary.

Four hundred and fifty-two miles to the south, the USS Bonhomme Richard lay in dry dock preparing to fit her island structure. Frank Knox sent word announcing the approval to rename this ship to the USS Yorktown, a fitting tribute to the former Yorktown whose workers from this shipyard had laid the keel on May 21, 1934. When the shipyard workers heard of the loss at Midway, they had immediately petitioned the War Department to rename the Richard to the Yorktown. It was now a reality.

The Lexington and Yorktown would live again to wreak havoc on the Japanese.

35. DALLAS, TEXAS

Lilly sat on her backyard porch swing with a silly smile, staring into the darkness.

"What is up with you, young lady?" asked her mother. "You have not stopped smiling since we got back from Phoenix."

"I know, Mom," said Lilly. "I just had so much fun talking to Charlie. I feel I have known him forever."

"Be careful, dear," warned her mother. "Your friend is going to war and no one ever knows how that will go."

That got Lilly crying.

"Now, there, there," consoled her mother. "I am sure Charlie will be fine. He is on a big ship and they are very hard to attack." Her mother wanted to protect her from the pain she was sure would come. War is very dangerous, and she was not positive Charlie would make it home. *This will be tricky*, thought her mother.

. . . . .

"And Brand wins another round," announced the instructor. The class completed another round of competing at finding and tracking contacts.

"This is fine," said Anderson, "but we are not out in the middle of the Pacific Ocean with Japs trying to sneak up on us."

Kent Anderson was from West Virginia and had been playing with radios as long as Charlie. Anderson was only three points behind Charlie in the competition.

"I know, Kent," Charlie said modestly. "I just got lucky."

"You watch out," warned Kent. "I am going to get you in the last round."

The radar gear sat in a room twenty-five yards from the concentric circles they had seen their first day of training. The competition was simple: finding the contact as quickly as possible, and correctly identifying the bearing and range of the contact.

The radar operator sat in front of the set, waiting for a contact to appear. The rest of the class was out in the hangar, riding the tricycles that emulated incoming planes, and operating the strings from the rafters that emulated the height and bearing of the incoming contact. The operator would use the dial on the set to sweep the antennae back and forth, looking for a contact. They would time each operator to determine how quickly he picked up the target, if he correctly identified the range, bearing, and altitude of the contact, and assessed his radio communications capabilities. In the last round, Kent and Charlie would face off to determine the winner of the competition. Kent was first. The door to the radar room closed, and the instructor signaled their readiness. The instructor pressed the stopwatch.

Kent performed a low-level sweep of the area in case the incoming aircraft were trying to fly under the radar. Ten seconds, twenty seconds, thirty seconds, nothing. Kent switched his set, sweeping higher until . . . He had a contact, but he would hold off until he could better determine the bearing, range, and altitude. Kent turned the selector on his second radar set and had everything he needed.

"Plot, Radar," called Kent.

"Plot, aye," responded the director. The instructor stopped the watch.

"Multiple contacts, bearing two three niner, range four four miles, at Angels fifteen," called Kent. He felt good about his performance.

"Stop exercise," ordered the director. "You may leave the room."

"I hope I did well," Kent said to the instructor.

"You correctly identified the contacts, Anderson," said the instructor. "That is half the battle."

They left the room.

The director waved the instructor over, and they conversed for five minutes. The class reset for the last contestant.

The director put on his headset and spoke to the men in the rafters, and one of them gave a thumbs-up. He placed an object on the line. Everyone in the hangar knew what was next.

"You ready, Brand?" asked the instructor.

"Yes, sir," responded Charlie.

The instructor signaled readiness and started the stopwatch

Charlie carefully swept, looking for incoming contacts. Ten seconds, fifteen seconds. *Got it*, thought Charlie. But another group of contacts appeared on the bottom of his scope. *Ah*, he thought.

"Plot, Radar," called Charlie.

"Plot, aye," responded the director. The instructor stopped the watch.

"Multiple contacts bearing one seven four, first group of contacts range three seven miles and the single contact at two two miles," called Charlie. "One group of three contacts at Angels fifteen, and one friendly contact at Angels ten."

"Stop exercise," ordered the director. "You may leave the room."

The director instructed everyone to go to the classroom where he would announce the final scores. The classroom was tense.

"Before I announce the results," began the director, "I want all of you to know that my staff is proud of every sailor in this class. All of you will graduate and help keep American sailors safe."

Charlie and Kent exchanged glances as they impatiently waited.

"Anderson," announced the director, "you correctly identified the targets in 46 seconds and accurately communicated those contacts to Air Plot. Your final class score is 481. Your lead over Brand is 19. Congratulations."

The students looked around. Both of the competitors were top notch, and they knew it would be an honor to serve with either man.

"Brand," continued the director, "you correctly identified both sets of contacts in 32 seconds and you identified the enemy *and* friendly plane. Before I announce your score, I have a question for you."

"Yes, sir," Charlie said sheepishly.

"What do you think was happening up there?"

"Well, sir," Charlie said with more confidence, "I saw the three contacts above the single contact. The single contact displayed on the bottom of my screen, so I knew this was one of our planes."

"Correct," said the instructor. "Continue."

"Well, sir," Charlie said more confidently, "those three planes were attacking our plane!"

"Correct!" praised the director. "In this scenario, we tested target acquisition in a real-life scenario. What will the Air Plot director do with your information, Brand?"

"He will ensure our plane knows he has three bogeys on his tail and direct CAP to engage the enemy, saving our plane."

"Correct again, Brand," said the director.

The class looked around in amazement.

"Class," concluded the director, "you are the eyes for the Air Plot director. The information you provide will save lives. Be calm, accurate, and concise in all of your communications."

"Yes, sir!" the class enthusiastically shouted.

"For your efforts, Mr. Brand," announced the director, "your final class score is . . ." The director paused. "Four hundred," he paused again, "eighty-six. Brand, you are the champion."

The class erupted in cheers. Kent was the first to offer his hand of congratulations.

"We will meet again, Charlie," promised Kent.

"I know," said Charlie. "It will be my honor to serve with you Kent."

"Congratulations to all of you," said the director. "Now, I must give you some bad news. While you attended this class, America lost two of her carriers to Japanese attack. The information and techniques you learned here will save lives. You are the best hope for America. As I call your name, come forward and receive your diploma and orders."

Every man in the class would immediately ship out to join the Pacific fleet supporting carriers, destroyers, and battleships. Charlie was the last man to receive his orders. The director pulled him aside.

"Brand," he began, "you have distinguished yourself here in San Diego."

"Thank you, sir," responded Charlie.

"You are the top radarman in this class," continued the director, "and the War Department will launch new carriers to replace those lost in the Pacific. As the top radarman, they will assign you to our newest carrier. You will deploy on the USS Lexington-CV16 and bring the fight back to the Japanese."

"Aye, aye, sir!" Charlie snapped to attention and saluted.

"The Lexington will not be ready until early next year," cautioned the director, "so we would like you to go to the Radar Lab to learn more about the new radar systems being installed on the Lexington over the next few months. I am very proud of you, sailor. You will do great things for our country."

The director extended his hand to Charlie, and they shook.

36. SAN DIEGO

"Hi, uh," stammered Charlie, "can I please speak to Lilly? This is Charlie, Charlie Brand from the train."

Charlie heard noises in the background and was unsure if they would allow him to talk to Lilly. Then, he heard loud footsteps running toward the phone.

"Charlie!" exclaimed Lilly. "I am so happy to hear from you. How did the rest of your training go?"

"Lilly, it is so great to hear your voice again," Charlie said emotionally. "It went well. I am shipping out to the Pacific soon, but they gave me some leave to see my family. I am making my plans and I am coming through Dallas in two days. It would be great to see you."

"Of course, I want to see you, Charlie," Lilly sweetly said. "How long can you stay in Dallas?"

"I will get in around 9:10 a.m. on Tuesday," said Charlie, "and I could wait to leave until the 6:42 p.m. train to Little Rock."

"That would be swell," gushed Lilly. "See you on Tuesday! Bye!"

Lilly hung up the phone and turned to see her mother staring at her.

"Were you even going to ask permission, young lady?" chided her mother.

"Oh, Mama," explained Lilly, "I am just so happy right now I could burst. Can I see Charlie this Tuesday, please?"

"I will talk it over with your father," promised her mother, "but I am sure we can work something out." Her mother was now smiling ear to ear as she could see the look on her daughter's face. She had once had that look.

Ellen Anderson, now Ellen Hope, met her husband when she was only seventeen. By the time she was twenty-one, she was married and had a baby on the way.

Ellen knew how Lilly was feeling, but she also knew she needed to protect her daughter from the possibility that Charlie would not come home from the war.

Tuesday came, and the Hope family waited at the train station to meet Charlie.

"Stop pacing, Lilly," scolded her father sharply. "It will not make the train arrive any sooner."

"I am sorry, father," Lilly said with some embarrassment. She stopped and turned her ear up the track. "I hear the train, Daddy!" she cried.

"I know, sugar," her father said sweetly. "I hear it, too."

Three minutes later, the train pulled into Union Station. Lilly strained to find Charlie, her head rotating left and right, almost in a frenzy.

"Hi, Lilly. Miss me?" asked a voice behind her.

"Charlie!" cried Lilly, and she threw her arms around Charlie as if they had known each other for years. "Absolutely I missed you!"

Charlie put down his seabag and shook hands with Mr. and Mrs. Hope. They walked the two blocks to where the Hopes had parked their green 1940 Ford De Luxe sedan. Charlie smiled when he saw the car.

"Are you a car man, son?" asked Mr. Hope. Henry Hope began tinkering with cars when he was a young man and fondly remembered working on them with his father.

"Yes, sir, I am," responded Charlie. "I believe you have an 85 horsepower 221 cubic-inch engine in your De Luxe, sir."

"So, you *are* a car man!" said Henry with a hint of smile.

Lilly beamed.

They drove up Preston Road into Highland Park, and arrived at a house twice the size of his own back in Little Rock.

Now, he knew he was out of his league. *How could Lilly possibly be interested in me?* he thought.

Lilly made plans with her parents to drive them back to their house where Charlie could freshen up, and then they would spend some time walking near Exall Lake.

"You must be hungry, Charlie," said Ellen. "Did you get breakfast in the train?"

"Well, ma'am," Charlie began, "I got a small bit of food, but it sure would be nice to have some homemade food again."

"Well, I will cook you up some eggs, bacon, and some grits," said Ellen. "How does that sound?"

"Wonderful," Charlie said, almost giddy. He could not believe how nice Lilly's parents were.

After breakfast and some time for Charlie to freshen up, Lilly and Charlie left to go for a walk around Exall Lake and Turtle Creek. Henry Lexall, the real estate agent responsible for the original purchase of the land from the Cole family that would become Highland Park, had dammed up Turtle Creek to create the lake that now carried his name. Originally named Philadelphia Place by some investors from Philadelphia, they envisioned an exclusive housing community that would cater to the more affluent families of Dallas just three miles from downtown. Unfortunately, financial constraints prevented the group from enacting their vision, and a new group of investors purchased the land in 1906. They named the new community Highland Park as it sat on high land overlooking Dallas. They hired Wilbur David Cook, who was the landscape designer for Beverly Hills, and George E. Kessler, the architect of Fair Park in Dallas, to design the community layout.

"Wow," said Charlie, "this sure is a beautiful lake. But not as beautiful as you."

Lilly blushed and reached for Charlie's hand. The two found a pecan tree and sat down. They talked for hours about their families and what they wanted to do after the war. With each moment spent gazing into Lilly's eyes, Charlie forgot the world around him. He forgot about the war and his resolve to bring the fight to the Japanese. He forgot about home . . .

"Charlie," Lilly breathed. "Charlie, where were you just then?"

"Wishing I did not have to leave today," Charlie said sheepishly.

Lilly smiled warmly. "I wish you could stay here, too. I do not want this day to end . . ." Lilly's voice trailed off.

"What?" questioned Charlie. "What's wrong, Lilly?"

"It is my mother," Lilly said, holding back the tears. "She does not want me to fall for you in case . . ."

"In case what?" asked Charlie, already knowing the answer.

"In case you do not come . . ." Lilly whimpered.

"Oh, my Lilly!" Charlie said as he held her close.

Lilly stopped crying.

"Lilly," assured Charlie, "I will be fine. I will be on a big ship and my job is to help keep our ship safe. As long as I do my job well, we should be just fine."

Charlie knew there was danger, but he did not want his Lilly to be afraid. Wait, he thought, *his* Lilly. He smiled, gently released Lilly from his embrace, and kissed her.

Lilly melted into his arms. He was hooked—this would be the reason he would come back from the war.

They stood and walked across the wooden bridge of Exall Dam. They walked down Knox Street and entered the Highland Park Soda Fountain.

"Hi Lilly," called the man behind the counter.

Joe Don Cole, his customers called him JD, was the co-owner of the Soda Fountain and knew all his regular customers. "Who is your friend?" he asked. "I am always glad to serve those who serve us."

"JD," Lilly motioned to the man behind the counter, "this is Charlie Brand."

"Nice to meet you, sir," Charlie said as he offered his hand.

JD firmly gripped his hand and motioned for them to sit down. "What can I get for you, Charlie, Lilly?" asked JD.

"I am really thirsty, sir," began Charlie. "I would like a Coca-Cola. Lilly, what would you like?"

"Charlie," said JD, "we call those soda pops Dallas."

"Huh?" Charlie had a quizzical look on his face.

"You see, Charlie," started JD, "they make the syrup for Coca Cola right here in Dallas, so we call that a Dallas. And they make the syrup for Dr. Pepper in Waco about hundred miles south of us. We call that drink a Waco. And, if you want both drinks, one for you and one for your lady, we call that a Waxahachie."

This still confused Charlie. Lilly stepped in.

"Charlie," offered Lilly, "Waxahachie is halfway between Dallas and Waco."

"Oh, I get it," Charlie said with some embarrassment. Lilly looked lovingly at Charlie, and they laughed, causing JD to laugh, too.

"Well," announced Charlie, "I guess we will have a Waxahachie, if that is alright with you Lilly." He looked to Lilly for approval.

"You read my mind, Charlie!" Lilly said gleefully.

"Do you like Chocolate Malts?" asked Charlie.

"I most certainly do," answered Lilly.

"Do you want to share one?" Charlie asked, hoping she would say yes.

"Yes," Lilly said coyly.

How will I ever be able to leave today? thought Charlie.

37. DALLAS, TEXAS

Charlie stepped up onto the train and turned to wave goodbye. This had been the greatest day of his life. He looked to see Lilly dabbing her eyes as her parents consoled her. He had promised to come home to her, and he intended to keep his promise. The train lurched forward, and he stuck his head out the window and called back to Lilly.

"I will be back—I promise!" called Charlie.

Lilly grinned and put her handkerchief up to dab her eyes. She waved and looked like she was saying something. Charlie could not hear her, but saw her mouth the words "I . . ." He could not make out the rest of what she was trying to say. He slumped down into the seat, feeling giddy and sad, all at the same time.

Charlie spent seven days with his family, and he told them about Lilly. They were happy for him, but warned not to lead her on. "You will be thousands of miles away from her, and you do not know what the war will bring." Charlie assured everyone that nothing would happen to him and he would be home soon after they beat the Japanese.

. . . . .

Charlie felt the train lurch to a stop.

"Boston Station," called the conductor. "Last stop. Everyone off the train."

Charlie grabbed his seabag and jumped off of the last rung of the train onto the gravel. He looked around.

"Brand, Brand," he heard someone call.

Charlie focused and headed toward the figure.

"Brand?" asked the military man.

"Yes, sir!" Charlie said with a salute.

"Great," said the lieutenant. "I am Lieutenant Saunders."

"Nice to meet you, sir" Charlie said, offering his hand.

"We have quarters for you at the Naval Air Station while you are here with us."

"Thank you, sir," said Charlie.

Charlie stowed his gear in his temporary bunk and headed to dinner. The next morning, Lieutenant Saunders met him in front of his barracks for the ride to the MIT Radiation Laboratory. Alfred Loomis greeted Charlie as he exited the Jeep.

"Brand, I assume," said Loomis, offering his hand. "I have heard good things about you. Come this way; let me introduce you to the team."

They walked up to the fourth floor where the team working on the SG radar awaited.

"Davidson, this is Radarman Second Class Brand," introduced Alfred.

Jeff Davidson led the team responsible for the development of the SG radar. "Nice to meet you, radarman," said Jeff with a wry smile.

"Nice to meet you too, sir," said Charlie, shaking his hand.

Loomis left to attend to other issues in the lab.

"We have heard much about you," said Jeff.

Charlie smiled in embarrassment. "I am not sure what you have heard about me, sir," said Charlie.

"Jeff," said Davidson. "Around here, you can call me Jeff. I am *not* in the Navy."

Charlie shook his head.

"Brand—" began Jeff.

Charlie put up his hand. "Charlie, please call me Charlie. Even though I *am* in the Navy." The team laughed. Jeff introduced the team to Charlie, and they sat around a small table to begin their training.

"Charlie," began Jeff, "we know about you because you completed your radar class in San Diego with the highest scores in the Navy. You are here because the USS Lexington, in dry dock at Fore River, will have the latest radar technology we have developed in our lab. That is why you are here, so we can tell you everything we know about these systems and make you an expert in just two short weeks."

Charlie gulped. He hoped he could live up to the expectation Jeff set before him. He felt uneasy.

"I am ready, Jeff," Charlie said, mustering as much confidence as he could.

Over the next two weeks, the Rad Lab team poured more theoretical and operational knowledge into the young apprentice. The team, most ten years older than Charlie, marveled at his ability to consume and assimilate the technical data of the new radar systems. On Charlie's last day at the lab, the team wanted to take him out for beer, but Charlie had to confess he was still not old enough to drink. He thanked everyone and headed for his ride.

"What have you been doing in there, Brand?" questioned Lieutenant Saunders.

"Just training, sir," Charlie said, smiling to himself. He was still under strict orders to not divulge his role in the war effort. A promise he took seriously.

"Well," shrugged the lieutenant, "command wants me to take you somewhere tomorrow."

"Where is that, sir?" questioned Charlie.

"It is a surprise, sailor," said the lieutenant with a bit too much sarcasm.

The next day, Saunders picked up Charlie, and they headed south toward the Fore River. Charlie had never been to Boston before, so he sat back and enjoyed the ride. How his life had changed in five short months.

Saunders stopped the Jeep and said, "There is your surprise, Brand."

Charlie exited the Jeep and looked around at the throngs of people surrounding a ship bigger than anything he had ever seen before. On September 23, 1942, the USS Lexington CV16 launched into the Fore River. This would soon be his home.

"Here," Saunders pulled out a card.

"What is this?" asked Charlie.

"Look at it, sailor!" chided Saunders.

"Wow," exclaimed Charlie, "what a great postcard, and I know exactly who I will send this to!"

• • • • •

"Lilly," called Ellen, "you have some mail!"

Lilly ran downstairs and took the postcard from her mother's hand. It was from Charlie!

The postcard had pictures of the USS Lexington CV2 and USS Lexington CV16 with the following text:

"FORE RIVER'S ANSWER TO JAPS AT CORAL SEA

THE LAUNCHING OF THE NEW USS LEXINGTON

Christened by MRS. THEODORE D. ROBINSON

(SPONSOR OF THE FORMER USS LEXINGTON)

BOTH CARRIERS LAUNCHED AT THE BETHLEHEM STEEL CO.

FORE RIVER YARD, QUINCY MA."

Lilly was excited to read the message from Charlie.

"My Dearest Lilly,

This is the ship I will be on in the Pacific. I still do not know when I will leave, but I am sure it will be soon. It was great seeing you and I cannot wait to see you again.

I will write as soon as I have the address you can send me letters.

Charlie"

38. GUADALCANAL

Hadaki jumped off of the troop transport onto the island. It was now his time to protect his emperor from the American dogs.

"Form up here," ordered his commander. Hadaki did not understand where they would go, but was eager to bring the fight to the enemy. Over the next three months, he worked to create their camp and helped dig the foundations for the airstrip that would rain terror on the American ships.

Hadaki heard much commotion and got up to see what was going on. Soon, his commanding officer came to assemble his team.

"Men," began his commander, "the American dogs are just off of the island preparing to land. We will withdraw to the hills and prepare a surprise attack on their inferior forces."

"Hai!" the men said in unison.

Over the next eight hours, the company moved their artillery and men up to the hills overlooking the airfield still under construction. The Japanese watched as the Americans landed on the island. Hadaki could hear much jeering from his fellow soldiers as the Americans struggled to land their forces. He wondered why they would not attack during the landing. He would soon see the plan, he was sure.

The next day, it was clear the Americans thought they had the element of surprise on their hands, unaware of the Japanese forces watching them, waiting for the optimal moment to engage.

Hadaki and his ammunition man Anso made their last preparations and waited for the order. The plan was simple: wait for the Americans to come onto the unfinished airstrip where they would be vulnerable, and then attack with overwhelming force.

"Banzai!" ordered his commander.

Hadaki had already picked out a spot where he would throw his first mortar. He loaded his mortar gun.

Thump. The projectile left the gun and landed within two feet of his intended target, blowing the legs off of one man and sending razor-sharp shrapnel through ten more.

"Finally," breathed Hadaki, "we take the fight to these dogs who think they can attack our islands."

"Here is another, Hadaki," offered Anso.

Hadaki reset his mortar gun, and let loose another round. Another direct hit. This time five more men met their doom.

"Forward!" ordered his commander. Hadaki grabbed his mortar and moved forward with his team. He set up for another volley. But he did not get a chance as the Americans returned a barrage of mortar and rifle fire to their position. They hit the ground.

"Anso, another round," called Hadaki. "Anso. Anso!"

Hadaki looked behind him to see his friend lying on his back. The bullets rang around him as he struggled to gain control of the mortars from his fallen friend. His command called for everyone to prepare to charge.

Hadaki had practiced this maneuver during his training. The front line of soldiers would place bayonets on their rifles and charge the enemy. The mortar teams would hold back and time their attacks until the enemy prepared to engage.

"Banzai!" called the commander, and his men sprang into action, racing across the airstrip to engage their mortal enemies.

The American battalion was ill prepared for the ferociousness of the Japanese forces. Most had never seen battle, and their preparations on the island of Java had not primed them for the battle discipline and bravery showed by the Japanese.

Hadaki waited for the correct time. *Thump, thump, thump.* The mortar guns lobbed their deadly projectiles forward of the charging Japanese infantrymen. Suddenly, a powerful gust of wind came up, blowing their mortars off course. The mortars exploded away from the enemy forces, and the Americans engaged his countrymen.

Hadaki sank as he watched his friends fall just feet from the American dogs.

Nightfall came over the battlefield.

His commanding officer sent three more attacks toward the enemy line, and they repelled each one. Hadaki heard the order to withdraw, and his heart sank. *How can we withdraw now?* he thought.

Over the next four months, Hadaki saw firsthand the unwavering commitment of his countrymen to their cause. They filled him with pride, and he knew Japan would prevail against the Americans. He longed for more opportunities to bring the fight to the enemy.

• • • • •

"Admiral Yamamoto," began Tojo, "I believe it is necessary for us to curtail our expansion efforts in the Pacific."

"I understand your position, Tojo-san," Yamamoto said with as much deference as he could muster. "I too am concerned we are stretching ourselves too thin. I believe a consolidation strategy would be prudent." Yamamoto studied his adversary. *Why would he be in consort with me related to this strategy? What is his end game? It is time to spring my trap and expose my apprentice.* Yamamoto spent the next ten minutes speaking to Tojo, discussing plans that would entice Tojo to engage Onishi to gather more details of the plan. *If Onishi brings up these plans, I will know he is the spy in my midst. I will grieve as I slit his throat myself.*

39. BOSTON SHIPYARD

"Brand," called the master chief, "they are flying in the SG radar now. Heads up!"

"Got it, sir," said Charlie as he ducked under the metal stairs of the island.

Charlie was on board the USS Lexington full time for one month as he worked with the construction crews on the installation of the radar equipment. Captain Felix B. Stump requested Charlie work with the technicians as they installed the new radar gear on his gleaming new carrier.

Born in 1894 in Parkersburg, West Virginia, Stump was appointed to the Naval Academy in 1913. He served with distinction during World War I and entered the flight program in Pensacola, Florida, in 1920. He served as a naval flight officer on the experimental carrier Langley and other commands during the period between the two World Wars. At the outbreak of World War II, Stump was back on the Langley, this time as her commanding officer. In January 1942, he transferred to the staff of the commander-in-chief, Asiatic Fleet, where he served with distinction. Now, as captain of the Lexington, he would exact revenge on those who destroyed her namesake.

Charlie watched the dockworkers crane in the new SG radar and attach it to the top of the mainmast. He remembered just four short months ago he was in San Diego, where he learned to operate all the radar equipment he helped install and configure. This was the complete compliment of the radar equipment on the Lexington:

Mark 4 fire control with the Mark 37 director: used to direct five-inch guns providing elevation, bearing, and range to target.

SM radar: fighter director radar including IFF. Not used as a search radar.

SG radar: used for low-altitude radar search.

SK-1 radar: air search radar with a range of 162 nautical miles

SC radar: air search radar with a range of 30 nautical miles

A feeling of pride welled up in Charlie. Not for himself, but for his country. All the people who worked tirelessly to make this ship, designed and built these radar tools, and those who supported the war effort in so many other ways—he could not let them down.

"Brand," called the technician, "I need your help up here!"

"Great," said Charlie with great dread. "Up the ladder again. I sure hope I get used to these heights one of these days."

Later that month came the day they had all been working for: commissioning day. The Lexington now had 80 percent of her crew compliment on board, and they were ready for sea trials. Charlie dressed in dress whites climbed the ladder to the flight deck. He took his position at the rail and stood at attention.

"On this day," started the secretary of the Navy, "February 17, 1943, we commission this great warship to wage battle against our mortal enemy, Japan. A short eight months ago, we lost her sister ship during the battle of Coral Sea. We will never forget the men who gave the ultimate sacrifice for this country. As we commission the USS Lexington CV-16, let us resolve to take the war to the enemy, to hunt down those who, though unprovoked, attacked our homeland at Pearl Harbor. Let our instruments of battle slice to the very core of our enemy so he may never again threaten this great nation or those we offer our protection."

The audience erupted in cheers and applause.

Now it was time to kick the tires and take this beautiful lady out for a test drive, Charlie thought.

40. COMBAT INFORMATION CENTER

Charlie entered the new Combat Information Center (CIC) on the second floor of the island structure. He had spent the past two months working with the technical team from Raytheon to help set up, calibrate, and test the new equipment that would change the face of war for years to come. In San Diego, he had learned how to identify, track, and communicate contact information to Air Plot, who would then send this information to the bridge. With the new CIC, all the radar sets, plotters, communications, and flight direction would be in the same air-conditioned room, the only air-conditioned space on the ship. Now, they could share information instantly and react faster to the changing environment of war than ever before. He could really see how this team would act more like a finely rehearsed orchestra, maybe like the Tommy Dorsey Orchestra, he thought.

"Afternoon, lieutenant," said Charlie as he sat down at his radar scope to begin his four-hour shift. The only light in the room was provided by the radar sets and the map plotting table.

"Afternoon, Brand," replied the lieutenant.

Lieutenant Joseph Hardin grew up in Texas, so Charlie felt a kinship with him. He completed his fighter director schooling in Georgia, where he finished top in his class. LT, as the enlisted men called him, had a calm disposition, and he seemed unflappable.

Lieutenant Hardin waited for the rest of the CIC staff to report to their duty station. Charlie began calibrating his radar sets. Calibration comprised validating the accuracy of the radar set against a known object, often another ship in the fleet.

"Radar operational," said Charlie. "We are ready to begin the simulation."

Behind Charlie and to his left, another radarman stood at a clear plastic board lit from the bottom, holding a grease pencil. His job was to write the contact information on the vertical plotting board so the fighter director could keep track of the contacts and their bearings. To reduce interference with the fighter director's vision, he would stand behind the board and write backwards so the text would appear correctly on the opposite side of the board. A skill Charlie had just mastered.

"Prepare to turn over your paper," ordered LT.

The radar operator was the only person other than LT with the script for this simulation. The goal was to communicate information to the team and stay attentive to the changing environment. LT created each scenario, and no one had prior knowledge of the scenario.

"Begin," ordered LT.

Charlie turned over his paper. "Contact bearing two niner two," called Charlie, "range eight five miles at Angels fifteen. Target identified bandit Zulu One."

Immediately, the second radarman wrote the information on the clear board. A man at the mapping table created a mark at the location of the contact. The mapping table had concentric circles around a center dot that represented the dead reckoning or current location of the carrier.

Charlie waited.

"Contact, scratch that," called Charlie. "Contacts bearing two eight six, range niner zero miles at Angels twenty. Targets identified Xray One, Two, Three, Four, Five, and Six."

"Very well," replied the LT.

"Flight OPS, CIC," called LT into his microphone, "scramble six Wildcats. CAP, bandits approaching at Angels fifteen and twenty. Vector niner four range to target eight fiver miles."

"Flight OPS, aye," replied the CAG.

"CAP, aye," replied the CAP leader.

"Contacts split," called Charlie. "Xray targets now bearing two six six, range eight two miles. Zulu target still on course, now seven niner miles out."

The team adjusted the contact information.

"Red Team, CIC," called the LT.

"Red Team, aye," was the reply.

"Vector to eight three, range to target seven two miles," ordered LT.

The radarman on the clear board now had thirteen individual targets on the board. The man on the mapping table used his ruler to determine vectors to the targets.

"CIC, Red Team," called the CAG.

"CIC, aye," responded LT.

"Splash Xray Two, Three, and Six," reported the CAG.

"I concur," responded Charlie.

The CIC team reacted to the report. The man on the clear board erased three contacts while the mapping table continued to adjust the location of the targets on the basis of the range and bearing information provided by Charlie.

"We lost Red six," reported Charlie.

The CIC team reacted.

"CIC, FOPS," called the CAG.

"CIC, aye," responded LT.

"Splash Zulu One, Xray One and Xray Five," reported the CAG.

The man on the clear board erased all the bandits from the board. The mapping table showed only friendlies.

"LT, we still have one contact," Charlie reported. "Xray Four."

"Stop simulation," ordered LT. "Men, we cannot make this kind of mistake! There is still one bandit on radar that could slip through our fighter screen and kill every man on this ship. All of us must keep his head in the game at all times. If you cannot commit to this, you can swab the deck and clean the head for the rest of the war."

The men of the CIC knew they had made a critical mistake, one that could prevent them from seeing their loved ones again. This was not just an exercise; LT meant it to prepare them for the tempo and intensity of a true battle situation.

LT ran a new simulation. It would not be long before they would have actual targets to track.

The Lexington left the next day for their shakedown cruise in the Caribbean. Charlie looked forward to warmer weather and a chance to test himself against real planes.

Over the past three months, Charlie had been all over the Lexington, exploring areas not part of his regular duty station. As much as he loved food, the mess on the carrier was passable. They enjoyed real eggs and meats while they were in port, but they warned him to not expect these luxuries when out to sea. Scattered throughout the ship, sleeping compartments held twenty-four men. Men placed their mattresses on the Navy version of a bedspring they had fashioned out of rope. Weaving the rope between suspended metal frames created enough strength to support a man and his mattress. The carrier had most of the comforts of home, including a dentist, laundry, barber, church, and best of all, a post office. Charlie especially loved mail call as he lived for letters from Lilly and his sister.

Charlie was apprehensive and excited as they threw lines and embarked for sea trials in the Caribbean. He prayed that God would save him from any seasickness. Secretly, he was sure that many of his new friends were unsure how they would handle the open sea. As Boston disappeared from view, they had their first taste of the open sea. With a length of 872 feet and weighing in at 27 tons, the Lexington was very steady in the seas of the North Atlantic. Two hours into their sea trials, Charlie experienced no seasickness. God had answered his prayers.

. . . . .

Fleet Radio Unit Pacific at Pearl Harbor, or FRUPAC, was the primary Navy code-breaking group. They had provided the intelligence leading to the victory over Japan at the battle of Midway.

"Flash traffic coming in, sir," said the ensign.

"What do we have here?" mumbled the commander. "Ham, Tommy," he called, "get over here on the double."

Ham and Tommy were the cryptanalyst heroes of the last Japanese code decryption exercise.

"Yes, sir?" said Ham.

"Look at this message, boys," said the commander. "We need some quick work on this one."

"We are right on it, sir," Tommy promised.

Eighteen hours later, they delivered the message to the commander.

"Well, I'll be . . ." the commander's voice trailed, his mouth agape.

The commander hurried to headquarters CINPCFLT to see Admiral Nimitz.

"Admiral," said the ensign over the intercom, "Commander Collins here to see you. He says he has something juicy for you."

"Send him in," instructed the admiral.

The commander did not even sit down before he gave the admiral the uncoded message.

"How fresh is this, commander?" asked the admiral.

"Eighteen hours, twenty-nine minutes, sir," replied the commander. This would surely endear him to the admiral.

"We must act on this immediately," said the admiral.

"I agree entirely, sir," said the commander sounding too agreeable. "If I may sir, I did some study of Japanese language and culture in Military College and I would recommend we go for it, sir."

"I am listening," said the admiral as he lit his pipe.

"The Japanese Military Command hold Admiral Yamamoto in the highest regard for his intellect, cunning, and charisma. He was the architect of the attack on Pearl, and any opportunity to take him off of the chessboard is worth the risk," concluded Collins.

"Thank you, commander, for your insight and recommendation," said the admiral. "I will let you know my decision."

Commander Collins left the office and could not help but smile.

The admiral took some paper and made a list of the pros and cons of specifically targeting a commander of enemy forces. He reviewed his list. He knew what they must do, and he buzzed his ensign.

"Yes, sir," said the ensign.

"Get me Admiral Halsey," ordered the admiral.

. . . . .

"Multiple contacts bearing two seven zero degrees," Charlie reported. "I see thirty friendly contacts headed our way."

Charlie knew these were friendly planes as they showed up on the bottom section of his A-scope. The incoming planes were all equipped with IFF beacons announcing their status as US war planes.

"That would be our Wildcats," replied LT.

The thirty Wildcats landed on the carrier without incident. Most of the pilots had never landed on the pitching deck of a carrier, causing some to land harder than expected. Some planes experienced minimal damage to the landing struts, but the plane captains quickly replaced the damaged struts, placing them back into service.

41. HENDERSON FIELD, GUADALCANAL

Admiral Nimitz informed Admiral Halsey of the plan, and they selected Rear Admiral Mitscher to lead the plan. Born in Hillsboro, Wisconsin, in 1887, Andrew "Pete" Mitscher had moved to Oklahoma City in 1889 where his father was a federal Indian agent and became the city's second mayor. Mitscher's appointment to the Naval Academy was short-lived, achieving 159 demerits and a forced resignation. On the insistence of his father, he reapplied and graduated 113th in his class in 1910.

The decoded Japanese message provided the complete itinerary of Admiral Yamamoto's upcoming trip to review the troops in Rabaul and Bougainville Island in Papua New Guinea. According to the message, Yamamoto's plane would fly over Bougainville on April 18, the one-year anniversary of the Doolittle raid.

• • • • •

"We are going to what?" said Major John W. Mitchell, commanding officer of the US Army Air Force 339th Fighter Squadron.

"We want you to shoot down the plane carrying Admiral Yamamoto," said the rear admiral, "even if you have to run into him. This is the guy who did Pearl Harbor."

"Oh, my God," breathed Captain Thomas Lanphier Jr., chosen as a shooter for the mission. "Consider it done."

The Lockheed P-38 Lightning was a high-altitude fighter, perfect for the mission. Capable of climbing to twenty thousand feet in six minutes, they could fit the P-38 with an extra-capacity drop gas tank, necessary to meet the extended mission parameters.

"We will need to fly four hundred miles around the Solomon Islands to avoid the Japanese," Mitchell explained. "Yamamoto is punctual as hell, so our window to intercept is maybe five to ten minutes tops. And we may have to contend with those seventy-five Zeros they have on Bougainville."

At 0710 hours, Mitchell and his team took off from Henderson Field. Mitchell would fly cover for the mission. Mitchell assigned Lanphier and Lieutenant Rex Barber as the shooters with First Lieutenants Besby Holmes and Ray Hine as the backup pilots. They would fly low over the ocean to avoid the Japanese radar and adhere to strict radio silence during the mission.

Flying over the smooth ocean, the pilots struggled to stay focused on the task at hand as the engines enticed them to doze. Flying just feet from the water, Mitchell wagged his wings slightly, signifying they were about to turn.

At 0810 hours, they turned to course 305° and made their last turn to the northeast thirty-eight minutes later. They ascended out of the haze that provided shelter from prying eyes and strained to locate their prey.

At two thousand feet, one pilot broke radio silence.

"Bogeys," he called, "eleven o'clock high!"

To his surprise, Mitchell saw two bombers, contrary to the intelligence briefing completed before the flight. This may be tougher than we hoped, thought Mitchell.

"Go get 'em, Tom," called Mitchell as he rose to overwatch position.

But before Lanphier could engage the Betty bombers, three Zeros descended from the clouds, ready for a fight. Lanphier engaged the Zeros breathing fire from the 20-mm cannon in his airplane's nose, splitting the formation. Barber had his shot.

The bombers dove for the deck.

"Going in," called Barber just as the bombers crossed his nose. He banked hard to starboard, falling in behind his prey where he unleashed hell from his four .50 caliber guns and 20-mm cannon. *Hit, hit, hit!*

"I got three Zeros on my six!" called Barber, but he did not waiver.

Lanphier saw his opportunity as they teamed to wreak havoc on the Betty bomber headed toward the treetops below. Lanphier banked hard right, and dove to engage the bomber he hoped would carry Yamamoto. He turned wildly in a last-ditch effort to line up his shot, but he was not in the optimal range to engage.

Lanphier fired, almost at a right angle to his target, hoping his aim was true. Rewarded and somewhat surprised to see fire from the right engine, he followed Barber closely.

"I think I got him, Mitch," called Lanphier.

Barber closed to within one hundred feet of their Betty, firing all the time. Flames erupted from the bomber, causing it to snap roll to the left, screaming toward the forest below.

"One bomber down," called Barber. "Verify it for me, Mitch."

Yamamoto was dead.

The rest of the Lightnings chased the remaining Betty bomber out to sea, where it impacted at full speed, disintegrating.

"Mission accomplished," called Mitchell. "Let's get home!"

Ray Hine never returned to Henderson Field.

. . . . .

The Joint Chiefs entered the Oval Office. President Roosevelt was already sitting on the sofa with his vice president.

"Good afternoon, gentlemen," said the president.

"Good afternoon, sir," responded the Joint Chiefs.

"What is the latest from the Pacific theater?" asked the president cautiously.

"First, Japan has now acknowledged the death of Admiral Isoroku Yamamoto," said Admiral King. "We believed we got him on Bougainville as I previously reported, but now we have confirmation from the Japanese government."

"What effect do you expect his death to have on the war in the Pacific, admiral?" the president asked.

"Yamamoto was an expert tactician," began the admiral. "We expect his loss to cripple the Japanese military for some time to come. This is a big win for us, Mr. President."

“Agreed,” said the president. “Send my congratulations to the team responsible for this operation.”

“Will do, sir,” responded the admiral.

The admiral then provided updates on the launching of the USS Lexington and USS Yorktown earlier that year and their readiness to join the war effort.

42. CARIBBEAN SEA

By the beginning of June, the crew eased into a daily routine. Flight operations began each day at 9:00 a.m., rain or shine, and continued throughout the day. Night flight operations were rare, but it was important to prepare the pilots to fly and land at night.

"Morning, sir," Charlie said as he sat down to calibrate his scope.

"Morning, Brand," said LT without looking up from his clipboard.

Captain Stump had high expectations for Charlie, and so far, he had met, at times even exceeded, them.

"I have calibrated the radar and I am ready to—" Charlie stopped.

"Brand," LT looked up, "what is the matter?"

"As I was validating the distance to my calibration object," Charlie said with concern, "I lost the object."

"What are you going to do about it, Brand?" asked LT, annoyed.

Charlie was already up on his feet, climbing the ladder to the top of the island structure. From there, he headed forward to the mainmast and climbed to the top, stepping onto the platform. He was careful not to step in front of the antennae in case another operator turned on the set in CIC.

"OK," Charlie said out loud, "what is the problem here?" He wiggled the coaxial cable that connected the antennae to the set in CIC. "What!" Charlie exclaimed. "How can this just come right into my hands?"

Charlie spent the next forty-five minutes reconnecting the cable to the antennae. It was clear to him that the technician did not check his work. He made a mental note to report this to LT and recommend that the Radar team validate the cable connections to every antenna and radar set on the ship. Mistakes like this could cripple the ship just when they needed the radar. Charlie climbed down retracing his path and walked back into CIC.

"Resolve the issue, Brand?" asked LT.

"Yes, sir," responded Charlie. "It was a loose cable. I reattached the cable, and we should be ready to go, sir. Recommend we check all cable connections as soon as possible, sir."

"Excellent," said LT. "Flight operations began twenty minutes ago."

Charlie settled into his chair when he saw concern sweep across LT's face.

"Brand," said LT, all business now, "I need a fix on those aircraft on the double."

"Aye, aye, sir," responded Charlie. "OK, sir I have them. Bearing one seven three, range two three miles."

"I want updated bearing and range every minute, sailor," ordered LT.

"Aye, aye, sir," Charlie said smartly. *Something bad is happening*, he thought.

"CIC, Green Six," said Ensign Kinnick.

Nile Kinnick was a celebrity aboard the Lexington. He had won the Heisman Trophy in 1939 while attending the University of Iowa and enlisted in the Navy three days before the attack on Pearl Harbor.

"CIC, aye," replied LT. He turned on the speaker in the room. He had a feeling this would be an important training opportunity.

"I have a serious oil leak and am sure I cannot make it back to the ship," reported Kinnick calmly.

"We have you, Green Six," said LT with no change to his inflection.

Charlie kept providing bearing and range information for the next three minutes.

"CIC, Green Six," called Kinnick.

"Go ahead, Six," replied LT.

"There is no way I will make it back to the ship," called Kinnick. "Ditching, ditching, ditch . . ."

"Brand, do you see Green Six?" asked LT.

"No, sir," Charlie said, trying to hide his emotions.

"Bridge, CIC," called LT.

"Bridge, aye," replied the XO.

"XO, one of our planes just went down about nineteen miles from the ship," reported the lieutenant.

"Any contact from the downed plane?" asked the XO.

"None, sir," replied LT.

Green leader circled the last known position of Lieutenant Nile Kinnick for forty minutes, but never found his plane or the pilot. On June 2, 1943, the USS Lexington CV-16 reported her first casualty of war.

In 1904, the United States took over the construction of the Panama Canal from the French after they experienced engineering difficulties. The canal connects the Atlantic and Pacific oceans across the Isthmus of Panama fifty-one miles through Lake Gatun. A series of locks lift vessels up to Lake Gatun from the Atlantic side and lower the vessels on the Pacific side. Using the canal shortcut, the Navy avoided the more dangerous route around Cape Horn on the southern tip of South America.

"Wow, I said I wanted it warmer," Charlie complained, "but this humidity is oppressive."

"You said it," agreed Gil.

Gilbert Rothchild grew up in Rhode Island and joined the Navy the same week as Charlie. Many people believed he was rich because of his name, but he told anyone who would listen that he never met nor did he know the Rothschild family, emphasizing the "s."

The friendship between Gil and Charlie quickly grew during operational watches, or shifts, in the CIC. Gil was responsible for the radar supporting the Mark 4 fire control system. The CIC staff operated using the four-hours-on-four-hours-off cycle. Charlie would move between the radar sets and the vertical plotting board depending on the needs of the fighter director. Charlie rose quickly to become the go-to enlisted man as he had a knack for finding contacts before anyone else in the division.

"This is going to take forever," complained Gil as the two left the fantail for the ship's mess. The fantail is below the flight deck at the rear of the carrier and is a favorite place for sailors to catch a quick nap between watches.

"Are you nervous, Gil?" asked Charlie, changing the subject.

"Nervous about what, Charlie?" replied Gil.

"We are in the Panama Canal headed toward the Pacific Ocean," Charlie emphasized, "where the Japanese Navy waits for us!"

"Yea, I guess," Gil said pensively, "but I trust you and my crewmates to keep me safe. That is all I have. I have to believe this, or I could not do my job."

"You see," Charlie confessed, "I have this girl back home in Dallas, real pretty. I really like her and think about her all the time, when I am not on watch."

"Lucky man," said Gil with a touch of envy. "What is her name?"

"Lilly, Lilly Hope. Funny thing is that I met her when I was on my way to radar school in San Diego," explained Charlie. "They were on their way to Phoenix, and we spoke for almost one day, non-stop."

"Wait, 'they'?" asked Gil.

"Her family," Charlie said, "her mom and dad. I think I could really fall for her," he added, his voice trailing off.

"Lucky man," Gil said again. "I will make sure you get back to her."

"Thanks," Charlie said.

"Now, how about we get down for dinner," prodded Gil. "Who knows how much longer we will have real meat to eat."

43. TOKYO, JAPAN

It was a rainy Saturday morning in June, and the funeral preparations to lay Admiral Yamamoto to rest were complete. The emperor ordered a state funeral and a week of mourning after the return to Japanese soil of the ashes of the revered admiral. The dense jungle on Bougainville had delayed the discovery of the Betty bomber crash site by the search party. Once discovered, they cremated Yamamoto's body and returned his ashes to Japan.

Brigades of military men, adorned in their dress military uniforms, lined the boulevard as the caisson carrying Admiral Yamamoto rolled majestically past the adoring crowds. A procession of naval officers, Prime Minister Tojo, and other military dignitaries marched solemnly behind the funeral procession. At the funeral tent, dignitaries, including Prime Minister Tojo, laid a flower on the cremains of Yamamoto, paying respect to the man who had brought great glory but also shame to the Japanese people. As an ultimate act of respect, each person approaching the cremains left without turning their back on their fallen admiral.

Onishi stood at attention, showing proper solemnity toward his former mentor. How long would it be before his traitorous deeds would find their way to his neck in the form of a knife or a rope? Was there a way to use this death to his advantage?

. . . . .

"Private come with me," said the lieutenant.

Hadaki looked up and followed the lieutenant as they headed toward their commanding officer. Hadaki gulped.

"Reporting as ordered," Hadaki said with a sharp salute.

"You will get your gear and follow this man," said his commander.

Hadaki wanted to know more. He wanted to know why he was leaving his team. What had he done?

"Hai!" Hadaki said as he bowed. He quickly gathered his gear and met the lieutenant as ordered. "May I ask where we are going?" asked Hadaki.

"No," was the curt reply.

They walked for miles until they came to a clearing. He could see a crew transport ship with many Japanese soldiers loading men and equipment.

"You will accompany these men and find Captain Isokawa," ordered the lieutenant.

"Hai!" replied Hadaki. *What is happening? Why am I leaving this battle zone? How can I honor my forefathers and bring the fight to the Americans?*

. . . . .

The crew of the Lexington lined the rails in their dress uniforms as she slipped into a berth at Pearl Harbor on August 9, 1943. Each man on the ship looked in horror at the remains of the USS Arizona. It only strengthened their resolve to seek revenge on the Japanese.

"I cannot believe what I am seeing," Charlie said, fighting back tears.

"I know," Gil said, also deeply moved.

"When are you scheduled for liberty?" asked Charlie.

"1200," said Gil, suddenly coming alive, "and you?"

"Same," said Charlie. "Do you want to explore together?"

"Sounds great," Gil said excitedly. "See you back here at 1145!"

"Deal," Charlie agreed.

Neither sailor had been to Hawaii before, nor had they experienced such freedom. Charlie, looking every bit his age of eighteen, and Gil, seven months past his eighteenth birthday, met at the rail and proceeded to the master-at-arms shack where he checked their leave cards and reminded them to be back on ship by 2000 hours or they would be absent without leave or AWAOL.

"What do you want to do?" asked Gil.

"I think it would be great to lie around at the beach for a while," Charlie suggested.

Both men had fifteen dollars in their pocket, and were eager to have a good time and forget the war, even for a minute. They loaded onto the train headed for downtown Honolulu.

"I heard about this great cafe," said Charlie, "right across from the armed forces YMCA called the Black Cat Cafe. I am told that they have great food, but there is usually a line to get in."

"Sounds good to me," agreed Gil. "We better hurry. I so want a steak!"

The men arrived at the Black Cat and found the expected line already forming. Within twenty minutes, they were inside, ready to have their first good meal in over four months.

"The prices are great!" Charlie exclaimed.

"Yeah, we can sure eat a bunch of food for real cheap," said Gil.

The two ordered the Porterhouse steaks with all the sides for one dollar. After they stuffed themselves, they walked along King street, playing pinball and shooting rifles at the arcade. But the best part of the day was taking photos at the photo booth. Charlie was looking forward to introducing Gil to Lilly through their picture. They arrived back at the ship by 1950 hours. They would be underway in two days, headed for who knows where.

44. OPERATION GALVANIC

The Marshall Islands are about twenty-one hundred miles west-southwest of Pearl Harbor. Comprising an archipelago of coral atolls hundreds of miles across, the island chain was essential to any plan to defeat the Japanese. The Japanese quickly invaded the Gilbert Islands to the south-southeast after hostilities began in late 1941 to create a buffer and protect the islands from direct attack.

Prior to World War I, war planners in Japan and the United States realized the high probability of war between the two nations. The key to both plans were the Marshall Islands. Operation Galvanic was a stepping-stone plan for any attack on the Marshall Islands, where the United States desperately needed an airstrip and logistics hub.

The training of the crew of the USS Lexington completed, they prepared to head into their first combat engagement. But they lacked combat experience. Three out of four pilots had not attended the Naval Academy in Annapolis, but were reservists commissioned from naval training bases around the United States. The Grumman F6F Hellcat, a replacement for the F4F Wildcat, was the new fighter plane on the Lexington. Faster than the Wildcat by 150 to 200 miles per hour, the Hellcat was more maneuverable and a better plane than the Japanese Zero.

The industrial might of the United States would soon change the face of the war. Within one year of their loss, the United States replaced two important carriers, while the Japanese could not replace one.

"What do you think it will be like?" asked Gil as he reached for his dinner roll.

"I do not know," Charlie said, remembering the mangled carnage of the USS Arizona. "I am sure it will be tough, but our training will see us through."

"Are you scared?" asked Gil, careful to not say this too loud.

"Sort of," Charlie said pensively. "I would say I am more apprehensive, because I do not know what it will be like."

"General quarters, general quarters, man your battle stations," called the voice over the intercom.

They ran to their general quarters post just outside of CIC. They arrived at their post to find it was another drill, the third general quarter drill called since they left Pearl Harbor. At least they would be ready.

"Secure from battle stations," called the voice on the hailer.

"All hands," called Captain Stump, "this is the captain. I can tell you now that we are safely out of port, the Lady Lex will get her first taste of battle. When we left Boston harbor, 95 percent of this crew had never served on a military vessel in their lives. You are all well trained and I know you will rise to the occasion. I have faith in each one of you and trust you with my life. That is all."

Charlie smiled to himself. Captain Stump had shown unusual interest in his progress as a radarman. Charlie could think of no man he would rather have as captain, the man who would shepherd his walk into manhood, thought Charlie.

Twenty days later, the Lexington prepared to enter the war.

"Status, Brand," ordered LT.

"Radar clear, sir," responded Charlie. "No contacts to report."

"Very well," said LT.

"CAG, launch our strike," ordered Stump.

"Aye, aye, sir," responded the CAG.

Ten minutes later, forty planes sortied toward Tarawa to soften the Japanese position in preparation for the upcoming assault.

"Keep a sharp eye out for trouble, Brand," ordered LT.

"Aye, aye, sir," responded Charlie.

"Form up, boys," instructed the team leader.

The bomber teams formed into an overall "V" formation made up of smaller groupings of three planes, also formed into "V" formations. Hellcat Fighters took up overwatch ten thousand feet above the bombers. Today's mission would inflict as much damage as possible on any ground-based airplanes and facilities on Tarawa.

"Friendly contacts have left the scope," Charlie reported. The attack force was out of radar range.

"Very well," replied LT.

"Keep your eyes open, boys," instructed the team leader. "Tarawa in sight."

The fighters engaged first, strafing the anti-aircraft installations below. The guns erupted, protesting the impending aerial onslaught. All but one fighter made it through the initial attack, and all of their targets took direct hits.

The dive bombers began their run. Pings of gunfire ricocheted off of the first wave of bomber's fuselage. Seven received extensive damage, but six released their ordinances against the enemy. *Hit, hit, hit, hit!* The island exploded into flames. The remaining bombers completed their runs, and the team formed up for return to their ship.

Flames engulfed twelve of twenty Japanese planes, and craters littered the island. The next wave from their sister carriers would not be far behind.

"Multiple contacts," called Charlie. "All friendlies!"

"How many, Brand?" asked LT with mild annoyance.

"I see thirty-five, sir," Charlie responded.

"I need you to find the rest of those planes, Brand," ordered LT. "Do your magic!"

"Aye, aye, sir," responded Charlie.

Thirty-five planes safely landed aboard the Lexington. Charlie stared intently at his scope, sweeping his radar back and forth across the horizon.

"Any luck, Brand?" asked LT.

"Well, sir," Charlie started, "I keep on seeing contacts, and then they disappear. I recommend trying to contact them."

"Blue team, Spartan." Spartan was the call sign for the Lexington.

"Blue team, aye," responded the commander.

"Health check, report status," said LT.

Silence.

"Spartan, Blue Twelve," called the commander.

"Spartan, aye," responded LT.

"We have Echo planes," called Blue Twelve, "limping along. Need guidance." Echo is the fifth letter in the military alphabet, and they needed a bearing back to the ship.

"Echo, aye," responded LT. "Brand, find me those five planes," he ordered with a sense of urgency.

"Aye, aye, sir," responded Charlie. "I have them."

"Where are they, Brand?" asked LT

"I have five contacts, one two zero miles out, bearing eight fiver degrees," reported Charlie.

"I want course and speed every minute," ordered LT. "Give me a bearing to bring these guys home."

"Got it," Charlie said, looking up to see LT give him a look. "Aye, aye, sir!"

Blackness engulfed the carrier.

"Plot course two four one, LT," called the man at the chart.

"Blue Twelve," called LT, "turn to arrow two three one. Supper is waiting." The remaining planes converted the bearing to true magnetic.

"Looking forward to it," responded Blue Twelve.

Twenty minutes later, the missing planes found their carrier and landed without incident. Inspection by the plane captains found an average of seventy bullet holes littering the planes. Four of five planes lost their radios, and the IFF systems were intermittent.

"I want to meet these people who got us home," said Blue Twelve during his debrief.

"I will make sure you get to meet them," the CAG promised.

Ten minutes later, Charlie and LT entered the ready room.

"These are the men who got you home," announced the CAG.

"How did you find us up there?" asked Lieutenant Jones, Blue Twelve leader.

LT and Charlie looked toward the CAG who nodded his head.

"Brand is actually the man who found you," said LT. "I was the voice on your radio."

The men swarmed Charlie and began thanking him and patting him on the back.

"How did you do it, Brand?" asked the lieutenant. "What is your first name?"

"Charlie. Well, sir . . ." Charlie stammered. He looked to LT for help.

"Guys, Charlie uses some top-secret gear," LT said carefully, "that allows him to see into the clouds."

"You mean radar, right?" asked Jones. Charlie nearly fell over.

The CAG stepped in. "Captain Stump read our pilots into the basics of radar technology before we launched," offered the CAG. "Some time, you can show some of our boys around your air-conditioned hideaway."

LT jumped in. "We will be happy to give them a tour, sir."

. . . . .

After the death of Admiral Yamamoto, the Supreme War Council appointed Admiral Mineichi Koga the commander-in-chief of the combined Japanese naval fleet. Born in Arita, Japan, in 1885, Koga graduated from the Imperial Japanese Naval Academy in 1905, ranked 14 out of 176. He quickly rose through the ranks, serving both at sea and as a naval attaché in Paris. He became vice admiral responsible for forces in the China Sea just before war broke between his country and the United States.

"Report!" demanded Admiral Koga.

"During the attack last night on Wake Island ," reported the captain, "our bases suffered extensive damage losing twenty-five planes and much of the island infrastructure."

"We must engage them now," Koga said forcefully. "Notify the fleet to sail to Eniwetok immediately."

"Hai!" responded the captain.

45. DALLAS, TEXAS

Lilly lay on her bed dreaming of Charlie and not paying much attention to her homework.

"Letter from Charlie, Lilly," said her mother sweetly.

Lilly raced to her mother trying not to grab the letter too quickly.

"Thank you, mother," Lilly said, hoping her mother would leave her to read in private. Her mother left her room, closing the door behind her.

Lilly carefully opened the letter and drank in each word like the finest glass of French wine. She lived for each letter from her Charlie. She could not wait to respond to his letters, and often stayed up late into the night putting on the last touches. She immediately penned her response.

My Dearest Charlie,

> Oh, how I long each day for your letters, hoping that today I will hear you are coming home to me. It is so nice to hear that you have a friend to be with on your ship. I enjoyed seeing the picture of you and Gil in Hawaii. What a life you lead. Is Hawaii as beautiful in person as the pictures I have seen?
>
> Mother and Father are doing well. Business is really booming for Father, and he needs to hire more employees to keep up with the customers. He has even asked me to help around the store occasionally.
>
> My girlfriends are so jealous of me that I have a real war hero boyfriend! I showed them the picture of you and Gil from Hawaii in your uniforms, and they love the picture as much as I do.
>
> With each letter you send me, I thank God that he is faithfully keeping you safe in His arms. I pray each day for your safety and that of

your crew. I am so scared that I will never see you or hold you again. But I know God has a plan for you, and so do I.

Charlie, I love you!

Lilly.

Lilly was thankful for each letter, but heartbroken that her man was not with her. She was already secretly planning her wedding, hoping that Charlie would soon be home, and they could begin their life together.

. . . . .

Hadaki looked in horror as his homeland came into view. Why was he here? How had he failed his emperor? Two hours later, he walked down the gangway to dry land.

"Yamatsumi," called a lieutenant, "Private Yamatsumi."

Hadaki raised his hand, wishing to find answers to his questions.

"Yes, sir," said Hadaki.

"Come with me," ordered the lieutenant.

"I am confused, sir," Hadaki said carefully. "Why was I removed from my unit on Guadalcanal?"

"I am ordered to bring you to command headquarters in Tokyo," said the lieutenant. "I do not know nor do I care to know why you are here. Your answers will come when our leaders believe you need to know. Stay quiet now!"

Hadaki shook his head meekly and waited for his arrival at headquarters.

Hadaki looked up and immediately knew where he was. He had seen pictures of this building before the war started. He was at the Imperial General Headquarters. He walked in and waited for someone to address him.

"Private," called the corporal at the reception desk, "why are you here?"

"Private Yamatsumi, reporting as ordered," Hadaki said as he snapped to attention.

"Sit over there," said the corporal dismissively.

Hadaki moved to the directed location and sat on a chair for the next two hours.

"Private," said an officer, "come with me."

Hadaki stood and followed the officer into a room next to the reception hall.

"You are Private Hadaki Yamatsumi?" asked the officer.

"Hai!" responded Hadaki.

"You are from Kawaguchiko in the southern Yamanashi Prefecture?"

Hadaki grew concerned. "Hai!"

"You have an exemplary record," began the officer, "just like your father."

A look of bewilderment crossed Hadaki's face. "How…" he tried to speak.

"I was your father's commanding officer," began the officer. "I am Commander Watanabe. Your father served bravely and died serving the emperor. I have only one question for you, private. Why did you lie to Japan?"

Droplets of cold sweat formed on Hadaki's forehead. "I would not lie to you or Japan," Hadaki responded indignantly. "I have served the emperor with honor."

"When the men came to your town to take men to war," reminded the commander, "you should have stayed home. You are the eldest male, which makes you exempt from serving in the war. Why did you lie to us?"

"My father came to me while I was on Fuji-san," responded Hadaki. "He told me it was vital that I enlist. My service to the emperor was necessary and I would bring the highest honor to my family."

"I see," said the commander.

"How did you find me among so many?" asked Hadaki.

"I went to Kawaguchiko looking for you," said the commander. "Your mother told me you enlisted. I have been searching through the records for months to find you. Japan cannot allow you to stay in the military; your family needs you back home."

"I beg of you, sir," pleaded Hadaki, "please allow me to continue to serve the emperor. Do not send me home!"

"I must take you off of the front line," said the commander. "I will place you in a training command through end of the war."

"Hai!" Hadaki said standing to attention. "Thank you, sir."

"Here are your new orders," responded the commander. "Dismissed."

• • • • •

"Operation Galvanic is proceeding according to plan, Mr. President," reported Admiral King.

The Joint Chiefs joined the president in the Oval Office, sitting on the sofa to his right. Henry Stimson sat in a chair across from the sofa, with the vice president sitting next to him.

"How are Admiral Turner and our boys fairing, Admiral King?" asked the president.

"Sir, our carrier forces softened up Tarawa for our landing and the Japanese moved their naval assets to Eniwetok instead of supporting our attack on Tarawa. Our attacks on Wake Island and the Marshall Islands earlier this year sure confused them. Even though Tarawa is heavily fortified, we are confident that we will prevail," Admiral King said confidently.

"Based on the losses at Guadalcanal, how can you be so confident?" asked Stimson.

"Well, sir," answered the admiral, "despite the heavy fortifications and ferocity of the Japanese fighter, our forces still prevailed. We learned much tactically from this battle, and our naval forces now outnumber those of the Japanese. We have the edge because of our industrial production and access to raw materials."

"It pains me each day as I review the casualty reports from the European and Pacific theaters," the president said empathetically.

"They brought the fight to us, sir," stated the admiral, "and we aim to finish that fight in Tokyo!"

• • • • •

"Our forces will begin their attack on Tarawa in sixty minutes, CAG," said Captain Stump. "We need to be ready to protect our boys from any air attacks."

"We have CAP up right now to protect the fleet, and we have air power up and ready to engage, sir," reported the CAG.

"Excellent," said the captain. "May God protect our boys today."

"I have two five contacts bearing five four degrees, range one one seven miles, flying Angels fifteen," reported Charlie.

"Very well," LT said calmly. "Plot me an intercept course, Johnnie."

John Baker grew up on a farm just outside of Cape Girardeau, Missouri, and worked the plotting map directly in front of LT.

"Intercept course one eight three," reported Johnnie.

"Green lead, Spartan," called LT.

"Green lead, aye," responded the lieutenant.

"We have two five bogies at Angels fifteen. Come to course one eight three and climb to Angels twenty," ordered LT.

"Green lead, aye," responded the leader.

Using the sun and clouds to disguise their approach, the squadron caught the Japanese attack force by surprise. The new Hellcat fighters had the edge and quickly reduced the attack force to twelve. The Japanese force lost seven more Zeros, retreating from the battle for their base in Eniwetok.

On Tarawa, the USS Lexington sorties continued to provide cover for the landing forces, allowing the marines a beachhead on the island. Throughout the next three days, the Japanese continued their attacks on the marines on Tarawa. Only two minor strikes on the US forces made it through the Lexington's air defenses.

46. KANTAI KESSEN

Before the beginning of World War II, the Japanese had adopted a military strategy stating a single decisive naval battle would win any conflict with an opposing nation. Influenced by naval historian Alfred Mahan, the Japanese called this Kantai Kessen, or the Decisive Battle Doctrine.

Prime Minister Tojo entered the War Council. "Admiral Koga," he said, "please proceed."

"Thank you, Prime Minister," said Koga. "For years, military planners believed the Kantai Kessen would save our nation from attack by our enemies. Recent events have shown reliance on our aircraft carrier dominance, a position held by Admiral Yamamoto, is not effective."

"What is your position on Kantai Kessen?" asked Tojo.

"I believe in this doctrine, as originally planned," began Koga, "the big guns of our destroyers can win any battle against the United States; we have just not correctly set the environment for this battle."

"Interesting," Tojo said. This comment intrigued him. "Go on."

"The Unites States is beginning their long crawl through the islands of each archipelagos toward the Japanese mainland," said Koga. "We need to prepare our forces for the final naval battle of our choosing. Guadalcanal is lost, and we will lose our position on the Gilbert Islands within days. We will require the Americans to take each island on the way to Japan, inflicting casualties that will cause the United States to lose their stomach for battle."

"Recommendations, admiral," said Tojo.

"With the recent loss of our battlecruisers *Hiei* and *Kirishima*," began the admiral, "we must withdraw our remaining battleships to a safe harbor and rely on our island-based aircraft to punish the United States at each island battle. We will meet them in the Philippine Sea where we will crush them so they will sue for peace."

The War Council considered Admiral Koga's plan for one hour before voting to approve it. The council adjourned.

. . . . .

Admiral Nimitz entered his conference room, and the officers stood to attention.

"Please be seated," said the admiral. "Commander, please present your plan."

"Thank you, sir," said the commander. "The Gilbert Islands campaign was successful, as was the attack on Rabaul, and it is time to finalize our battle plans to arrive in Tokyo Bay. The decision to split into southern and northern task forces will stretch the Japanese forces to their breaking point. The Japanese expect our allied forces to attack each island on our way to Tokyo, but we have a better plan. We have the element of surprise on our side and the Japanese are now on the defensive. By selecting only key island strongholds to attack, we minimize our casualties and can attack with superior forces every time."

"What is our timeline, commander?" asked Nimitz.

"Sir, we will begin our next northern offensive in Kwajalein by the beginning of February. From there, we expect to go directly to attack the Japanese base at Eniwetok by the end of February and begin our offensive on the Marianas by the end of July."

The command staff discussed the plans, finalizing ship movements and defining objectives.

. . . . .

Charlie lay on his bunk, trying to sleep. The humidity in the air hung like an unwelcome wet blanket, encouraging sweat to seep from his body. This was the reason most of the ship's crew slept out on deck, except during flight operations. He had grown accustomed to the smell of fuel permeating every area of the ship, affecting the taste of their food. He looked forward to his air-conditioned watches as they were his only respite from the oppressive heat. Charlie also enjoyed watching flight operations. His relationship with the airedales was unique. They relied on him to keep them safe, directing their attacks on the enemy and shepherding the lost back to the ship. But he was only a radarman, an enlisted man. Charlie was in awe of their knowledge and skill. It amazed him every time he watched flight operations: the choreographed dance of the planes as they prepared to launch from his ship to pinpoint precision, blindly grabbing the arresting wire, preventing a plane from sliding into the ocean. They talked to him, made him feel special. They were of the few who really knew the impact he had on the operations of this ship. A secret shared, but never discussed with anyone.

"General quarters, general quarters," was the call over the loudspeaker, "man your battle stations."

Charlie jumped down to the deck, trying to pull his cloths through the stickiness. He ran to his battle station and waited for instructions. The door to the compartment opened.

"Charlie," said Gil, "LT needs you on the set."

Charlie was happy to be in the air-conditioned room, ready to do his job. Charlie found the CIC buzzing with activity.

"Brand," said LT, "you have ten bogies out there. I want them tracked; nothing gets through to the ship. Got it?"

"Yes, sir," responded Charlie.

The most dangerous time for a carrier is during night operations. It was nearly impossible to identify enemy or friendly contacts. Even aircraft identification through the A-scope could be difficult during dogfights as contacts moved around the radar screen.

Just six hours ago, Charlie was on watch, helping direct his airedale friends for their raid on Kwajalein. The Lexington air group raid scored thirty aircraft kills, two damaged cruisers, and damage to a cargo ship. Now, the Japanese were again attacking at night, believing he would not be able to detect their presence.

"Contacts now bearing three two seven, range two zero miles," reported Charlie.

"Keep an eye on them," ordered LT. "Bearing and range every thirty seconds." LT seemed concerned.

“Contacts holding steady on same bearing,” reported Charlie. “Range one four miles.”

The Lexington would normally open fire on targets at this range, but any anti-aircraft fire from the ship would expose her position.

Two flares illuminated the night sky. They were in trouble.

Flames jumped from the quadruple 40-mm guns as they searched the night sky for targets. Two Betty bombers fell, eight remaining. CAP downed two more bombers, six remaining.

“We now have six contacts, same bearing,” reported Charlie trying to remain calm, “four miles out.”

Ten minutes after the flare sighting, the Lexington’s stern jumped into the air.

“Damage report,” ordered Captain Stump.

“Torpedo hit, starboard side,” reported the executive officer. “We lost our steering.”

“I need that steering!” ordered the captain.

“Aye, aye, sir,” responded the XO. “Damage parties working on it!”

The Lexington settled five feet to stern, circling to port. Suddenly, smoke bombs used to provide a protective blanket during battle exploded, spreading their acrid darkness throughout the ship. The crew braced for another hit; a feeling of impending doom raced through the crew.

“This is the captain,” Stump said over the loudspeaker, “we have been hit by a single torpedo on the starboard side. The hit ignited many of our smoke bombs causing the discomfort you are now feeling. There is no cause to worry. If there is any worrying to be done, I as your captain will do it. If God is good to us, we will go safely to Pearl Harbor, under our own power, and be back to give the Japanese more hell. That is all.”

To a man, the crew put aside any worry and worked to repair the damaged steering. Twenty minutes later, a temporary repair in place, the Lexington and her crew slipped from the battlefield on her way to Pearl Harbor.

As the Lexington secured from general quarters, the captain again addressed the crew. "This is the captain," began Stump. "I have received a message from the admiral complimenting me on my seamanship and leadership of this crew. When we left Boston for the battlefield, we were all strangers, civilians with no experience or business aboard a battleship. Today, I responded to the admiral, 'Thank You, Negative.' Today, you became a crew, my crew. A fighting force destined for greatness. I am proud to call each of you my crew and I would sail to Hell and back, without stopping to load any ice. That is all."

Every man beamed with pride, basking in the praise from their captain. The Lexington made Pearl Harbor for emergency repairs, and sailed on to Bremerton, Washington, for full repairs.

47. KAWAGUCHICO, JAPAN

Hadaki opened the door to his childhood home, full of anticipation for the warm welcome he expected to receive. Yet, concern about the actions of his *haha* during the visit from his *otosan's* commanding officer consumed him. Why would his *haha* betray him? He would soon have his answers.

"*Kon'nichiwa*!" called Hadaki.

Yoshi bounded around the corner into Hadaki's arms, followed closely by his *haha*.

"Oh, my *musoko*," cried his mother, "how I have missed you. I will make you lunch."

"Tell me you are home to stay," pleaded Yoshi.

"No," Hadaki said sweetly, "I can only stay for lunch and then I must return to my unit. Now, please go and play while I talk to our *haha*."

"OK, I will go," said his sister sadly. "I want to show you my new doll later."

"I look forward to seeing your doll," Hadaki said.

Yoshi left the room, and Hadaki turned to see his mother placing rice into a bowl, topping it with dried fish.

"We have missed you, my son," said his mother trying not to cry. "I have worried every day for your safety."

"I was on Guadalcanal," Hadaki said tersely, "fighting with my unit. Bringing honor to my family and then . . ." His voice trailed off.

"What?" asked his mother, empathetically.

"They took me off of the island and brought me to Tokyo." Hadaki's anger grew.

"Oh?" his mother said demurely, placing the bowl before her son.

"I met my father's commanding officer," Hadaki's tone was more direct. "He said you told him I enlisted. Why would you betray our family?"

"Betray?" Hadaki's mother was now growing angry. "You left us here. You are my firstborn; your place is here with us. What should happen if you die? I will lose everything! Your family will lose everything!"

Hadaki stopped chewing.

"Oh, my mother," Hadaki said emotionally, "I would never leave you here alone if it was not vital. I serve our emperor. Remember, our ancestors told me I must serve."

"Our ancestors will not be here to save our family farm if you die," said his mother tersely.

"Your fears are unwarranted, Mother," Hadaki said. "They transferred me to a training post here in Japan. I am no longer in danger."

Hadaki held his mother as she cried.

"You will still bring honor to our family, my son," wept his mother.

. . . . .

A fresh snow blanketed the wandering prairie, sheltering her fertile soil from the grips of the early winter frost. Charlie struggled to push down his emotions still raw from the attack on his beloved ship. The perilousness of war became very real to him that night. Even though he was in the CIC, protected from the terror suffered by the crew, it reminded him of the tenuousness of life. His dreams, love, what he still wanted to accomplish. As he gazed out the window of the train, geometric crystalline frost encroached his view of the scenic North Dakota landscape, enticing him to daydream. The bright brittle blue sky caused him to squint, sundogs creating magical rainbows beside the morning sun. He immediately thought of Lilly, and a sense of calm enveloped him like the blanket of snow outside his window.

What would he tell her about the war? He wanted to protect her from the reality of his choice to serve. To her, he was a hero. Charlie knew he was just a man, answering a higher call from God and his country, nothing more. Yet, the danger he just faced caused him to realize, for the first time in his life, he may not survive the war. He was not invincible. Ongoing repairs to his ship showed America's resolve to stay the course, to win the war at all costs. For America, there was no choice. To him, the torpedo changed his life forever.

The train pulled into Union Station in Little Rock; no military band played the national anthem. No cheering crowds met him as he left the train. This was just fine with Charlie. On the way to his house, a few people recognized him, asking how he was doing and about his time overseas. He turned the corner onto his street, and the pace of his stride quickened. The door flung open, and his sister ran toward him at full speed. Charlie dropped his seabag, preparing for the hug he expected would knock him to his knees.

"Charlie!" she cried. "How I have missed you!"

"I have missed you too, sis," Charlie said, fighting back the tears. "I sure missed your cooking!"

Doris Ann kissed him all over his face. "You must be exhausted," her voice still high-pitched. "Come in and relax!"

"Sounds great," said Charlie. "It has been a long train ride from Seattle."

"Is everything alright, Charlie?" she asked. "You are not hurt, are you?"

"No," Charlie assured her, "I am fine. My ship is having some work done to her." "Work," Doris Ann said, concerned. "Is your ship hurt?"

They gave the crew strict instructions not to disclose anything to their families about the attack on the ship or why she was in dry dock.

"Uncle Sam decided I needed some time with my family for Christmas," Charlie lied.

Doris Ann gave Charlie the look. She always knew when he was telling her a story, but she also knew there were things he could not tell her until this awful war was over.

Doris Ann cooked Charlie's favorite meal, and they retired to the front room to catch up.

"Before you ask, sis," Charlie began, "there are things I cannot tell you about what I do or where I have been. I am under strict orders not to talk about the war."

"Who wants to talk about war?" Doris Ann lied. "I want to talk about love," she said, elongating the "ove" in her best Arkansas drawl.

"You mean Lilly," Charlie said coyly.

"Yes, I mean Lilly," Doris Ann chided. They laughed.

"As I told you in my letters," Charlie said, "I met her on the train ride out west for school. We really hit it off, talked almost twenty hours straight!"

"Sounds promising," said his sister.

"I went to Dallas to see her before I came home last time," Charlie confessed.

"Really," Doris Ann said, slightly annoyed.

"I spent the day with her," Charlie said, his voice trailing off. "What a day."

"Wow, Charles," his sister said.

Charlie perked up. His sister only used his given name when he was in trouble.

"I have never heard you speak of a girl like this," she said sweetly. "You must really be hooked."

"I guess I am," Charlie confessed.

Doris Ann smiled sweetly. Her marriage was in two months and she would miss having her brother there to celebrate. They stayed up late talking about everything, but mostly Lilly.

48. DALLAS, TEXAS

After spending Christmas with his family in Arkansas, Charlie took the train to Dallas where the Hopes offered him a room in their home until he returned to his ship.

"Charlie!" cried Lilly as she ran across the platform.

Lilly stopped just short of Charlie. Charlie beamed.

"I missed you so much," Charlie said, tears forming in his eyes.

"I was so worried I would never see you again!" Lilly began to cry.

Charlie took her in his arms and kissed her deeply, his mind capturing every detail of the moment, the smell of her hair, the warmth of her skin, and the feel of her lips against his. He knew now he could make it home from the Pacific. He had to. Time stopped for Charlie, the passion of the moment overwhelming his senses, causing all thoughts to vacate. He was deaf to the noise of the platform, consuming the love pouring into his soul.

"I am so glad to see you again," said Mr. Hope.

Charlie broke his embrace, dazed. A welcoming hand reaching for his, he struggled to gain control. "Thank you for the invite, sir," summoned Charlie, still dazed.

"We are happy to have you," said Mrs. Hope, taking over the conversation to protect the moment.

Charlie offered his hand to Mrs. Hope, only to find a welcoming embrace.

Twenty minutes later, they walked into the Hope home. Charlie looked at the Christmas tree in the front room and felt a sense of dread filling his stomach. The Hope Christmas tree was nine feet tall and was the most beautiful he had ever seen. Glass ornaments adorned the aromatic pine tree as silver tinsel shimmered like the North Dakota snow. How could Lilly ever be happy with a man like him?

"Your tree is beautiful," Charlie complimented. "I think it is the most beautiful I have ever seen."

"Thank you, Charlie," said Mrs. Hope. She could sense his uneasiness and knew she needed to talk to her daughter. Henry and Ellen exchanged a glance.

"Charlie," said Henry, "come with me and I will show you where you will be staying."

"Thank you, sir," said Charlie as the two disappeared up the stairs.

"Lilly," Ellen gently said, "I think Charlie is uncomfortable here."

"Uncomfortable?" Lilly asked, her voice rising.

"Yes," Ellen said. "I get the impression that his family in Little Rock does not have the lifestyle we have here in Dallas. We need to make him feel welcome and show him we are just like his family back home."

"Oh, Mother," Lilly whimpered, "I love him so much!"

"I know you do, honey," Ellen reassured. "I can see it all over your face."

"You can?" Lilly responded.

"Yes, Lilly," said her mother. "I remember how I felt about your father when I first met him. I was not much older than you and fell hard for him."

"How long till dinner, Ellen?" asked Henry, entering the kitchen.

"Dinner is at 6:00 p.m., sharp," Ellen replied.

"Good," said Henry. "Charlie, I want to ask your opinion about something on the car."

"Yes, sir," replied Charlie. "Happy to help in any way I can."

Charlie and Henry walked out the back door to the garage.

"Charlie," began Henry, "how are things going with the war?"

"Well, sir," said Charlie, "me and my crew are giving it to the Japs any time we can. We are making them pay for what they did to us at Pearl Harbor."

"What actually do you do on your ship, Charlie?" asked Henry.

"Well, sir," Charlie said carefully, "I support our pilots."

"So, you work on the planes?" asked Henry.

"No, not really," Charlie was trying to dodge this line of questioning. "My captain says I can tell no one what I do on the ship."

Henry pondered this for a moment. Few people would have the guts to refuse his questioning, especially those interested in his daughter. It took guts to volunteer to serve the country, and Henry was thankful. He had a newfound respect for Charlie; he approved of his daughter's choice in this man and would be proud to show Charlie around while he was here.

"I understand," Henry lied. "Are you safe out there in the Pacific?"

Charlie measured his response again. "I would say I am safer than the guys fighting for us on the islands." Charlie was proud of himself. He knew this question would come up from her parents, but it surprised him Mr. Hope brought this up so early in his stay.

"What did you want to ask me about your car?" Charlie asked, changing the subject.

The two fiddled with the car for twenty minutes and entered the kitchen to wash their hands. Ellen and Lilly were sitting at the kitchen table talking. Ellen noticed a change in her husband's demeanor. She would ask him about that tonight before they went to bed.

"Do you know how to play Pinochle?" asked Ellen.

"Yes, ma'am, I do," Charlie replied. "The guys in my section like to play Pinochle after a watch."

"A watch?" Lilly asked.

"Sorry," Charlie offered. "On our ship, we work for four hours and then we are off for four hours. We call those watches."

"I hope they are letting you sleep and giving you plenty of food," Lilly said.

"I am well cared for on my ship," assured Charlie. "Now where are those cards?"

They chose teams and played until dinner. After they ate, they retired to the front room where Lilly played their grand piano. Lilly impressed Charlie in so many ways. She was beautiful, thoughtful, caring, and now she played piano better than anyone he knew. Lilly played for an hour, and then she and Charlie went outside to sit on the porch.

"I am cold, Charlie," she cooed. "Hold me. Do not let go until you have to leave for your ship."

Charlie kissed her. "Does this help warm you up?"

"Sure does," she could barely speak. "I feel safe in your arms."

Over the next three days, the Hopes entertained Charlie showing him the sights of Dallas. Henry Hope took Charlie to his store, where he fit him for a new suit. He would pick it up the next time he came to Dallas. Lilly introduced Charlie to all of her friends, and they went to see a movie at the Majestic Theater.

"I just love going to the picture show," declared Lilly. "I have been waiting to see this movie all month!"

Lilly wanted to see the musical comedy "This is the Army." Charlie did not much care for movie musicals, but he would do anything to be alone with her in a dark theater. The lights dimmed, and a newsreel describing the victory at Tarawa came on the screen. Charlie gulped; he was not sure he wanted Lilly to see this newsreel.

The images mesmerized Lilly. Charlie felt her tremble as she clung to him.

"Were you there?" whispered Lilly.

"My ship supported those men, but I was far away from the battle," Charlie assured.

They held hands as they watched the movie, occasionally stealing a kiss. After the show, they went for ice cream before heading back to Highland Park. They stopped to sit on the porch.

"I am so scared for you, Charlie," Lilly was suddenly very serious.

"I promise you, Lilly," Charlie said, "my pilots are in far more danger than I am. I do not even carry a rifle."

Charlie hoped this would assuage her fears. It did not.

"Charles Brand," scolded Lilly, "I want you to tell me the truth!" Now Lilly sounded like his sister.

"I am telling you the truth, Lilly," protested Charlie.

"Then why will you not tell me what you are doing on your ship?" she demanded.

"Because the captain of my ship will not allow me to tell anyone not in the military what I do," Charlie offered. "I can tell you that my job is very important to my team and the war effort."

Lilly smiled, her face glowing like a full moon over the Pacific Ocean.

"I am so proud of you, Charlie!" Lilly said, cuddling up to Charlie.

49. USS LEXINGTON

Charlie lay in his bunk dreaming of Lilly and hoping this feeling would never end.

"Charlie, Charlie," Gil was standing next to him, gently shaking his shoulder. "Charlie, get up," Gil cajoled. "They are serving mystery meat tonight."

"Humph," Charlie complained. "I am not hungry."

"Charlie, you are always hungry," chided Gil. "Now get up!"

"Alright, alright," Charlie relented." Maybe the mystery meat will be a big fat steak!"

"You looked happy before I woke you," said Gil. "Were you dreaming?"

"I sure was," Charlie said, his voice trailing off.

"Lilly?" asked Gil.

"Yeah," Charlie said. "I miss her so much!"

"I know you do, buddy," Gil said comforting his friend the best he could. "We need to stay focused so we can get us back home."

"I know," said Charlie, resigned to his fate. "So where is this big steak?"

Loneliness was a constant companion on their ship. Even on a ship of twenty-five hundred, it was amazing how alone a guy could feel. The mutual support system Charlie and Gil developed had worked so far, and Charlie prayed every day that he would not lose Gil. Preparing for battle through their regular training drills helped them forget what they left behind, but the time alone, when they had time to think about their family, that was when the demons of loneliness spoke. And they had a lot to say.

"Greetings, my fellow orphans of the Pacific," a familiar voice emerged from the loudspeaker. "It is your old friend Orphan Ann. How are you today?"

"I hope Tokyo Rose plays some good music today," said Charlie.

"I heard she looks like a geisha girl," said Gil.

Tokyo Rose was the name the Americans called Iva Toguri, an American citizen stranded in Japan just before war broke out. She struggled to find any means of supporting herself during war time and turned to working in a steno pool for an English paper in Tokyo. Her ability to speak perfect English landed her a spot on the radio transmitting Japanese propaganda to the troops in the South Pacific.

"I do not know about that, Gil," Charlie responded, "but it is always nice to hear music from home."

"We are so concerned about your welfare, my fellow orphans," said Tokyo Rose, "we want to remind you that our men do not want to hurt you; we are only protecting our homeland from your political leaders."

"Right," Charlie sneered, "tell that to the men on the Arizona!"

"Your political leaders have forgotten about you. We are fellow orphans, alone and missing our home. Our condolences to the families of the USS Lexington who went down at sea in December. We would like to play for you 'Sunday, Monday, or Always' by Bing Crosby in honor of your fellow orphans," concluded Tokyo Rose as the song played.

Men around the mess looked at each other in amazement.

"You look fantastic for a dead man," joked Gil.

"I guess I need to send a letter to Lilly explaining my untimely death," Charlie said gravely.

The music stopped.

"This is the captain," announced Captain Stump. "As you just heard, Tokyo Rose has announced that they sank us just before Christmas. Reports of our demise are greatly exaggerated."

The ship erupted in cheers.

"We are back from the grave and very much alive," continued Stump, "and like a blue ghost, we will wreak havoc on the Japanese anywhere we find them. We will avenge our premature demise! That is all."

Cheers continued for ten minutes. Captain Stump knew how to get a rouse from his men. They sent many letters home that night.

Five days later, they arrived at Majuro in the Marshall Islands, rejoining Task Force 58. Taking command of the Fast Carrier Task Force 58 in early January, Rear Admiral Marc Mitscher had tested his forces on the impenetrable Japanese stronghold of Truk. Attacking from behind a weather front, an early dawn attack scored fifty-six kills in the air and destroyed seventy-two aircraft on the ground. Task Force bombers destroyed multiple warships including three auxiliary cruisers.

Rejoining Task Force 58, Mitscher chose the Lady Lex to be his flagship. Mitscher now had the most battle-tested task group in the fleet, eager to engage the Japanese fleet, ready to deliver the crushing blow that could win the war.

50. USS LEXINGTON

Charlie turned the corner to find himself face to face with Captain Stump. As per military protocol, he stepped to the side allowing the captain to pass.

"I was hoping to run into you, Brand," said the captain.

"What can I do for you, sir?" Charlie said warily.

"I am sure you have heard the scuttlebutt," said Stump. "They are moving me to command Task Force 52. You will have a new captain very soon."

"Congratulations on your promotion, sir," Charlie said, his face showing some concern.

"What is it, sailor?" asked Stump.

"You have been very important to me and the crew, sir," said Charlie.

"Brand, you are so important to this operation," responded Stump. "I know the new Captain very well, and I have told him of your gift on the radar set. He will rely on you as I have so many times before."

"Thank you, sir," Charlie said with a smart salute. "Given 'em hell, sir!"

"Always, sailor, always," Stump said with a wry grin.

Charlie continued through the passageway and climbed the ladder where he entered the CIC.

"Afternoon, LT," Charlie said warmly.

LT was like the brother he never had.

"Morning, Brand," LT said crisply.

LT called no one by their first name while in the CIC. Everything was strictly business.

"Calibration complete, sir," announced Charlie.

“Very well,” responded LT.

“Admiral Mitscher has ordered a strike on Mili in the Marshall Islands,” informed LT. “Brand, you keep a close eye out for any bandits that may try to ruin our little gift to the Japanese stationed there.”

“Yes, sir,” Charlie responded, and he began his slow sweep looking for enemy planes. His job was to look in front of the sortied planes for oncoming danger. Other than finding lost planes, this was his specialty.

“Multiple contacts bearing three zero two, range one two zero miles, flying at Angels twenty,” reported Charlie.

“Very well,” said LT. “What is your best guess on the number of bogies, Brand?”

“I believe we have six, sir,” replied Charlie.

“I want bearing and range every minute, sailor,” ordered LT.

The CIC sprang into action. The team placed the contacts on the board and dead reckoning table.

“Contacts bearing holding steady, sir,” reported Charlie. “They appear to be circling, sir.”

“VF Leader, Spartan,” called LT, “welcoming party range six zero miles out, Angels twenty.”

“Spartan, VF Leader,” responded the fighter leader, “roger.”

“Keep your eye peeled for those bandits,” ordered the VF Leader.

Commander McDaniel led the fighter group off the Lexington. VF referred to his Hellcat squadron responsible for protecting the VB group, or the bomber group, headed to wreak more destruction on the little atoll of Mili. American forces had cut the supply lines to the atoll two months earlier, leaving the remaining forces to starve. This would be good practice for the newer members of the VB group, he thought.

“OK team, we have the sun to our backs,” said the commander. “We should have a better-than-average chance of sneaking up on those patrol planes.”

The fighter squadron responded with a roger.

“Contacts still same bearing but they are now five zero miles out, sir,” reported Charlie.

"VF Leader, Spartan," called LT.

"Spartan, aye," responded Mitchell.

"Bogies on the move," said LT. "Expect contact in two minutes."

"Just saw them, Spartan," replied Mitchell.

"VF team, climb to Angels twenty-five," ordered Mitchell. "Use the sun to our advantage. Maybe we can surprise them for a change."

The Zeros did not see the Hellcat fighters until they began their attack run. Within five minutes, the VF team dispatched all six Zeros, clearing the way for the VB group. The VF group attacked first, strafing the remaining compound on the atoll. The VB group followed immediately, destroying the anti-aircraft facilities and small buildings not destroyed by previous raids.

. . . . .

"Prime Minister," interrupted his assistant, "I have an emergency communication for you."

Tojo reached for the paper, and as he began to read, each word caused the blood to drain from his face.

"Assemble the War Council," ordered Tojo.

Four hours later, Tojo entered the room. "Gentlemen, I must inform you of the death of Admiral Koga," he announced. "His plane went down in a typhoon. Admiral Toyoda is next in line to replace Koga."

After a brief discussion, the council agreed and named Admiral Soemu Toyoda as the commander-in-chief of the Combined Fleet. Toyoda, once a member of the War Council, held the minority view that war with the United States was unwinnable. Following disagreements with Tojo and other members of the council, they demoted him to command of the Yokosuka Naval District.

. . . . .

Admiral Nimitz entered the conference room for the briefing.

"Proceed, commander," ordered Nimitz.

"As I recently briefed you," began the commander, "while trying to fly around a typhoon, the Japanese lost one of their command aircraft. Admiral Koga was on that plane and we now have confirmation of his death. We have additional information related to the loss of Koga. There was a second plane that went down because of the typhoon; it crashed in the Philippines. Guerrilla forces captured Admiral Koga's staff and extracted plans for the next attack against our forces."

"Do we have the plans, commander?" asked Nimitz.

"Yes sir, we do," said the commander. "The Japanese plan to draw us into a single battle where they expect to inflict such overwhelming damage to our forces that we will sue for peace. Several Japanese fleets will attack our flank simultaneously using carrier-based planes and then refuel on island airstrips. They plan a second attack on their return to their carriers. Admiral Toyoda is waiting to see where we will strike next."

"As usual," began Nimitz, "this plan is overly complicated, and the splitting of his fleet will not allow coordinated support during the battle. We too have planes that can attack."

"Yes sir, we do," agreed the commander.

"What we need, gentlemen," offered Nimitz, "is a diversionary plan where we take advantage of their desire to surprise us on our flank."

"How will we know from which direction they will attack?" asked an officer.

"Our search planes found them at Midway," offered the commander.

"Exactly," Nimitz said slapping his hand on the table. "We are already planning to attack at Biak in New Guinea next month so Toyoda should move much of his land-based planes and other naval assets to protect this island. Once they show their hand, we move Task Force 58 up to the Marianas and surprise the Japs."

The team completed their tactical plans and sent orders to Admiral Spruance who was preparing to support the attack on Biak.

51. MARIANAS TURKEY SHOOT

PRELUDE

In late April of 1944, reconnaissance photographs of Truk Island showed the successful rebuilding of much of the infrastructure destroyed in the February attack. Task Force 58 prepared to launch another strike against the impenetrable atoll. Fighters and bombers from the task force attacked Truk, decimating the anti-aircraft facilities and planes on the ground. The task force aircraft destroyed three light carriers, four destroyers, three patrol crafts, and thirty-six merchant ships and auxiliaries. Of greater importance, Japan lost 270 aircraft including fighters and bombers, and the airfield at Truk became unusable. Japan would abandon the once impenetrable island fortress, making way for the last major carrier battle in the war.

"Contacts bearing one niner seven, range eight one miles, flying at Angels twenty-five," reported Charlie.

"I need to know how many, sailor," demanded LT.

"Working on it, sir," Charlie stalled. "OK, got it. Best count is twenty-nine, sir."

"Bridge, CIC," called LT.

"Bridge, aye," responded the XO.

"We have twenty-nine bogies incoming," reported LT. "CAP is going to need some help up there, sir."

"Launch our fighters," ordered the CAG, "and notify the other carriers."

The gong of general quarters screamed from the loudspeakers.

"Pilots to your planes," called the announcement over the intercom.

Within twelve minutes, thirty-five Hellcats rose from the Lexington, prepared to destroy anything in their path.

"I need range and altitude, Brand," ordered LT.

"Still the same bearing and altitude," Charlie reported. "Range now six eight miles."

"I need a vector," ordered LT.

"Vector fiver four degrees," offered the officer.

"VF Leader, CIC," called LT.

"VF Leader, aye," responded the commander.

"Recommend intercept vector fiver four degrees, climb to Angels twenty-eight," ordered LT. "You have two nine incoming bogies."

"Roger," replied the commander.

"OK, boys," said the commander, "be ready to engage immediately upon contact."

"I see them," called VF Nine, "one o'clock low."

"Tally-ho!" ordered the commander.

The fighters peeled off of the formation, immediately engaging the incoming fighters and bombers. Over the past year, the Japanese had lost most of their experienced fighters, while the VF squadron from the Lexington overflowed with confidence. Ten Zeros split from the formation to draw fire away from the Val bombers.

"Seven, watch your six!" called the commander. A Zero was lining up for a shot.

VF six did a quick snap roll to the left while the commander lined up his shot. Seconds later, the blazing wreckage of the Zero hit the ocean. Five minutes later, the squadron claimed ten Zero kills and seventeen downed Vals. The remaining Vals unloaded their bombs in the sea and headed back suffering major damage. The Val bomber pilots would again report the sinking of the Lexington.

The Japanese culture does not tolerate failure in any form. This would explain why Japanese pilots often exaggerated their wins while minimizing their losses. A practice that would not serve the emperor during the upcoming battles.

. . . . .

JAPAN WAR COLLEGE

Admiral Toyoda stood as the emperor entered the room. Everyone bowed.

"Welcome to our war game exercise, emperor," Toyoda said deferentially.

The emperor waved his hand to proceed.

"This will be the last exercise to test our plans," began Toyoda, "before we execute Operation *A-Go* for Kantai Kessen. Proceed."

"We will draw the American naval forces including Task Force 58 into our zone of decisive battle, the Palau Islands, part of the Philippine Sea, where we will attack them from multiple locations," said the Naval War College president.

"Describe the location and strength of our attacks," ordered the admiral.

"Vice Admiral Ozawa will command the First Mobile Fleet against the American Navy," began the president. "We have 440 aircraft on 9 carriers, while the Americans have an estimated 905 planes and 15 carriers. Although the Americans have more ships and planes, we will destroy at least one-third of their carriers using our 500 land-based aircraft."

"You are positive we will prevail against their new Hellcat planes?" asked Toyoda.

"Our projections are very clear, admiral," said the president. "We will attack with great ease and our superior pilots will destroy one-third of the American carriers."

"Describe the organization of Vice Admiral Ozawa's fleet," prompted the admiral.

"Vice Admiral Ozawa has organized his fleet into three units," said the president. "A-Force will be under the direct command of Vice Admiral Ozawa, built using the assets from Carrier Division 1. B-Force will be commanded by Rear Admiral Joshima, built using Carrier Division 2, and C-Force will be commanded by Vice Admiral Kurita, using the assets from Carrier Division 3."

"How do you expect to gain surprise against the enemy?" asked Toyoda.

"Admiral," said the president, "we have a one-hundred-mile advantage in our attack range, and we expect their radar will not spot us until it is too late. Our superior planes will win the day."

"Describe the air strategy," said Toyoda. "How do we organize our attack?"

"Admiral," began the president, "our carriers will launch in waves attacking the American fleet and then proceed to Guam for refueling and repairs as needed. The wave will return to the carrier group attacking the American fleet a second time. Our strategy will force the Americans into a constant alert state, creating havoc and an inability to recover and relaunch their planes. We estimate the first complete set of waves will complete in four hours with the returning waves overlapping the first waves. We expect the time between attacks will be less than thirty minutes."

"What if we experience unexpected losses?" asked Toyoda.

"Admiral," answered the president, "despite the disparity in force strengths, the constant wave of attacks will wear down the American forces causing fatigue and chaos."

"Damage estimates," demanded Toyoda.

"Admiral," stated the president, "conservative estimates expect one-third of the carrier force and half of the planes destroyed."

"Excellent," said Toyoda. "Proceed with the exercise.

For the next three hours, the war games continued toward a predetermined conclusion. Toyoda had his cover. Even the emperor could not question his direction or timing. The plan was set. Now all he had to do was wait for his prey. He knew it would not be long.

52. THE PHILLIPINE ISLANDS

"Send this communication to Admiral Toyoda," ordered Ozawa. "McArthur has attacked Biak Island off the New Guinea coast. I suggest this is our opportunity to lure the American carrier force into the zone of decisive battle. Recommend sending Admiral Ugaki to lead a small force to split their forces. We expect the US to respond in force to protect McArthur."

One hour later, Ozawa had his answer. They would detach Vice Admiral Matome Ugaki from the First Mobile Fleet with a force comprising two battlecruisers, one light cruiser, and six destroyers.

Matome Ugaki graduated ninth out of a class of 144 in 1912. He had served in many capacities for twelve years until attending the Naval Staff College where he graduated twenty-second. In August 1941, Yamamoto appointed him to be his chief of staff, a position he held until Yamamoto's death. Ugaki accompanied Yamamoto on the ill-fated review of his troops in Bougainville and was on the second plane shot down in the April 1943 attack on Yamamoto's party. His plane crashed into the water at high speed where he was one of three survivors. In February 1944, he assumed command of the First Battleship Division, now part of the First Mobile Fleet under Ozawa.

. . . . .

JUNE 11, 1944

The plan to draw out the Japanese was now in motion. Admiral Spruance's five-hundred-ship fleet packed with one hundred twenty-five thousand troops prepared to land on the Island of Saipan.

Admiral Mitscher sat on his couch in the Flag Bridge as Commander Gus Widhelm and his deputy lieutenant commander Johnny Myers sat down.

"Admiral," began the commander, "we have this plan for our next attack on Saipan."

"Really," said the admiral with some trepidation.

"You see, sir," Myers piped in, "we have been doing the same thing for a while now and we believe we should spice it up, catch the Japs off guard."

"You have my attention," said Mitscher getting annoyed. "Now get to it!"

"Our previous attacks have been early morning," began Commander Widhelm. "We suggest we change our approach from the morning, so we attack at dusk tonight after their planes are on the ground."

"We will catch them off guard, admiral," concluded Myers.

"So, what is the code name of this operation, gentlemen?" asked Mitscher.

"Plan Johnny," said Lieutenant Commander Myers.

"With an important addendum called Plan Gus," Widhelm quickly added.

The admiral eyed his senior staff officers wryly as a crooked grin flashed across his face. "Prepare the orders, gentlemen."

"Aye, aye, sir," the men snapped to attention, turned, and disappeared down the corridor.

At 1530 hours, the fleet prepared for Plan Johnny/Plan Gus. At 1740 hours, just before dusk, the Lexington squadron approached the northern Saipan airfield.

"Visual of target," called the commander. "Prepare to attack."

"Tally-ho!" called the commander.

The fighters dove to strafe the airfield, but found no planes. Dive bombers leveled all support structures around the field. The squadron assembled for the flight back to the Lexington, dejected and demoralized.

"I guess we now know why we missed the welcome party," said a lieutenant junior grade. The squadron landed safely aboard the Lexington, and all reported their ordinance usage and targets destroyed to the intelligence officer. Over the night and into the next morning, reports trickled into the Flag Bridge.

"I really thought we laid a big egg on this one, admiral," confessed Commander Widhelm.

“Your plan worked better than we could ever have hoped,” said Mitscher enthusiastically.

An ensign delivered a communication to Commander Widhelm. “Here are the final numbers, admiral,” began the commander. “Our other carrier attacks bore more fruit. The final tally for our plan, 124 Japanese planes destroyed to just 11 of ours.”

“Hot damn!” exclaimed the admiral.

. . . . .

“Message for you, sir,” said a young ensign.

“American forces attacking Marianas. Attack American forces at Marianas. Activate Operation A-Go. Adm. Toyoda”

“Recall Vice Admiral Ugaki,” ordered Ozawa. “It appears the Americans did not take the bait.”

. . . . .

“Con, Sonar,” called Seaman Second Class Douglass.

“Bridge, aye,” responded Captain Cutter of the USS Seahorse.

“I have multiple contacts bearing three niner fiver, range two thousand yards,” reported Douglass.

“Very well,” said the captain. “Are they headed our direction, seaman?”

“No, sir. Range now twenty-two thousand yards,” responded Douglass.

“Well, let’s get a better look at who we have up here,” said the captain. “Make your depth five zero feet, Mr. Anderson, periscope depth.”

“Five zero feet, aye,” said the executive officer. “Control, one zero degrees up bubble. Make your depth five zero feet.”

“One zero degrees up bubble, aye,” said the seaman. “Depth five zero feet.”

“Con, Control,” reported the seaman, “leveling off at five zero feet.”

"Very well," said the cutter. "Up periscope."

"Up periscope, aye," was the response.

Captain Cutter spun around and peered through his eyepiece. "They are definitely part of the Japanese fleet, but there are no flat tops visible. I expect this is Vice Admiral Ugaki."

Captain Cutter grabbed his communications pad and wrote:

"Detected Admiral Ugaki headed north from New Guinea"

"Mr. Anderson, send this message to Admiral Spruance immediately," ordered Cutter.

"Aye, aye, sir," responded the XO. "Comms, send this message to Admiral Spruance."

"Aye, aye, sir," responded the lieutenant over comms.

Admiral Spruance received the communication, and one from the USS Flying Fish reporting the easterly movement of the First Mobile Fleet. He sent orders to Mitscher to reform Task Force 58 and prepare to attack the Japanese fleet.

53. MARIANAS TURKEY SHOOT

DAY 1, JUNE 19, 1944, 6:30 A.M.

"I believe they have found us, LT," said Charlie. "I have multiple contacts bearing seven fiver degrees, range niner six miles."

"Bearing seven fiver degrees, aye," responded LT. "Bridge, CIC," called LT.

"Bridge, aye," responded the XO.

"Multiple contacts bearing seven fiver degrees, range niner six miles," reported LT.

"Seven fiver degrees, range niner six degrees, aye," responded the XO.

Mitscher stood and walked toward the captain who was conferring with the CAG.

"We have a sighting of Ozawa's fleet to our east about three five zero miles," began Mitscher. "We have a report that we just shot down a torpedo plane on our western picket. We need to launch fighters to investigate these contacts to our east. I expect we will be very busy today."

Thirty fighters launched, heading toward Guam. When the Hellcats arrived, planes were still taking off from the airfield below. Japanese reinforcements had arrived at Guam by 0800 hours from Truk and Yap islands to fend off the American attack. The Hellcats engaged the Japanese aircraft and quickly destroyed thirty zeros and five Jill bombers without the loss of a single American plane.

At 0830 hours, sixteen fighters, forty-five bombers, and eight Jill torpedo bombers took off from Force C carriers headed toward Task Force 58. At 1000 hours, the Lexington radar discovered the attack force.

"Multiple contacts bearing two eight niner, range one fiver zero miles," reported Charlie.

"Give me your best count, sailor," demanded LT.

"Best guess is about fifty to sixty planes, sir," Charlie responded.

"Bridge, CIC," called LT, "at least sixty contacts bearing two eight niner, range one fiver zero miles."

"Looks like we have our fight," said Mitscher. "Launch fighters. Recall our fighters from Guam!"

The CAG gave the order to launch forty fighters. "VF-1, Spartan, Hey Rube!"

"Spartan, VF-1," responded VF-1, "roger wilco."

"Looks like they need us back home, boys," called VF-1 to his squadron. "Come to course two four three."

"I see friendlies leaving Guam, LT," Charlie reported.

"Very well," said LT. "Give me updated bearing and range every minute, Brand."

"Aye, aye, sir," said Charlie. "Bearing remains constant, range now one zero zero miles." He felt a calm come over him, the same calm he had felt during other enemy engagements. LT could be very intense, but he created a calming atmosphere, something Charlie had grown to appreciate.

"Signal all carriers to have Hellcats up and ready to support CAP should the Japanese get through the defense," ordered Mitscher.

Mitscher and the CAG organized fighters in a stack formation between Angels seventeen and twenty-three. Stacking fighters created a vertical screen to prevent any planes from penetrating unnoticed.

"Range now seven two miles," reported Charlie. "Friendlies stacking from Angels seventeen to twenty-three."

"Very well," responded LT. He provided validation of Mitscher's order to the bridge. "VF-10, CIC," called LT, "Radar reports you should be right on them now."

"CIC, VF-10," called the squadron leader from the Enterprise, "we are scanning, and we do not—"

"VF-10, VF-16," called the fighter pilot, "I see them 4 o'clock low."

"Tally-ho!" called VF-10 Leader.

All Hellcats dove to meet the attacking Jill bombers and Zeros splitting the formation. The Zeros banked high to get behind the attacking Hellcats. The Zeros, still more maneuverable than the Hellcats, engaged the Americans looking for an opening. Suddenly, four Jill bombers exploded, falling frantically to the ocean below. Through experience, the Hellcat fighters understood the best form of attack was a slashing quick attack across a group of Zeros. Three Hellcats broke high, unnoticed by the Zero leader, and slashed across a group of Zeros preparing to engage their brethren. One Zero started a flat spin toward his doom, while another exploded, nearly killing the diving Hellcats.

The Japanese attack force was in chaos, but slowly reformed only to meet a second American defense line. The Hellcats decimated the remaining Zeros and Jill bombers. A few planes carrying bombs penetrated the second defensive shield and found their target. The USS South Dakota took a hit at 1049 hours from a Jill bomber thought to have been downed by her gunners. The eight-by-ten-foot hole in the deck killed twenty-four and disabled a 40-mm gun mount.

None of the prime targets, the US carriers, took any enemy fire, although one of the Jill bombers exploded to stern of the Lexington, accompanied by great cheers from the crew. Final toll for this engagement was forty-two of sixty-nine Japanese planes lost.

The second wave, this time from Force A, launched at 0856 hours comprising fifty-three Judy dive bombers, twenty-seven Jill torpedo bomber, and forty-eight zero fighters. Just after takeoff, a Jill torpedo pilot lost a torpedo and eight more pilots turned back because of engine trouble. Force C gunners, confused by the armada of planes in the area, opened fire on the formation, hitting two and badly damaging eight more. Because of mechanical issues and the fog of war, the original 128-plane attack wave was now a mere 109 planes.

At 1107 hours, Task Force 58 radar found wave two.

"Multiple contacts bearing two fiver fiver, range one one fiver miles," reported Charlie. "This is double the size of the last contact group."

"Very well," answered LT. He reported the contacts to the Flag Bridge and Flag Plot, where Mitscher stood poring over charts.

"Another wave," began Mitscher. "Based on intel, I expect we will see two more before this is over."

During the lull between attacks, carrier Hellcat fighters refueled and continued air patrols. Attacks on Guam continued to eliminate the possibility of land-based attacks on their flank.

"I need a vector to intercept," ordered LT.

LT communicated the vector to VF-16 Leader. By 1107 hours, the Hellcats met the second attack wave sixty miles out. By 1139 hours, the Hellcats claimed seventy planes. At noon, six Judy bombers formed to attack the fleet. Immediately, Hellcats dove from the clouds and four Judys disappeared from the battlefield. A small group of Jill torpedo bombers lined up to attack the Lexington, head on. Only two dropped their torpedoes, but both passed harmlessly to port. However, Lexington guns and those of the support cruisers inflicted heavy losses on the remaining Jills. Out of the 129 planes launched from Force A, only 11 survived. Two Judy bombers escaped to the east, one headed for Guam and the other to Rota.

Wave three launched from Force B comprising fifteen fighters, twenty-five Zero bombers, and seven Jill diver bombers at noon. Miscommunication sent the third wave north of Task Force 58; twenty-seven planes returned to their carrier.

"Another wave contact bearing two three, seven," reported Charlie. "Range one fiver four."

"Are they inbound to attack the fleet?" asked LT.

"Range is still one fiver four," Charlie answered. "The range should have reduced if they were inbound."

LT reported the contacts to Admiral Mitscher, who ordered reports every five minutes.

"Contacts now one zero zero miles, bearing three four eight degrees," reported Charlie.

LT relayed the new range and bearing of the attack force along with vector coordinates to the incoming bogies.

Forty Hellcats intercepted the remaining twenty planes of Force B. The Hellcats shot down seven planes, and the remaining thirteen returned to the Force B carriers.

Wave four launched from a combination of all Force carriers. Launched from 1100 to 1130 hours, thirty zeros, nine Judys, twenty-seven Val dive bombers, ten Zero bombers, and six Jills formed Forces A and B. Miscommunication again sent the attack force too far south where they could not locate Task Force 58. They turned back for home.

"Contacts bearing two one one, range four five miles," reported Charlie.

"How did we miss these planes, sailor?" barked LT.

LT relayed the contacts along with the intercept bearing for the forty Hellcats. The Hellcats came in at Angels twenty-five behind the attacking Japanese planes. They caught the fighters by surprise and downed five. Another group of Hellcats joined the attack, accounting for nine more planes down. Forty-nine planes made a break for Guam, jettisoning their bombs.

"At least forty-five contacts bearing one four six," reported Charlie. "Current bearing will bring them to Guam in four three minutes."

"Very well," responded LT. "VF-16, Spartan."

"Spartan, roger," responded VF-16.

"Bogies headed back to Guam," said LT. "Pursue!"

VF-16 was now in command of the remaining twelve Hellcat fighters in his division. The Hellcats intercepted the Japanese planes ten miles out from Guam, attacking from Angels twenty-eight. The Hellcats surprised the remaining Japanese wave running on fumes. They destroyed thirty of forty-nine planes.

Lieutenant Junior Grade Ziegel "Ziggy" Neff entered the ready room, making a beeline for the intelligence officer.

"Report," said the intelligence officer, almost bored.

"I downed a Jill around noon sixty miles from the task force and then, on my second mission in midafternoon, I bagged a lone Jake floatplane and a pair of Zeros," reported Ziggy. "Hell, this is like an old-fashioned turkey shoot."

The Battle of the Philippines was now the Great Marianas Turkey Shoot. Ozawa never heard the report of the complete failure of his forces that day. Ozawa lost 243 out of 373 planes during combat operations. With 65 percent of his planes destroyed, Ozawa's mobile force would never rule the skies over any battlefield again.

Ozawa's misery extended to his carriers as well. At 1152 hours, the US submarine Cavalla spotted the dreaded Shokaku from the attack on Pearl Harbor. Six torpedoes screamed from the Cavalla, hitting the Shokaku four times. The Taiho experienced a similar fate around 0900 hours when a torpedo found its mark. Both the Shokaku and Taiho succumbed to their mortal injuries, reducing the Japanese fleet by two mighty carriers.

Now the Americans attack, thought Ozawa.

54. MARIANAS TURKEY SHOOT

DAY 2, JUNE 20, 1944

Charlie heard reveille and tried to ignore the call to get up. As usual, Gil was at Charlie's bunk, waiting for him to get ready for breakfast.

"How did you sleep, Charlie?" Gil asked.

"Pretty solid," Charlie said as he dropped to the floor. "Was a long day. LT asked me to stay around on the set most of the day. I expect the same today. How was your night? Did you get any sleep?"

"I had a night watch in CIC," Gil said as he stretched. "That is why I am here waiting for you." Gil was always cheery in the morning, even after he worked overnight.

Charlie pulled on his trousers and headed off for breakfast. Charlie and Gil stood in line listening for scuttlebutt.

"I hear the Japs are on the run after the licking we gave them," said a sailor.

"Yeah," added another sailor. "I hear he is on his way back to Japan to hide." Everyone around them laughed.

Gil and Charlie knew more than the average swabbie, as Admiral Mitscher relied heavily on their work, especially Charlie's. The two took their food and sat down away from the other sailors.

"Pretty intense yesterday," said Gil.

"Sure was," Charlie replied. "LT was really intense, especially as the waves continued. This was the longest group of attacks I have experienced so far."

"I could see that," said Gil. "You barely noticed me when I came on watch. I think we really handed it to them yesterday."

"We sure did," agreed Charlie. "I ran into some airedales as I made my way to dinner. They sure appreciate what we do!"

"You are the best in the fleet, you know," Gil said.

"I am just lucky," Charlie said modestly.

Charlie and Gil shared a look. Charlie knew how God had blessed him with exceptional skills on his radar set, and Gil knew Charlie did not believe he was anything special.

"Nice work yesterday," said LT as Charlie sat down at his set.

"Thanks, LT," Charlie said.

"We must find those Japanese carriers before they disappear for good," said LT. "The admiral does not want another repeat where they are attacking us. It is our turn now!"

"Aye, aye, sir!" Charlie exclaimed.

Charlie calibrated his set and began looking for the enemy. The dead reckoning board showed the fleet moving to the west-northwest. Charlie spent most of his sweeps searching between 80° and 95°. He did not want any unwanted guests sneaking up to take any pot shots on the fleet.

Charlie got off the set just in time for lunch, and was back on it just after 1300 hours. He was about to leave when a report came across the radio at 1605 hours.

"Sparta, VS-1," called a search plane.

"VS-1, aye," responded the XO.

"Contact flattops. Full fleet bearing two niner niner, range two eight fiver," called VS-1.

"VS-1, roger," responded the XO.

"We cannot wait," said Mitscher. "I want to finish this, now! Prepare to launch attack force."

. . . . .

"Intercept from American search plane," said the captain of the Zuikaku. "The Americans know where we are."

"Discontinue fueling operations," ordered Ozawa. "Set course one eight five, speed twenty-four knots. We will outrun their fighters."

"As I reported, admiral, we suffered significant losses yesterday," reminded the captain. "We could not contact our bases on the Mariana Islands."

"I am sure that our attack forces landed safely," Ozawa said, trying to convince his subordinate, "and they are preparing to attack the Americans. We attack again tomorrow."

"Hai!" responded the captain.

. . . . .

"We are firing our bolt," said Mitscher to his command staff. "A single shot to finish this thing."

At 1621 hours, the carriers turned into the wind and launched seventy-two dive bombers, fifty-four torpedo bombers, and eighty-five fighter escorts in ten minutes. The Hellcats and Helldivers carried an extra belly tank to extend their range.

"I am sure you saw the board," said the VF Leader. "The Japanese fleet is sixty miles further than we thought. Not sure we have enough to get back home."

The sober reminder did not deter the pilots from their mission.

At 1820 hours, they spotted Japanese fleet.

"The tankers and destroyer are trailing," called VB-1 to his squadron. "Light is getting low, boys. I would say we have twenty minutes to say *sayonara* to their fleet."

His team responded with roger.

"The fleet is in a single line," called VT-1 to his team. "Watch that flak; it will be intense!"

His team also responded with a big roger.

Seventeen torpedo bombers moved into attack formation against the three tankers and three battleships. They hit two of the tankers and were rewarded with massive explosions that would later cause the scuttling of the tankers. Ten bombers and twenty torpedo bombers attacked the Hiyo. Leaking aviation fuel caused an immense explosion, and the captain gave the order to abandon ship, going down with 250 of his crew.

Dive bombers hit the Zuikaku, Junyo, and Chiyoda, but all survived, and by 1920 hours, the Americans headed home after sinking two tankers and one carrier.

Charlie lay in his bunk dreaming of his Lilly. He had just finished completing three watches in a row, a short two hours ago.

"Up and at 'em, sailor," said a familiar voice. "Brand, I need you in CIC, on the double."

Charlie rolled over to see LT staring right at him intensely. "Brand, our boys are on their way back and it is pitch dark out there. They need you to guide them home."

"Aye, aye, sir," Charlie barely said as he dropped to the floor. "I am on my way, sir."

Within five minutes, Charlie was entering CIC, ready for another grueling turn at the scope. At least he had an idea where his boys were coming from, he thought.

"Calibration complete, LT," announced Charlie.

"Find those planes, Brand," said LT, "and be sure to keep an eye out for bogies. We do not want any unannounced guests ruining recovery efforts."

"Yes, sir," replied Charlie. "Scanning between two seven zero and three eight five," he reported. It had been over two-and-a-half hours since the launch of the attack force. He should get them on radar in about fifteen minutes, Charlie calculated.

Sixteen minutes later, Charlie saw contacts on the bottom of his scope showing friendlies with IFF.

"Contacts bearing two niner fiver," announced Charlie. "We got 'em, sir!"

"VF Leader, Spartan," called LT, "status."

No response.

"VF Leader, Spartan," called LT, "status."

No response.

"Range to contacts," ordered LT.

"Range one seven eight," reported Charlie. "I repeat, one seven eight."

LT put his hand on his left earphone, straining to hear.

"Spartan, VF-5," reported the lieutenant junior grade, "we read you 5X5. VF-Leader lost his communications during the attack."

"Roger, VF-5," responded LT, "I am sure you are bingo." Bingo meant being close to no fuel.

"Roger, Spartan," replied VF-5, "most of us are too close for comfort."

"Give me a vector for our boys," ordered LT.

"Turn to two three four," recommended the lieutenant.

"VF-5, come to course two three four," ordered LT. "Spartan should be visible in one six minutes."

"Roger wilco," responded LT-5.

"Good job, Brand," praised LT. "They would have flown by us to the north if you had not found them."

"Thank you, sir," Charlies said modestly. Gil entered the CIC just in time to hear LT praise Charlie. He smiled to himself, thanking God that Charlie was part of *his* team.

"Range now one two one miles," reported Charlie.

"Spartan, VF-5," called VF-5, "we are losing airedales. Requesting pickup service."

"Bridge, CIC," called LT, "did you get that, sir?"

"CIC, monitoring your communications," responded the XO. "Admiral is already moving assets for pickup."

"Range now eight six miles," reported Charlie.

"VF-5, Spartan," called LT, "we see you eight six miles from home. You should be able to see us in seven minutes."

"Spartan, VF-5," called VF-5, "our boys are getting antsy up here. No joy, I repeat no joy." The returning pilots could not see Task Force 58. Darkness enveloped the moonless night, and pilots strained for any glimmer of light to guide them home.

"Range two zero miles," reported Charlie.

"VF-5, Spartan," called LT, "visual in two minutes."

"Roger, Spartan," replied VF-5, "we lost more airedales."

"CIC, Bridge," called the XO, "attack force can land on any available flattop."

"Roger," replied LT.

"Range now one one miles, sir," reported Charlie. "They should have visual by now."

"VF-5, Spartan," called LT, "do you have visual?"

"Spartan, no joy," called VF-5, his voice now more intense. "I repeat, no joy!"

Admiral Mitscher rose from his couch and looked out his window, straining to see any sign of his men. "Turn them on, captain," ordered the admiral.

"Sir?" questioned the captain. "You mean light it up?"

"That is exactly what I mean," the admiral stated tersely. "I refuse to lose any of those brave pilots. Light up the Task Force!"

A glow arose from the immense blackness. A sense of hope filled the returning pilots, most having resigned themselves to spending the night with the sharks.

"Spartan, VF-5," called VF-5 with a noticeable lift in his voice, "thanks for the light show!"

Admiral Mitscher had taken an enormous risk turning on the lights of his Task Force. Any patrolling enemy submarine would have had no issue picking it out as the prime target; fortunately, the destroyers reported no submarine activity that night.

An intense struggle to land anywhere overcame the frantic pilots. Any flat area long enough to land a plane became prime targets for the weary warriors. Some lost their fight and ditched into the ocean, many just feet from their safe harbor.

"I am going topside, sir," said Charlie. "I love to watch them come in."

Charlie walked out onto the landing just in time to see one of his brave friends cut his engine, landing on the deck, captured by the arresting wire. A choreographed ballet moved the plane up the deck, preparing for another weary soul to land. Charlie watched as Paddles directed another pilot to safety.

Suddenly, Paddles motioned in a way Charlie had not seen. Charlie saw the plane. He was obviously too high and would miss the arresting wires. This would not end well.

Paddles waved off the pilot, but he continued, cutting his engine a moment too late. The tail hook of the plane missed the arresting wires and careened unimpeded toward the bow where the returning unsuspecting pilots exited their planes. The plane, propeller still rotating, crashed into a plane, slicing viciously into the rear gunner of a torpedo plane and instantly killing him. Ten minutes later, they pulled another lost soul from the mangled wreckage, a deckhand who left a wife and a new baby boy at home.

Death is an unwelcome companion in war. The next morning, the entire crew assembled to honor their fallen friends as they entombed their bodies in the deep dark stillness of the Marianas Trench, each man remembering their friends, thanking God they were one day closer to seeing their loved ones again.

55. TOKYO, JAPAN

Vice Admiral Onishi read the after-action reports from the Kantai Kessen battle. Losing most of their experienced pilots during the attacks on the Americans would prevent Japan from future domination of the skies. Japan was losing the war. What Japan needed was another divine wind to save the great nation.

In the autumn of 1274, around nine hundred Mongol ships carrying almost forty thousand men attacked Japan. While in Hakata Bay, a typhoon consumed the flotilla, killing thirteen thousand and sinking almost one-third of their ships.

The Mongols returned seven years later, but found new walls preventing beach landings. Before they could find a suitable landing location, another typhoon destroyed the fleet, saving Japan from another Mongol invasion. The Japanese called this the "Divine Wind," or kamikaze.

This is what Japan needs, Onishi thought. He must recruit new men to bring the fight directly to the enemy, to bring such terror and destruction, the Americans will lose their will to fight. He needed men like those of the samurai of old, men who would go to their death without question.

"How could you be so stupid?" chided Lieutenant Hadaki Yamatsumi. Taking the switch in his hand, he beat the soldier for the next ten minutes. "Now you will use this weapon with the accuracy demanded by our emperor."

"Hai!" responded the cowed infantry man.

Commander Watanabe took a special interest in Hadaki and pushed through an officer's commission. Hadaki excelled as an officer, but he now beat his subordinates just as they beat him. This was not how his ancestors would want him to act toward his fellow soldiers, he thought.

"Lieutenant Yamatsumi," called another officer from across the compound, "come here!"

The disruption annoyed Hadaki, and he strolled to the officer in defiance.

"You have an exemplary record, lieutenant," said the captain. "The high command has noticed your work."

"Hai!" responded Hadaki. "Thank you, sir!"

"We have another assignment for you," said the captain. "Have you ever wanted to learn to fly?"

. . . . .

President Roosevelt rolled into CINPAC Headquarters, and up to the second floor where Douglas MacArthur and Admiral Nimitz were waiting in the admiral's conference room.

"Good morning, Mr. President," the admiral said cordially as both men stood.

"Good morning, gentlemen," responded the president. "Now, we need to discuss our next steps in the Pacific. The Joint Chiefs are not providing a unified plan for our next campaign, so I want each of you to present your best case. General, please proceed."

"Thank you, Mr. President," MacArthur began. "At the beginning of the war, the Japanese forced America from the Philippines. This left seventeen million Filipinos at the mercy of the Japanese tyrants. It is unconscionable that we would not make every effort to liberate these islands as they are crucial to our plans to drive the Japanese back to Tokyo, taking the gains achieved during their first months of the war. We must avenge those who suffered and sacrificed during the Bataan death march. America needs to see this through. When I left in 1942, I said I would return, and by God, this is the right time to do so, Mr. President."

"Admiral Nimitz?" prompted the president.

"The decision here," began Nimitz, "is very clear. Avoiding the Philippines in favor of attacking Formosa is purely a matter of geography. Formosa is closer to Japan and provides an excellent base for attack against the Japanese mainland. This will force the Japanese to sue for peace and will cost our country less in talent and treasure."

As this was a presidential election year and Roosevelt had just accepted the nomination of his party, he calculated that traveling to Pearl Harbor to mediate a dispute between his commanders in the Pacific would show that he and he alone was running the war. Also, there were rumors that Douglas MacArthur may become the nominee of the Republican Party. The public would see MacArthur as subordinate to the president, creating an immediate advantage for Roosevelt.

"Gentlemen," announced the president, "I have made my decision. Thank you both for your thoughtful presentations. I must agree with General MacArthur that an attack on the Philippines is the prudent course of action."

The Joint Chiefs later ordered MacArthur to occupy Leyte by the end of 1944.

• • • • •

"Brand reporting as ordered, sir," said Charlie as he snapped to attention.

"At ease," ordered the captain. "Come over here, Charlie."

Charlie? I did not even think the captain knew my first name, he thought.

The captain brought Charlie to a more private area on the bridge. What he had to say would not be easy.

"Son," began the captain, "I do not know how to tell you this. There was an accident on the rail line in Arkansas and I am so sorry to tell you this. Your father died in the accident. Unfortunately, we received this letter today, and the funeral was two weeks ago."

Charlie's knees nearly buckled. His father? How could this be?

"Here is the letter," said the captain. "I relieve you of your duties until 0600 hours tomorrow so you can grieve your loss. I am sorry we could not get you home for this, Charlie."

"I understand, sir," Charlie barely said out loud.

"Dismissed!" said the captain, and Charlie turned to leave the bridge, numb and confused.

• • • • •

"Mama!" screamed Lilly. "Mama!"

"What is it, Lilly?" Ellen said, racing to the side of her daughter.

"Charlie's letter . . ." stammered Lilly. "His father . . . died!" Lilly wept.

"Oh, no!" exclaimed Ellen. "How did it happen?"

"Charlie just said it was an accident on the rail line where he worked," Lilly said, trying to regain her composure.

"What was his job on the railroad?" asked Ellen softly.

"He was a conductor," Lilly remembered. "Charlie said he spent many hours on the train with his father during summer vacations. He was very special to Charlie. I just do not know what I would do if I lost Daddy!" Lilly wept again.

56. TOKYO, JAPAN

Hadaki boarded a train headed to Kasumigaura Airfield, where he would begin his pilot training. He felt honored that they would choose him for such an important mission. He thought back on his life back in Kawaguchico and how proud his forefathers must be right now, an officer, and soon to be a pilot. The rolling hills gave way to flat lands as he approached his destination.

A captain entered the train. “On your feet!” he ordered. “Come with me.”

Ten men on his train immediately grabbed their bags and followed the captain onto a large truck. Hadaki evaluated his fellow officers, many new recruits who did not know of the horrors of war. Hadaki longed to bring the war back to the enemy. Now he could serve his emperor in a way to honor his ancestors, he thought. The truck entered the airbase and stopped next to a dilapidated building.

“Everyone out,” ordered the captain. “Be ready in five minutes for inspection.”

Four minutes later, Hadaki, along with the other men, formed in a single line, prepared for the beating he surely would receive.

“I am Captain Yamato. You are here because the emperor needs men like you. Your country needs you, even if this means your sacrifice. It is your greatest honor to serve and possibly die for your emperor. They shall call you men of great courage, heroes, the chosen.”

The captain continued for twenty minutes describing the lore of the famous samurai who protected and ultimately died for their country against the invading Mongols.

“Here,” he concluded, “you will learn to fly. Just as each samurai had a sword, your plane will be your sword. A mighty sword it is. You will inflict great harm on our enemy, and the very sight of you will strike fear in their hearts.”

Hadaki listened intently, taking in every glorious word. He was the oldest and heir to all of their possessions, *but my ancestors told me I would be great and bring honor to my family so I must continue*, he thought.

Until the beginning of the war, the Nakajima Ki-27 served as the primary fighter plane for Japan. The lack of Zeros because of losses in the Philippines had forced the high command to bring the Ki-27 out of retirement. Over the next two weeks, Hadaki learned the basics of flying. His skill surpassed all expectations of Captain Yamato.

"Lieutenant Yamatsumi," called the captain.

"Hai!" responded Hadaki as he ran to the captain and dropped his head in deference.

"Your flying skills are unmatched within this training group," praised the captain. "You are ready to learn how to fight. I am sending you to Mabalacat Airfield, where you will complete your training and bring honor to our emperor."

One week later, Hadaki found himself 350 miles from his last combat assignment, confident he would now bring the fight directly to the enemy.

. . . . .

Charlie stood on the fantail looking out, thinking about his father and how easy it would be to just drop over the side. The pain permeated every fiber of his body, causing him to drop to his knees. He wanted to cry but not in front of his crew; he was too proud. A hand gently touched his shoulder, tugging him back to reality.

"There you are," Gil said tenderly. "I thought I might find you back here. How are you holding up, my friend?"

"I am not," Charlie confessed. "If I was going to be honest, I was looking over the side and thinking how easy . . ."

"Hold on there," Gil said, holding tighter to Charlie's shoulder. "You must remember all you have to live for. Lilly? And then there is me. What would I do for fun around here without you? Who could I watch pack away inedible food if you are not here?"

Charlie stood and smiled briefly. "I have so many regrets, Gil."

"A wise man once told me," Gil pointed to Charlie, "that having regrets is only punishing yourself for the life you were too afraid to have. You had a significant life with your dad; you shared so much important time together."

"But he never met Lilly," Charlie said, his voice trailing off. "When this is all over, I *am* going to marry that girl!"

"That is my boy," Gil lightened the mood, "and I know she *will* say *yes*!"

Charlie felt better, almost.

"Who will I go to for advice?" Charlie asked to no one in particular.

"You can always ask me," Gil offered. "I will always answer your letters. We will stay close when all of this is over. You just wait and see."

"Thanks," Charlie said with gratitude. "I do not know how I could make it out here without you."

"Me?" questioned Gil. "We rely on each other; that is the only way we will make it through this war alive. We watch out for each other!"

An announcement came over the hailer: mail call!

Charlie and Gil made their way to their post office, and as usual the officers cut in front of the enlisted.

Charlie had only one letter, a letter he waited every minute of every day to get, a letter from Lilly.

"See you at chow," said Charlie. "Gil . . ."

"I know, Charlie. Me too," said Gil.

Charlie found a spot on the deck away from everyone and opened his letter.

"Dear Charlie," began the letter. This was not from Lilly; it was from her father.

Ellen and I are sad for you, as is Lilly. Losing a parent is a terrible thing. I lost my father around the same age as you, but I could attend his funeral. I am so sorry for you, Charlie. I know you must feel lost and confused, who can I turn to if I have questions, or need advice? Please know that I would be happy to fill this role for you. I have the feeling you will be a permanent fixture in our family after the war.

Be safe out there and know that you have another family ready to welcome you back, welcome you home.

Charlie dropped the letter and thanked God for His providence, for bringing him hope for the future.

. . . . .

"So, you are the pilot Yamata sent us," said the commander. "He speaks highly of you. We will see if his trust in your skills matches mine."

"I am only here to serve the emperor," Hadaki said, believing every word. "I know I will learn much from your leadership."

"I am sending you up with my best pilot," said the commander. "We will see soon enough if you are worth the time it will take to make you ready for battle. I will not waste a perfectly good plane on a pilot with no skills. How many hours do you have in your trainer?"

"Fifty-five, sir," said Hadaki with as much confidence as he could muster.

"That is not nearly enough to go up against our enemy," the commander chided. "You will show me today before I will waste any more time on you."

"Hai!" Hadaki shouted as he saluted.

"Lieutenant," called the officer, "I am Tagata. Are you ready to go?"

Five months with the air group, First Lieutenant Tagata had quickly distinguished himself as an excellent pilot. During the battle of the Philippines, he had downed two American pilots and fought in battles over Truk and Saipan.

"Flight pre-check complete," said Hadaki to his plane captain. "Ready to take-off when you are, sir."

Hadaki and Tagata moved toward their take-off positions. Tagata took off first, and Hadaki quickly followed. Once in the air, Tagata banked hard right and leveled off.

Let us see if he can fly in formation, thought Tagata. Hadaki moved into position off of Tagata's left wing, a little too close for comfort for Tagata.

"Back off, lieutenant!" Tagata said with disgust. "Are you trying to die in your first hour with us?"

"No, sir," Hadaki said. "Yamata trained me to fly in formation before I left his command."

"I see," said Tagata. "Alright, form up with me. Second position."

Hadaki reduced his speed and flew to the right of Tagata, taking up the second position.

"Very good," said Tagata. "Now I want you to begin an attack to your right. Now!"

Hadaki banked right slightly faster than expected and had to correct his position before he hit the right wing of Tagata. Hadaki expected a complaint from his instructor.

"Good correction," said Tagata. "You have very good instincts."

Twenty minutes later they landed.

"You are young and aggressive when you fly," said Tagata, "but I see you have natural abilities we can use. I will report to the commander you can stay, for now."

Tagata smiled. Hadaki relaxed, and both men walked to the headquarters where Tagata made his report.

57. MABALACAT AIRFIELD

Hadaki banked hard and dove to attack his prey. He knew he could score this kill.

"Got you!" Hadaki called. He knew this would please the commander, as he had just scored a kill on his best pilot.

"Very good, lieutenant," said Tagata. "Your skills are now ready to engage our enemy."

The pair landed and met as they walked toward the headquarters.

An ensign ran to meet them. "Sir," he said, "the commander urgently needs to see both of you."

"Thank you, ensign," said Tagata.

"Reporting as ordered, sir," Tagata said as both officers saluted.

"Admiral Onishi will visit our base in the morning," the commander said. "Tagata, I need you to review this list of pilots. I need the best we have on this list."

Tagata reviewed the list. "I concur with your list, sir, but I would add one more name."

"Yes, who?" questioned the commander.

"Sir," began Tagata with some trepidation, "I respectfully suggest Lieutenant Yamatsumi."

Hadaki's knees buckled, but he stayed upright.

"Yamatsumi?" the commander bellowed. "He has not seen one day of combat and you would put him on this list. No!"

Hadaki breathed, and both men left the office.

"Sorry, Hadaki," Tagata said. "I really believe you can do this. You will get your shot soon. Then you will show the commander your skills. He will see what I see."

"Thank you, sir," Hadaki said smiling to himself.

The next morning Vice Admiral Onishi addressed the squadron.

"As you must know by now," began the admiral, "our country has suffered terrible losses this past year, and we must consider plans to change the tide of the war. Our plans must be bold, like those of our famous samurai warriors who gave their lives while facing overwhelming forces."

Hadaki leaned in closer.

"The US carriers," continued the admiral, "with their planes are the targets we must destroy to win this war. Our plan is so bold that I do not think there is another way to carry out this operation without the supreme sacrifice, one all of you swore to give when you became pilots."

What can he be asking of us? Hadaki wondered.

"So," concluded the admiral, "I am asking for volunteers to join a special attack force. You will load a 250-kg bomb to your plane and crash into one of the American carriers, disabling her for at least a week. I will not order you to volunteer, but you know that your country is asking for this sacrifice."

Hadaki quickly looked around at the men he knew were on the list. Twenty-two raised their hands. They still needed two more men to make this squadron. Hadaki's mind flashed to Mount Fuji where he had met his ancestors for guidance before he volunteered to serve in the military. Then, a red fox flashed in his mind, and he knew what he must do. Hadaki instinctively raised both hands, not thinking of the ramifications to his family.

The commander noticed Hadaki and raised his eyebrow.

Should they select me, how will my haha survive? They will lose everything. My ancestors were clear, though—you will do great things as part of this war. They will provide for his family.

Admiral Onishi smiled as he reviewed the men with both hands raised high. This will be the only way to inflict such terror on the US Navy that they will have to withdraw from the Philippines, he thought.

"Lieutenant Yamatsumi," called the commander, "you will come with me."

"Hai!" answered Hadaki as he ran to meet the commander.

"Lieutenant Tagata speaks highly of you," said the commander. "This is the second person I trust to speak this way about you."

"Thank you, sir," Hadaki said with lowered head.

"I will ask you this only once," said the commander with great gravity. "Are you ready to volunteer for this special attack force?"

Hadaki slowly raised his head, looking directly in the eyes of his superior officer. "Yes, I am."

"Very well then," said the commander. "I will grant your request. Admiral Onishi, we have our last volunteer."

Hadaki turned to join his new attack force. There would be much to discuss and prepare before their first mission.

. . . . .

Following the meeting with President Roosevelt in Hawaii, General MacArthur and Admiral Sprague planned for the invasion of the island of Leyte, part of the Philippine Islands. Admiral Halsey would command a mobile force tasked with supporting the invasion unless an opportunity to destroy the Japanese fleet presented itself.

. . . . .

Operation: *Sho-Go* was another overly complicated Japanese plan designed to lure the US fleet to a battle far away from the expected US invasion location. Admiral Ozawa would command the Northern Force, with orders to sacrifice every ship to keep the US fleet occupied. Once occupied in battle, a Japanese battle force would attack the invasion force from the sea, cutting all support from the infantry on the island.

On October 23, US submarine forces attacked Admiral Kurita's Japanese forces on their way to attack the Leyte invasion force. They damaged two battle cruisers, forcing them to retire from the battle. Undeterred, Kurita's forces continued south to engage the American fleet.

On October 24, Admiral Halsey's Third Fleet, minus two carrier groups, detached to resupply and refuel, prepared to engage Kurita's forces. Admiral Onishi directed over 150 planes in three waves to attack Admiral Halsey's Third Fleet. CAP destroyed 90 percent of the Japanese planes. However, a dive bomber penetrated the air defenses, sinking the USS Princeton and causing the loss of 233 men and damaging two battleships supporting the recovery efforts.

Sorties from Halsey's carrier air groups hit the battleships Nagato, Yamato, and Musashi. The heavy cruiser Myoko sustained severe damage, causing her to withdraw to safe harbor. US estimates exaggerated the damage to Kurita's forces, negatively effecting Admiral Halsey's decision to support Admiral Sprague and MacArthur's invasion force. The discovery of the Northern Force enticed Halsey to abandon his supporting role and follow Admiral Nimitz's direction to destroy the Japanese Navy if the opportunity presented itself.

. . . . .

Hadaki sat with his unit discussing the correct angle of attack needed to inflict the greatest damage on a US carrier. The special attack force organized into four units of six planes: Unit Shikishima, Unit Yamato, Unit Asahi, and Unit Yamazakura, a patriotic death poem inspiring the naming of each unit. They assigned Hadaki to the Yamato unit, meaning the spirit of old/true Japan. Hadaki swelled with pride at his selection.

"Unit Shikishima will make the first kamikaze attack on the US Navy," announced the commander. "They attack on 25 October."

Alternating waves of envy and relief washed over Hadaki. The gravity of his decision to die for his emperor was now weighing heavily on his heart. He would not see his siblings ever again. But his *haha*—what had he done? Surely his name will be great in his prefecture, but his family will certainly suffer because of his decision. It was too late; he could not change this even if he wanted to. His life would end in the next few days.

. . . . .

Charlie sat at his station, trying to remain focused. Grief washed over him like thousands of cuts to a surfer dragged over a coral reef after a wipeout. He fought to drive his emotions down. Thousands of people counted on him to look for the ever-present enemy.

"Multiple contacts bearing three four four," called Charlie. "It is a large force flying at Angels twenty-four. I am working on the estimated strength and distance."

"Contacts bearing three four four, aye," responded LT. "Get me those estimates, sailor." LT needed Charlie on his best game. Too many lives were at stake.

"Estimated strength of attack force is between seventy and seventy-five," called Charlie. "Range one one one miles."

"One one one miles," responded LT. "Force strength between seventy and seventy-five, aye. Nice job, sailor!"

Charlie smiled to himself.

Overnight, Admiral Halsey transferred tactical command to Admiral Mitscher, and Mitscher ordered 108 aircraft to attack the Japanese force before the Northern Force, under the command of Ozawa, could even launch their attack. They would not survive.

LT vectored the CAPs who quickly downed all but five of the enemy aircraft. No US ships sustained a single hit from the attack. At 0800 hours, Mitscher's attack force engaged Ozawa's Northern Force.

"CAP orbiting twelve o'clock high," called the VF Leader. "Split into teams and engage. Tally-ho!"

The fighters, outnumbering the Japanese CAP three to one, broke into teams of three and picked off the patrol force like a skilled marksman at a shooting gallery. They destroyed the CAP in six minutes. It was now time for the bombers to impose their will on the unprotected Japanese fleet.

Over the next eight hours, Mitscher's task force flew 527 sorties against the Japanese Northern fleet, striking the Zuikaku, Chitose, Zuiho, Akizuku, and the Chiyoda, destroying the core of the Northern Fleet. However, Toyoda's plan to draw Halsey's forces away from their invasion support role worked fabulously. At the beginning of the attack on the Northern Force, emergency calls came from Admiral Sprague's Seventh Fleet describing their dire situation.

MY SITUATION IS CRITICAL. FAST BATTLESHIPS AND SUPPORT BY AIR STRIKES MAY KEEP ENEMY FROM DESTROYING CARRIERS AND ENTERING LEYTE GULF

Admiral Halsey did not receive this message for two hours, delaying the vital help required to save the lightly armored ships of the Seventh Fleet. Admiral Halsey's forces contained the latest aircraft and fully armored battleships needed to protect the invasion force from Kurita's encroaching armada.

On Oahu, Admiral Nimitz, careful to allow his field commanders the latitude necessary to prosecute a battle plan, grew concerned about the fate of the Seventh Fleet.

"Send this message immediately," ordered the admiral.

TURKEY TROTS TO WATER GG FROM CINCPAC ACTION COM THIRD FLEET INFO COMINCH CTF SEVENTY-SEVEN X WHERE IS RPT WHERE IS TASK FORCE THIRTY FOUR RR THE WORLD WONDERS

Padding communications to the fleet with extra words disguised the message from the Japanese cryptanalysts, causing critical delay during decryption. The decrypted message without padding read like this:

FROM CINCPAC ACTION COM THIRD FLEET INFO COMINCH CTF SEVENTY-SEVEN WHERE IS TASK FORCE THIRTY FOUR THE WORLD WONDERS

During the decryption of Admiral Nimitz's communication, three extra words inadvertently remained: "THE WORLD WONDERS." Admiral Halsey read the communication and believed Admiral Nimitz was criticizing his leadership. Halsey reacted with sobs of rage for three hours until his chief of staff rebuked him, snapping Halsey back to the task at hand. The admiral ordered Mitscher to turn his forces south to help the Seventh Fleet. It was too late. By the time Task Force 34 arrived, all that remained of Kurita's forces withdrew to safe harbor.

58. UNIT SHIKISHIMA

"We are twenty miles from the US fleet near Leyte," called First Lieutenant Tagata. "We will split to engage the fleet concentrating on their carriers."

Each man in the unit understood the importance of their mission. They knew this was a one-way trip. Soon they would cross over to death in a glorious explosion designed to terrorize and demoralize the American navy. The first kamikaze air attack in history was eight miles from their targets.

Anti-aircraft guns exploded, and flak dotted the morning sky as if God tore holes in His creation, leaving blackness in its wake. The kamikaze pilots skillfully avoided the flak and prepared to launch their attack.

The Japanese employed two strategies when preparing to attack the US fleet. One tactic sent the kamikazes high into the cloud to protect them from discovery by US CAP until it was too late. The second tactic sent the pilots low to the water to mask their advance from the radar they knew would discover them in time to launch an offensive against them. Using smaller attack groups also aided their deception, minimizing the number of radar targets. Today, Tagata chose the first tactic.

"Tora, Tora, Tora!" called Tagata as the kamikaze pilots prepared to unleash an attack never seen to this point in the war. The pilots peeled off of formation and concentrated their efforts on the small, lightly armored aircraft carriers of Admiral Spruance's Seventh Fleet.

The turbulence of the flak caused the first pilot to lose control and hit the port catwalk of the USS Kitkun Bay, cartwheeling into the sea. Two kamikazes dove on the USS Fanshaw Bay, but expert anti-aircraft fire took them down before they could reach their target. The remaining pilots dove on the USS White Plains, but missed to port. However, one kamikaze, trailing smoke, broke off the attack and targeted the USS St. Lo.

Laid down on January 23, 1943, the USS St. Lo was a Casablanca-class escort carrier. Originally named the USS Midway, they renamed her in July 1944 to the USS St. Lo to free up the name for a new attack carrier entering the fleet. The name change would forever prevent the tarnishing of the name Midway, the battle that turned the tide of the war for the Americans.

Lieutenant Tagata, trailing smoke and losing control of his aircraft, aimed his human bomb toward the flight deck of the St. Lo. Sailors on the St. Lo watched in utter disbelief as Tagata crashed his plane into the deck at 1051 hours on 25 September. His bomb continued through the flight deck where it exploded on the port side of the hangar deck. With operations to refuel and rearm her aircraft underway, the explosion ignited the aviation fuel and the fire quickly spread to the planes causing multiple explosions. The last explosion detonated the torpedo and bomb magazine, and thirty minutes later, she sank, the victim of the first planned kamikaze attack of World War II.

Admiral Kurita reported the results of the successful kamikaze attack to Admiral Onishi, who sent congratulations to the commander on Mabalacat Field. The day before the attack on the St. Lo, Lieutenant Tagata flew to other airfields recruiting pilots to join their cause. He recruited seventy pilots willing to make the ultimate sacrifice for their country, flying to their death, leaving their families distraught and alone.

By the end of the next day, fifty-five kamikaze pilots contributed to the carnage from the first attack. They hit seven carriers and forty other ships, sinking five, inflicting heavy damage to twenty-three, and moderate damage to twelve. Admiral Onishi considered the damage report and recommended expanding the kamikaze fleet. It would be the last best hope to save his beloved Japan.

The battle of Leyte Gulf was the last recorded battle ever between battleships. Japan lost three battleships, one large carrier, three light carriers, six heavy cruisers, four light cruisers, and eleven destroyers. The United States only lost one light carrier and two escort carriers, making this the decisive naval battle of the war. The United States now had supremacy in the air and on sea. The Japanese still had terror to deliver. The kamikaze threat would prove difficult to defend.

59. USS LEXINGTON

Ten days after the Battle of Leyte Gulf, Charlie completed his twelfth consecutive eighteen-hour day supporting cleanup operations against the retreating Japanese fleet. He lay on his bunk, trying to relax. The sound of the catapult above his head meant another night of restless sleep, if any at all. He thought of the letter sent by Henry Hope and his generous offer to step in as his substitute father. No one could ever replace his father, but Henry shared many of the traits Charlie admired most about his father.

Shhhhhhhwwwooooooooook. Another plane exiting the carrier. He might as well get up and watch the night operations. As he headed topside, he approached the ladder from the bridge.

"Make way," called a voice he knew well. The captain appeared at the bottom of the ladder. "Brand," greeted the captain, "how are you doing these days? Any easier to sleep?"

"Thank you for asking, sir," Charlie responded. "Sleep is a sometime thing, but work keeps me from dwelling on my loss, sir."

"Good to hear," said the captain warmly. "Keep up the outstanding work, sailor."

"Thank you, sir," Charlie said. *What a man*, he thought. *He really cares about his men. I am just a radarman, one of many, and he takes the time to ask how I am doing, wow! He has so many other things to take up his time, Japanese attacks, planning attacks on enemy positions, but he still . . .*

"What are you doing up, Charlie?" Gil asked from behind.

"Sleep is still difficult," Charlie confessed. "I have even lost some weight; not much interested in food these days."

"That is my biggest concern with you, Charlie," Gil said plainly. "You need to keep up your strength if you are to be of any use to LT. How about seeing if there is something to eat."

"I guess it would not hurt to try," Charlie agreed.

. . . . .

The day had come. Unit Yamato would take off in the morning. The finality of the order weighed heavily on Hadaki's heart as he prepared to say goodbye to his *haha*.

My dearest Mother,

How I have failed you and our family. Tomorrow, I will enter battle against our enemy, something I freely did with the design to inflict such terror and damage they would withdraw from battle, never to return. This action is just, but I know our family will suffer for my actions.

I am sorry that I did not stay to protect our family, that I served even though I was exempt. I will miss you and my siblings. Remember me fondly as I go to meet my Father and our ancestors. Tell my siblings I did this for the honor of our family.

Your son,

Hadaki

This was the hardest letter he ever wrote. He did not want to die; he did not want to leave his family with nothing. This was the act of a selfish man, Hadaki concluded. He had no choice; he was a man of principles and he could not—would not—go back on his word. The emperor needed him to make this sacrifice. There was no other option.

. . . . .

The ship was only 873 feet long, so it did not take him long to get from one end to the other. There was no privacy or any place to get away when you lived on a carrier. Charlie needed to think about his life. *When the war is over, I will have no reason to go back to Little Rock; both of my parents are dead and Doris Ann is married*, Charlie thought. *How much I have missed for this war.*

Charlie headed to the fantail, his favorite spot to think. He walked out the door and found many people had the same idea; he turned to find another spot. Close to Admiral Mitscher's old battle perch, a secluded balcony overlooked the flight deck. No flight operations in progress, Charlie could contemplate his life and plan for the future.

Twenty-six hundred officers and men on the USS Lexington, and I feel isolated and alone for much of my day, Charlie lamented. He knew he suffered from depression, a common part of the grieving process. *It is incredibly hard to grieve when I have no family around to talk to or remember the good times with my father. Gil has been great since I heard the news, but he never knew my father.*

. . . . .

Hadaki stood at attention as his commander rallied Unit Yamato to victory over the evil American forces. His head shaven except for the top, he resembled a fourteenth-century monk preparing to pray. Instead, he would partake in the most ancient and revered rituals in the Japanese culture: suicide.

"Today," began the commander, "you will join Japan's greatest fighters as you inflict such pain and terror on the enemy, that the mere sight of a Japanese Zero in the air will bring them to their knees. Through your actions today, you show for all to see the tenets of a Japanese officer: your obligation to loyalty, the propriety of your life, how you esteem military valor, your righteousness, and the simplicity of your life."

One man stepped out from behind the commander and moved behind the men of Unit Yamato.

"We now mark you with this one-thousand-stitch headband to remind you of the samurai who went before you," announced the commander.

The man tied a headband on each member of the unit. The commander stepped forward to each man. "Take this sip of sake to ensure success in your mission," said the commander.

The commander poured the sake, made with fermented rice, into a bowl so each man could have a drink. After serving the last of Unit Yamato, the commander stepped back from the line.

"You will now take the fight to our enemy," he concluded. "The destruction and terror you inflict will break their will to fight, and save Japan. You are the heroes Japan will celebrate for millennia. Banzai!"

"Banzai!" the unit cried.

. . . . .

"I thought I would find you here," Gil had a knack of finding Charlie just when he needed him.

"I suppose you are here to make sure I eat," Charlie joked.

"You still look like a rail to me, mister," Gil replied with a wry smile. The two laughed. Charlie realized this was the first time he had laughed since the news. Charlie quietly thanked God for giving him a friend like Gil. It made the hell of war easier to bear.

Four minutes later, they were in line for lunch and quickly sat down with their sandwiches.

"Do you think she will say yes?" This was Gil's favorite question if he wanted Charlie to smile.

"For the millionth time," Charlie said, playing along, "of course she will. How could she deny a man in uniform?"

They laughed even harder. The plan was working better than Gil hoped.

"Hey," said Charlie, changing the subject, "you have never mentioned a girl back home. Anyone special?"

"There was," Gil confessed, "but she was afraid to get a Dear John letter from the Navy after I enlisted, so she decided it would be best to hold off on anything until

I get back from the war. I told her not to worry because my name is Gil, not John. They only send those letters to guys named John."

Charlie was snapping out of it. He seemed like his old self, thought Gil.

"General quarters, general quarters, man your battle stations!" the loudspeaker exploded.

Charlie and Gil shared the same duty station in the CIC, but neither were on duty that day. They also shared the same battle station, fifteen feet from the entrance to CIC. They scurried up the ladder and across the hangar deck, where they climbed their last set of ladders to the second deck of the bridge structure. Charlie turned the corner and headed for the door to their compartment just as the five-inch guns erupted. Charlie stumbled, but Gil fell flat on his face, busting his nose. He tried to get up but could only turn over and force himself up against the wall to a seated position.

All in the compartment heard the sound at the same time; it was all too familiar. The faint whine of a Japanese Zero, and it sounded like it was speeding up.

Hadaki emerged from the clouds to find a carrier directly below. He assumed attack position, diving at a 45° angle to increase the zone of destruction. Flak burst around him as the explosions created turbulence that nearly shook his hands from their death grip on the stick of his plane. He could make out people now, pilots running from their planes.

Hadaki felt it strange that people would stop to look up at his plane, mouths agape. He aimed his human missile at the bridge structure, where he would . . . *Haha*!

Charlie looked around the compartment and could not see Gil. He raised to his feet and reached for the door . . .

The explosion knocked Charlie to the floor where his head bounced off the bulkhead, giving him a large welt on his forehead. The exterior wall shook, and the rivets holding the steel wall plate in place twisted in pain, groaning against the tons of aircraft pressing against its skin. Smoke filled the room. One person reached for the door to open it.

"Stop," warned Charlie, "do not open that door! We may have more fire outside our door and even more smoke. Our Damage Control crews should be here momentarily." Just as Charlie finished his sentence, the door opened, and LT entered.

"Everyone good here?" called LT.

"Yes, sir," responded Charlie as he tried to stand.

LT walked out the door and gasped. This cannot be good, thought Charlie.

60. USS LEXINGTON

The Japanese Zero approached from the stern of the ship, crashing into the port island structure, bursting into flames. Two tons of mangled plane compressed the steel protective skin of the carrier, pushing the steel to its limit. During general quarters, all interior and exterior hatches must be closed to protect the ship from flooding; the hatch to the second floor was not closed. The fire flashed into the island structure, crawling up the ladder, searching for fuel to feed its voracious appetite.

It turned the corner at the top of the ladder, on the prowl for prey, and found its next victim. It attacked, burning the entire right side of Gil's body and 60 percent of his face, leaving sinews of flesh to cover the cartilage. The flames retreated as quickly as they came, satisfied with its feast.

"Gil!" screamed LT. "Medic!"

Charlie flew around the corner and stopped cold.

"Gil," Charlie breathed, "not you, God not you!" Charlie reached to hold Gil's mutilated hand.

"Stop!" ordered LT. "Do not touch him! Go get help, on the double." Charlie raced to the stairs, determined to save his buddy. As he rounded the corner, he placed his hand on the ladder rail and recoiled in pain; the metal was still hot from the fire. He took his shirt off, wrapped his hand, and descended the ladder.

Charlie found two corpsmen and sent them to attend to Gil.

As they arrived at Gil, they shared a knowing glance.

"Respiration fifteen, pulse thready," said one of the corpsmen.

They carefully lifted Gil and placed him on a stretcher and raced to the sick bay.

The corpsmen entered the sick bay and placed Gil on a metal table.

“Who do we have here?” asked the doctor. Hank Thurston, a graduate of Harvard Medical School, had volunteered to serve in the Navy in 1942, and was now on his third deployment.

“Radarman Gil Rothchild,” said one of the corpsmen.

“Cut his clothes off of him,” ordered the doctor.

The corpsmen began cutting the remaining cloths from Gil’s body, ripping off charred flesh fused to the garments.

Gil moaned.

“Morphine!” ordered the doctor. “Respiration’s ten. I have no pulse!”

Dr. Thurston began chest compressions, continuing for three minutes, stopping only to check for a pulse. The doctor halted the compressions and looked at the clock.

“I am calling it,” he said. “Time of death, fourteen twenty-two.” He took off his gloves and moved to another patient, hoping for different results.

Within twenty minutes of the kamikaze attack, Damage Control contained all fires. The ship began normal flight operations after clearing the flight deck. Sixty-five men died because of the attack, none more important to Charlie than Gil Rothchild.

When they found Charlie, he was still sitting outside the sick bay, his head down.

“Come on, sailor,” said the chaplain, “we need to talk.”

Charlie and the chaplain walked to the chapel, finding a quiet place away from those praying.

“It has been a tough few weeks for you, Charlie,” the chaplain said quietly. “How are you processing all of this?”

“Gil was my rock on this ship,” Charlie began. “He was the one person I could count on to keep me going when it got tough.”

“You are a man of faith?” asked the chaplain.

Charlie and Gil had spent many Sundays in the chapel, not uncommon for those facing death most every day.

"I am," Charlie said with as much conviction as he could, "but you sure have to wonder, why God would take him?"

"This is a terrible war, my son," said the chaplain. "Our ship has experienced its share of death and misery. Is this the first time to lose such a close friend on the ship?"

"Yes, it is," Charlie said, fighting back the tears welling in his eyes. "How will I go on?"

"God provides paths through our misery," said the chaplain. "His ways are true and just. Trust in Him and He will comfort and minister to you according to your need."

Charlie tried to speak, but the chaplain prayed for him. After they prayed, Charlie left the chapel and went to the fantail to think.

Three days later, the Lexington arrived at Ulithi, an atoll southeast of the Philippines, recently liberated by US forces. Repairs on the Lexington began immediately, and the captain allowed his crew the opportunity to decompress.

"Watch Brand out there," said the captain to the XO. "I need to know if he needs a change of scenery."

"Aye, aye, sir," said the XO.

Charlie spent most of his time on the beach, alone and disconnected with the rest of the crew. After two days with no improvement, the XO reported to the captain.

"I believe Brand needs a new home," said the XO. "I sure hate to lose him; he has the best eyes and ears in the fleet."

"Find a new home," ordered the captain. "The Yorktown will arrive from Pearl in two days; make a trade with them."

"Aye, aye, sir," said the XO.

Three days later, Charlie found himself on another ship, questioning, *Why me?*

The USS Yorktown CV-10 was an Essex class carrier, just like the USS Lexington, so the transition to his new ship was made easier.

As Charlie settled into his new bunk space, he heard a voice he knew. *This cannot be true*, he thought. He turned around.

"How ya been, slim?" asked Ed Steiner. "Bet you never thought you would find me way out here!"

"How is this possible, Ed?" asked Charlie, still in shock.

"When you left for the war," began Ed, "I finished up high school and then volunteered. I knew you went into the Navy, so I thought, why not?"

"Wow, what is your MOS?" asked Charlie, curious to know his childhood friend and partner in crime's military occupation specialty, his job aboard the ship. He looked at Ed's shoulder patch. "No . . ." Charlie said in disbelief, "you are a radarman?"

"Sure am," said Ed. "Been following you around the Pacific for the better part of a year. During radar school in San Diego, I kept hearing about this sailor who was a natural, the best they had ever seen come through the school. I almost lost my lunch when they told me it was you!"

Charlie stood there, stunned. He nearly forgot about his grief. Charlie spent the next three hours telling Ed about Gil, how they would have loved spending time in Hawaii together.

"Let me introduce you to our new lieutenant commander," Ed offered. "He is in CIC right now settling in."

Charlie and Ed entered CIC and Charlie stopped. For the second time today, he found himself unable to speak.

"LT?" asked Charlie. "Err, I mean Commander Hardin!"

"You know him?" asked Ed in disbelief.

"We served on the Lexington together," Charlie said. "Nice to see you again, sir. Congratulations on your promotion."

"Speaking of promotions," said the commander, "this is long past due, sailor. I am proud to inform you of your promotion to Radarman, First Class."

"Thank you, sir," Charlie said modestly.

"You earned it!" praised the commander. "Now, I need you to step up here and get this section in shape. I am counting on you."

"Aye, aye, sir," Charlie said, both men saluting.

Two weeks later, the Yorktown left Ulithi to join Task Force 38, part of the Third Fleet supporting air strikes on the island of Luzon.

"Sir," said Charlie, concerned.

"What is it, Brand?" said the commander.

"You need to see this, sir," Charlie said, motioning for the commander to look at his radar screen.

"Is that a land mass?" asked the commander.

"No, sir," Charlie said. "This echo is the wrong location to be land. If I had to guess, I would say this a hurricane."

"A typhoon," corrected the commander. "In the southern hemisphere, they call them typhoons."

"It sure is big," Charlie commented. "I would not want to be in that storm."

Typhoon Cobra was the twenty-third storm and last of the season.

"This is the captain," the voice said over the hailer. "It is going to get rough over the next day. Typhoon Cobra is on her way, and we are going to be right in the middle of it. Seas are building now, and we expect a bumpy ride. Secure your belongings and wait for further orders. That is all."

"Oh, boy," breathed Charlie.

One of the strongest storms of the season, Typhoon Cobra battered the Third Fleet, sinking three destroyers and damaging another thirty ships. Radar became unusable as the storm raged. On the Yorktown, sailors suffered bruises and a few broken bones as the ship rolled wildly, sometimes as much as 55° side to side. Many sailors, including the captain, questioned the wisdom of subjecting the fleet to such punishment. The typhoon later became known among the fleet as Halsey's Typhoon, as he had ordered the fleet into the storm rather than searching for safe harbor to ride it out. After an inquisition, they determined Admiral Halsey was not derelict in his duty but did display bad command judgement. In February, Admiral Sprague relieved Admiral Halsey from the command of the Third Fleet.

61. KAWAGUCHICO, JAPAN

Two men entered the village, searching for the home of a hero. They turned the corner to find the Yamatsumi home. They knocked on the door.

Hadaki's mother looked out the window to see men in uniform. Men like these had visited this village before, bringing news of death and despair. Today would be no different.

She opened the door.

"We bring you news of your son, Hadaki," said the officer. "Your son gave his life gloriously to honor our emperor and save this great nation. You should be proud to call him your son." They gave her Hadaki's letter.

She wept. She was alone. How would she support her family, she thought. She composed herself enough to speak.

"What is to become of us?" was all she could muster.

"As you know," said the officer, "your son was the heir to his father's land. You will need to give up this land and move to a city where the government will care for you till you meet your husband and son again."

She knew this day would come, from the day Hadaki announced he would join the military. Anger burned against her country. How could they let her son become a kamikaze? They knew he was the firstborn. How could they take him from his training command and send him to his death? *The emperor is truly a heartless man.*

The men left her to contemplate the life she once knew, full of hope and optimism. Now despair consoled her heart, broken for a second time. How cruel her ancestors were. What will become of her children? What life will they have?

. . . . .

Admiral Matome Ugaki returned to headquarters in Tokyo, where they had assigned him the commander of the Navy Fifth Air Fleet on Kuyushu, the third largest Japanese island. He arrived two days later, determined to avenge the losses suffered by the Japanese fleet during the Battle of the Philippine Islands. Kamikaze attacks were his only option.

Ugaki knew he needed more pilots, and an airplane easy enough for inexperienced pilots to fly. They chose the Nakajima Ki-115 or the Tsurugi. It was a single-engine wooden frame aircraft that could be easily constructed from spare parts. They ejected the non-retractable set of landing gear after takeoff to prevent the pilots from returning to base.

He recruited pilots from other branches of the military, not fully disclosing the full nature of their mission. Pilots received forty hours of flight training, along with brutal corporal punishment. The brutality of the beatings left many incapable of flying. Pilots were told that their officers were instilling the will to fight, leaving many with no remaining feelings of patriotism. Upon completion of their flight training, they gave the pilots a piece of white paper with three options: volunteer out of a strong desire, simply volunteer, or decline. Many enthusiastically volunteered, while others felt the immense pressure of their peers to volunteer.

The kamikaze pilot manual described the tactics they would use to attack their target and provided guidance on how to think and prepare for their mission:

> *When you eliminate all thoughts about life and death, you will totally disregard your earthly life. This also enables you to concentrate your attention on eradicating the enemy with unwavering determination, meanwhile reinforcing your excellence in flight skills.*

. . . . .

Commander John Thach entered Vice Admiral John McCain's cabin.

"Reporting as ordered, sir," Thach said, sporting a sharp salute. Thach had recently become the admiral's operations officer.

"What are we going to do about these damn kamikaze attacks, commander?" asked the admiral. "We have seen almost five hundred attacks since November! These attacks are causing too much damage to our ships, not to mention the loss of life."

"That is what I hoped to speak to you about, admiral," Thach said.

"You have a plan then?" asked the admiral.

"Yes, sir," began Thach. "I believe we need earlier warning of these attacks, sir."

"Is that not what our radar is for?" the admiral asked tersely.

"Yes, sir, it is," responded the commander. "To augment our radar efforts, I believe we need to provide dawn-to-dusk combat air patrols, creating a net to catch them before they can get too close."

"Ok, I get your plan," said the admiral. "How far out are you thinking?"

"That is the second element of the plan, sir," Thach continued. "We would move our picket of destroyers out to fifty miles from the carriers and fly the CAP missions over the picket. If any kamikaze attack penetrates our first line of defense, we have enough time to pick them off with our radar-equipped proximity munitions."

"Excellent plan, commander," praised the admiral. "I will send this to Admiral Sprague for approval."

One hour later, the fleet enacted what they would call the big blue blanket.

. . . . .

"The Americans grow close to our homeland," Admiral Toyoda said gravely. "Present your plan to thwart this progress."

"Admiral," began a commander, "we believe that our only remaining option would be to use kamikaze tactics with our surface vessels."

"Commander," said the admiral, "kamikazes fly planes into our enemy. Are you suggesting a suicide mission with our remaining surface vessels?"

"Sir," continued the commander, "the Americans are preparing to invade Okinawa. We must send out surface ships to act as a barrier to the invasion force."

"What are you suggesting, commander?" asked the admiral, understanding the futility of the mission. "The emperor expects the Navy to perform a miracle to save Okinawa."

"We recommend the Yamato and her escorts sail to Okinawa where they will attack the US fleet," continued the commander. "Our attack force will fight their way through the enemy line and beach their ships near the middle of Okinawa, between the villages of Higashi and Yomitan."

"I see," said the admiral, contemplatively.

"Our fleet will fight like shore batteries," concluded the commander, "until they can fight no longer."

"We have limited fuel to support this attack," reminded the admiral.

"That is correct, sir," said the commander. "Each ship will receive just enough fuel to reach Okinawa. We suggest naming the operation *Ten-Go Sakusen* (Operation Heaven One)."

"This is our only hope, commander," agreed the admiral. "Prepare the operation immediately."

"Hai!" responded the commander.

62. TOKUYAMA, JAPAN

The officers and enlisted men gathered in the tradition of the samurai and kamikaze.

"Men," began Admiral Ito, "we embark on our last mission. We are the last line of defense against the invading Americans. Soon, they will begin their bombing raids against our beloved Japan, terrorizing our families and destroying our crops. Our families will starve if we are unsuccessful! You are the last hope for Japan. We must stop the invasion of Okinawa! You will inflict such damage on the US fleet, invading Japan will not be possible. Just one more victory by our forces, and we will turn the tide of the war. This is what you are fighting for. You must be ready to make the ultimate sacrifice. You must have the spirit of our samurai ancestors. Only you can save your families. Banzai!"

The admiral shared sake with his officers and enlisted men as they made their last preparations to depart for Tokuyama. Defying standing fuel allocation orders, the Tokuyama personnel gave most of the remaining depot fuel to the armada. Everyone at the deport and those on the ships knew that, even with additional fuel, they would never return.

As Operation Heaven One made way through the Bungo Channel, American submarines Threadfin and Hackleback detected the departing Japanese forces. The American subs shadowed the force until they pulled away, the Balao-class submarines only able to make 8.75 knots while submerged. Once clear of the Japanese coast, they came to periscope level and contacted fleet headquarters.

"Flash message, sir," said the communications officer. "The Yamato and nine other ships, including a light carrier, departed Tokuyama on course to Okinawa."

"Very well," said Admiral Mitscher, who monitored all fleet traffic in case an opportunity presented itself. He lifted the phone.

"I need to see both of you in my quarters," ordered the admiral.

Commander Widhelm and Lieutenant Commander Myers knocked on the stateroom door.

"Enter," said the admiral.

"Reporting as ordered, sir," said Widhelm.

"At ease," said the admiral. "Have a seat, gentlemen."

"An opportunity has presented itself to us," began the admiral. "A kind of gift, you might say. Have a look."

The admiral passed the communications to his senior staff members.

"Oh, God," breathed Widhelm. They smiled.

"What does Admiral Sprague have to say about this?" asked Myers.

"Our communications officer intercepted this message. The admiral has not sent orders. That is why you are here."

"Preparing our own strike?" asked Widhelm.

"Absolutely!" the admiral almost shouted. "We have been looking for an opportunity to destroy the flagship of the Imperial Japanese Navy, the Yamato, and I am going to take it."

"And Admiral Sprague?" asked Myers, knowing the naval history of rivalry between carriers and surface battleships.

"Admiral Sprague," responded the admiral, happy to get the upper hand, "will order a surface attack using overwhelming forces. Old school! This is an operation designed for carriers."

"How many planes are you thinking?" asked Widhelm.

"Four hundred should do," said the admiral with a wry smile. "The attack force should have no air cover. Prepare the plan and have it to me in two hours."

"Aye, aye, sir!" both men said, saluting smartly.

"I want planes up there looking for the attack force," ordered the admiral, "immediately!"

Five planes launched from the USS Bunker Hill.

"Brand," said the commander as he entered CIC, "I need your expert skills."

"What can I do to help, sir?" asked Charlie.

"The Yamato is on its way to Okinawa," said the commander. "I want you to find her first before our search planes."

"Sir," Charlie said, "they are at least 400 miles away from us, sir. Best I have ever seen for surface ships is 124 miles."

"Keep an eye out, Brand," ordered the commander. "Get it done!"

"Aye, aye, sir." Charlie said. *What is he thinking? How am I going to find the Yamato?* Charlie trained his radar to sweep between 0° and 15°. He turned the gain of the set to maximum and found the five planes launched from Bunker Hill.

"How is it going, Brand?" asked the commander.

"I have our five search planes, sir," reported Charlie.

"Oh, boy!" Charlie said, not realizing he said this out loud.

"Speak up, sailor," ordered the commander. "What did you find?"

"Multiple contacts inbound bearing one niner niner," reported Charlie. "Range two one three, flying at Angels fifteen."

"Get me the number of contacts, sailor," ordered the commander.

"I believe we have one zero fiver contacts, sir," reported Charlie.

"Bridge, CIC," called the commander.

"Bridge, aye," responded the XO.

"One zero fiver incoming bogies, range two one three," reported the commander.

"More kamikaze, I assume," said the admiral.

The Big Blue Blanket, now fully operational, prepared to welcome their guests. The kamikaze attack force numbered 115, but immediately lost 100 planes to the expert CAP fighters and destroyer fire. Fifteen kamikaze planes chose their targets.

The guns of the destroyer picket rumbled to life, swatting at the kamikaze planes like annoying mosquitos. Three more exploded, falling harmlessly to the ocean.

"Commander," called Charlie, "we have one headed straight for us, sir."

"Does your radar director have this one?" asked the commander to the operator of the gun director.

"Yes sir," said the operator. "We got this one."

Those on the deck of the Yorktown scrambled for safety. Suddenly, fire exploded from the Japanese Zero's engine. An ensign on the bridge reported he saw the pilot wide-eyed, mouth agape, struggle to keep the plane in the air. The kamikaze pilot missed the bridge, diving into the ocean, ten feet off the starboard bow. The crew cheered!

"Plane gone," reported Charlie. "Looks like he missed us."

The American fleet reported no damage due to the kamikaze attack.

"Great work, everyone," said the commander. He wondered how long the Yorktown could avoid a direct hit from one of these lunatics. Charlie and the commander exited CIC.

"Commander," called Charlie, "I have a question, sir."

"What is on your mind, Brand?" asked the commander.

"Why did you ask me to find ships hundreds of miles away?" Charlie asked. "You know as well as I do the range for these radar sets, and these ships were at least two times the capable discovery distance."

"You are a smart guy," said the commander. "What do you think?"

Charlie pondered the question. "Well," he answered, "I guess you needed me engaged in my work, after all of the loss I have suffered recently."

"Exactly!" praised his commander. "That is why I ensured your promotion; you are very smart. You would have made a good officer, Charlie."

"Thank you, sir," Charlie said graciously, "for everything."

Mitscher sat on the couch waiting for news from the search planes.

"Superman, VS-1," called search plane one.

"VS-1, Superman, aye," responded the XO of the USS Indianapolis, flagship of Admiral Spruance.

"We have visual of target, bearing one eight seven degrees, two six four miles," reported the pilot.

"Bearing one eight seven degrees, two six four miles, aye," responded the XO. "Remain on station."

"VS-1, aye," responded the pilot.

. . . . .

On the Yamato, radio operators heard the transmission from the search plane. In response to hearing of the discovery of his armada, Admiral Ito ordered the forward guns of the Yamato to fire their 460-mm bow guns loaded with special beehive shells, but the ordinances fell short of their target. VS-1 and VS-2 remained on station, waiting for an attack force, providing updates every fifteen minutes.

. . . . .

"There it is," said Admiral Mitscher, as he rubbed his hands together. "Launch our planes in two waves. This will put an end to the debate if air power alone can prevail over surface forces. We will end this debate here and now."

The carriers of Task Force 58 launched four hundred planes in two waves of two hundred each. Included in each wave were Hellcat fighters, Helldive bombers, Corsair fighters, and TBF Avenger torpedo bombers. On the Indianapolis, Admiral Spruance prepared to order Task Force 54, his modernized battleships, to cut the Japanese armada off before they could reach Okinawa. Hearing of the launch from Mitscher's carriers, Spruance agreed to the air attack plan.

Two hours later, the first wave of aircraft arrived over the armada, finding no Japanese Zero protection.

"Ocean Wave, VF-1," called the Hellcat fighter leader.

"VF-1, Ocean Wave, aye," answered the XO of the Yorktown.

"Targets unprotected, no patrol," reported the Hellcat Fighter leader. "Recommend coming in hot, immediate attack."

"VF-1, roger wilco," answered the XO.

The first wave circled their prey like a pack of hungry wolves on an unprotected deer. Hellcat and Corsair fighters began their runs, engaging the Japanese anti-aircraft guns while strafing the armada. The attack design expected the gunners to concentrate their firepower on the agile fighters, leaving an opportunity for the Helldivers to attack, almost at a 90° angle, toward the Yamato. The Avengers, requiring a low altitude attack, relished all the distractions the fighters could garner as they approached from the port side. Their textbook plan did not disappoint.

The light cruiser Yahagi suffered a torpedo hit to her engine room, decimating the engines and her crew. She remained dead in the water, rife for continued attacks. Six more torpedoes and twelve bombs hit her, and she succumbed to her injuries. The destroyer Isokaze attempted to render aid, but the second wave heavily damaged her and she sank.

The Yamato sustained two armor-piercing bombs through her steel deck and one torpedo, despite her evasive maneuvers. Still able to sustain flank speed, a fire aft of the superstructure, caused by a bomb, burned uncontrollably. The second wave scored eight torpedo and fifteen bombs hit on the struggling Yamato, damaging the gun directors, requiring manual aiming and firing of her anti-aircraft guns. The Yamato listed to port, unable to control her impending capsizing. Admiral Ito and her captain ordered the crew to abandon ship, but refused to leave the bridge where they met their doom.

The Japanese lost the destroyers Asashimo and Kasumi to bomb strikes, but the Suzutsuki made the port of Sasebo, minus her bow that was blown off during the attack, steaming in reverse to avoid sinking. Destroyers Fukutsuki, Yukikaze, and Hatsushimo escaped relatively unscathed, saving over fourteen hundred sailors.

The United States lost only ten aircraft and twelve men because of enemy fire. Losing the mighty Yamato rendered the Japanese navy impotent throughout the rest of the war.

American forces landed on Okinawa on April 7, beginning the final land-based operation of the war. The fight to take Okinawa and the suicidal actions of Operation *Ten-Go* convinced the Joint Chiefs that there would be no invasion of the Japanese mainland; the calculated human cost was too high. On July 21, 1945, Allied Forces secured Okinawa from Japanese occupation.

The Japanese culture reveres its warriors and values selfless and often futile acts of bravery. A poetic name often used for Japan is Yamato. Many equate the loss of the battleship Yamato as a metaphor for the end of the Japanese empire.

63. WARM SPRINGS, GEORGIA

On April 12, Roosevelt complained of a severe headache while sitting for a portrait. By 3:45 p.m., he was dead from an intracerebral hemorrhage; he was just sixty-three years old. A flag-draped coffin held the body of their fallen leader as he traveled in the presidential train back to Washington, DC. After a White House funeral, the next day, the president made his final journey to his birthplace at Hyde Park, New York. They buried Roosevelt on April 15 in his Springwood Estate's Rose Garden.

Harry S. Truman, just three months into his first term as vice president, assumed the office of president of the United States. The full weight of the war upon him, his most difficult decision was still ahead.

On a hot summer afternoon on July 16, 1945, years of work by hundreds of people would change the outcome of World War II. On the barren Alamogordo missile range, 210 miles south of Los Alamos, with the "gadget" loaded, the "Trinity" test would alter the balance of world power and set the United States on a path designed to break the will of the Japanese rulers. At exactly 0530 hours, the United States ushered in the nuclear age.

The USS Indianapolis, recently repaired from a kamikaze attack, made way for Hunters Point Shipyard in Mare Island, where they loaded the special cargo into the hold of the ship. Captain McVay read his orders:

> *You will sail at high speed to Tinian where your cargo will be taken off by others. You will not be told what the cargo is, but it is to be guarded even after the life of your vessel. If she goes down, save the cargo at all costs, in a lifeboat if necessary. And every day you save on your voyage will cut the length of the war by that much. You will not share the horizon with any ship.*

At 0800 hours, the Indianapolis made way for Pearl Harbor, arriving seventy-four-and-a-half hours later, a new speed record. She took on fuel and made way for

Tinian in the Mariana Islands, arriving on 26 July, the day when President Truman ordered the use of the first atomic bomb.

Tragedy struck the ship and crew of the USS Indianapolis as two torpedoes sank her, shot from Japanese submarine I-58. She lost three hundred men. By 31 July, the bombs were ready for deployment, pending favorable weather reports, Typhoon Eva driving the site selection.

On 6 August, three B-29 Flying Fortress bombers left Tinian, destined to change the face of war. Arriving over their target, Hiroshima, just after 0900 hours, Tinian time, the Enola Gay, named after the mother of the mission commander, prepared to deploy the world's first atomic weapon. At 0915:17 hours, the bomb dropped, and the pilot executed an emergency escape maneuver: a dive and a maximum speed turn. Detonation of the bomb occurred 45.5 seconds later, and shock waves jolted the plane one minute later.

Radiation and the bomb blast killed about one hundred and twenty-six thousand civilians and twenty thousand military personnel. Among the dead civilians was the family of the captain of submarine I-58. The Japanese retaliated by killing twelve US prisoners of war: eight by the blast, two by execution, and two by stoning by a crowd.

On 8 August, the United States dropped leaflets over cities in Japan:

> *America asks that you take immediate heed of what we say on this leaflet. We are in possession of the most destructive explosive ever devised by man. A single one of our newly developed atomic bombs is actually the equivalent in explosive power to what 2,000 of our giant B-29s can carry on a single mission. You should take steps now to cease military resistance. Otherwise, we shall resolutely employ this bomb and all our other superior weapons to promptly and forcefully end the war.*

Japan did not respond. Again, weather would determine the date of the next bombing mission. On 9 August, the B-29, codenamed Bockscar, departed for Kokura, the site selection for the second atomic bomb. Bad weather over Kokura, a relatively heavily defended city, forced the team to move to Nagasaki, the backup site. Bad weather over Nagasaki almost caused the United States to abort the mission, but at 1201 hours, a hole opened in the clouds, and the second atomic bomb exploded over Nagasaki, killing about eighty thousand civilians and one hundred fifty military personnel.

At precisely noon on 15 August, a phonograph recording of Emperor Hirohito notified his loyal subjects that Japan would surrender. For many, this was the first time to hear the voice of the emperor. For the Mother of Hadaki, his words rang hollow in her heart..

On Kyushu, Matome Ugaki listened carefully to his emperor's instruction to cease hostilities. Writing in his diary that as he had yet to receive the formal cease-fire order from Tokyo, and taking full responsibility for losing the war, he would fly one more kamikaze mission. Ugaki and three of his officers boarded a Yokosuka D4Y, headed for the Philippines to inflict one more attack on the victors. The plane never made an attack on the US Fleet or returned to Japan.

In his quarters, Takijiro Onishi committed *seppuku* (ritual suicide) on 16 August. In his suicide note, he apologized for sending almost four thousand pilots to their death.

On the USS Yorktown, the crew was unclear if the war was over, although they canceled all strikes planned for 15 August. Later that month, she received orders to proceed to Honshu, providing air cover for the occupying forces.

On 2 September, representatives from the United States, Japan, and all allied nations observed the formal surrender of the Japanese and the end of World War II on the deck of the USS Missouri. The Yorktown sailed under the Golden Gate Bridge and docked at Alameda Naval Air Station on 20 October after ferrying two thousand soldiers back home, victorious.

"Charles Brand to CIC, Charles Brand to CIC," the voice called over the hailer.

"Radarman Brand, reporting as ordered, sir," said Charlie, saluting.

"Charlie," said his commander, "let me be the first to tell you, you are going home. The papers are being signed as we speak. Your service on the Lexington and Yorktown has earned you many accommodations."

The commander read five accommodation letters and pinned the ribbons on Charlie's chest. Charlie tried to speak, but his commander put up his hand.

"It has been *my* honor to have you in my command," said the commander, fighting off his emotions. "You survived more tragedy than most in this war, and I know you will continue to do great things for our country."

"Thank you, sir," Charlie said extending his hand.

They shook hands and found themselves in a hug.

"I will never forget you, sir," Charlie said in a faint whisper.

Five days later, he arrived in Dallas.

"Charlie!" cried Lilly, accompanied by her family. "Welcome home!"

Charlie dropped his seabag and ran, not caring who saw the tears falling from his eyes.

"I missed you so much, my love," Charlie said, his voice cracking. "I am never letting you go."

They kissed. His mind flashed to the last time he had kissed his Lilly. This time the intensity of the moment overwhelmed them both. They broke their embrace, incapable of standing without the aid of the other. Charlie regained the strength in his legs and moved toward Henry, waiting patiently a few feet away.

"Welcome home, son," said Henry. "Well done! We are all so proud of you!"

Charlie could not speak, but looked into Henry's eyes. Henry knew.

"I meant everything in that letter, Charlie," Henry said, ever stoic. "Anything you need from me, I am here for you."

Charlie tried to speak again. This time, he wanted to ask Henry a question.

"Of course, Charlie," said Henry with a smile, reducing the volume of his voice, "you have our blessing."

Two hours later, Charlie and Lilly sat down under their pecan tree near Lexall Lake.

"It was painful being away from you for so long," Charlie said, "but the memory of your touch, your smell, and your beauty gave me the strength to go on when all I wanted to do was die."

"You wanted to die?" Lilly looked deep into his eyes, desperate to see the man she fell in love with so long ago.

"What I have seen," began Charlie, "it can change a man, harden him away from ever loving another."

Tears formed in Lilly's eyes.

"But not me, Lilly," Charlie said, smiling broadly. "Thinking of you is what saved me, what kept me going during my toughest hours."

Lilly smiled sweetly.

"I wish you could have known Gil," said Charlie pensively. "We watched out for each other. He became the brother I never had."

Lilly looked deeply into Charlie's eyes, this time seeing the man she knew. She beamed.

"Gil and I talked of this moment all the time," said Charlie, now nervous. "I hope I do not mess this up." He stood up, reached into his pocket, and grabbing a box, dropped to one knee.

Lilly gasped.

"Lilly," Charlie said, his voice strengthening with each word, "the day I met you on the train, I knew God sent me an angel. I did not want our talk to end. Then, walking with you by this lake, kissing you for the first time, I knew. I knew God's plan for my life would be to take care of you, for the rest of my life. You told me *you* have a plan for me."

Lilly's breathing increased.

"Well, Lilly Hope," Charlie concluded, "I have a plan for you. Would you make me the happiest man in the world? Would marry me?" Charlie opened the box, displaying a one-carat diamond ring.

"Yes!" screamed Lilly. "Oh, *yes*!"

Charlie put the ring on her finger. He would not sleep for the next twenty days!

They kissed deeply.

. . . . .

On a summer day in 1965, an elderly British man drove down the Pacific Coast Highway with the top down on his new 1965 Shelby GT350 Mustang, enjoying the sun and sea air. He did not notice the California Highway Patrol officer on the motorcycle, but the officer noticed him. The motorcycle pulled behind the Mustang and flashed his lights.

The elderly man pulled over, flustered at his predicament.

"Good afternoon, sir," said the officer cordially. "Are you aware the speed limit is forty miles per hour on this part of the highway?"

"I believe I know that officer," said the British man, embarrassed by his situation.

"License and registration, please," said the officer.

The British man reached into the glove box and presented the requested documents.

The officer reviewed the license. "Mr. Watt," began the officer, "if you promise to watch your speed, I will give you a warning today."

"Thank you, officer," said Watson-Watt. "I will be more careful."

The irony of the situation did not escape Robert Watson-Watt. Back in 1938, he was the first man to create a demonstration showing the potential of a new technology, radar. And now, his invention had caught him in a speed trap in the United States, after his country gave them the key to help win World War II. Arnold would certainly have a pleasant laugh.

Many years had passed since he thought of that meadow and what they had accomplished. He had led an extraordinary life, one his father would have been proud of, he thought. He looked over his shoulder, shifted into first gear, and deliberately pulled onto the highway.

EPILOGUE

Since Robert Watson-Watt and Arnold Wilkins successfully tested the use of radar to detect airplanes, many inventions have improved our lives.

In 1945, Percy Spencer invented what he called the Radarange. We know this today as the microwave oven. Spencer discovered that his chocolate bar melted in his pocket while around an active radar set. After further experiments to ensure the validity of his first observation, Raytheon patented the invention, making the microwave oven the most used kitchen appliance in today's homes.

Another invention keeps us safe when we fly and during severe weather events: pulse Doppler radar. Air traffic controllers manage thousands of planes every day in airports around the world. Pulse Doppler radar was first used in fighter aircraft in the 1960s for determining the range to enemy targets. Now, the same technology guides thousands of planes each day safely to their destination. For the past fifteen years, meteorologists have used Doppler radar to gain greater velocity definition of severe weather outbreaks. Doppler radar saves thousands of people each year through early, specific warnings.

Medical diagnostic tools like sonograms, ultrasounds, and CT scans all use radar technology to display images on a screen. Physicians order millions of these tests each year for successfully diagnosing cancer, knee injuries, pregnancy, and so much more.

Advances in circuit design have directly led to the development of the computers we use today. Pulse forming networks, pulse counting circuits, and memory circuits from World War II drove the need for the invention of computer technology. The technology we use today has its origins in the weapons used to defeat the Japanese.

Radar-guided weapons deliver missiles and bombs to targets miles away. Modern warfare is now about pinpoint delivery of ordinances to targets, thus minimizing errors.

We owe so much to the men and women who fought during World War II, truly the greatest generation. By 1945, over twelve million men and women served the United States Armed Forces, over three million in the Navy. Of all US servicemen, 38.8 percent volunteered, with 61.2 percent drafted into service. The average enlisted man made $71.33 per month, while their commanding officers took home $203.50 per month.

Women played an important part during World War II, serving directly in the military as Women's Amy Corps (WAC), Navy Women's Accepted for Voluntary Emergency Service (WAVES), Women's Airforce Service Pilots (WASP), and nurses caring for the wounded.

The United States lost 407,316 brave soldiers, airmen, marines, and navy men. America entered the war because of the attack on Pearl Harbor, but the industrial might and ingenuity of the men and women of the United States were what paved our way to victory. The gift from Great Britain, the technology to create our secret eye, saved countless pilots and ships, ensuring military victories and generations of families.